BROTHERS

BROTHERS

HAIG TAHTA

To my dear friends
Rolf and Audrey
with love.

Haig

BLACK
APOLLO
PRESS

First published in Great Britain by
Black Apollo Press, 2013

Copyright © Haig Tahta

ISBN: 9781900355766

A CIP catalogue record of this book is available at
the British Library.

For information regarding our other titles, please
go to our website:
www.blackapollo.com

Contents

Chapter 1

Harriet

Harriet Tate was an only child. Her father – Alan Tate – was born in India in the little town of Darabad in the province of Bihar in the summer of 1897. Alan was the son of an indigo planter, who had himself inherited the plantation from his own father. On the somewhat dubious grounds that it was in some way more genteel and higher up the social scale in the invisible hierarchy that constituted British India, Alan's father had sold the plantation and switched to the business of importing cotton goods from Lancashire. He had not made any more of a success in this business than in that of being a planter. Alan had remained an only child.

When war broke out in Europe in 1914, Alan was already over 17 and could not wait to get away from his stuffy home life in Darabad to join in the 'great adventure' of the war which seemed so attractive to so many bored young men all over the British Empire. So it was that the day after his 18th birthday, he joined the Indian army. He was given only the most cursory training before joining a regiment as a junior officer. In April 1915, after only a short time of training together, this new regiment embarked at Bombay on a mission to reinforce the hard-pressed Indian army contingent which continued to hold Basra.

Alan was fortunate in that he had been just too young to have gone with the original Indian forces in the invasion of the Ottoman Empire at Basra. A substantial part of this original force, commanded by a British Regular Army General – General Townsend – had advanced too far down the Tigris, outrunning their supplies. Then, on the arrogant assumption that Ottoman power had already been broken, this force had continued on towards Baghdad where it was eventually surrounded, forced to retreat and form themselves into a fortress under siege. Two proud empires, both due to fall and be displaced within the next forty years, faced up to each other. This was an army of Indian soldiers, officered largely by the British, facing an army of Arabs, officered largely by Turks. After several attempts at relief had failed, including a rather dishonourable attempt to bribe the besieging Ottoman General, this Indian army had eventually been forced to surrender at Kut-al-Amara.

In fact, throughout the War, the Ottomans were never quite the pushover imagined by the British. The invasion at Gallipoli had got bogged down almost immediately against fierce Ottoman resistance. In Mesopotamia, although the Turks were never able to recapture Basra, the surrender of a whole British force to an Asian army was unprecedented, and was the worst British military disaster since the retreat from Kabul in the previous century.

Alan Tate survived the war and expected to return to India to be demobilised as soon as the Armistice was declared. But from the very moment of the signing of the Armistice of Mudros, ending the war against the Turks, the leaders of the British Empire in London attempted to manipulate the extraordinary situation left by the collapse of the Ottoman Empire in the Middle East. Eager young men, both those in the Arab Bureau in Cairo and those in the corridors of power of the Foreign and Colonial Office in London, were happily drawing boundary lines over the whole area of the dying Empire. They paid scant regard to the history of the region, or to the ethnic diversity and religious sensibilities of the people living there, treating the whole of the Middle East as a 'tabula rasa'. Only two aspects were important to them. First, to arrange matters so as to 'do down' the French, and second, to get a hold on as much as possible of what was then believed to be only small reserves of oil known to be in the region. The French, of course, were playing exactly the same game in the opposite direction. Meanwhile, threatening all the time to upset this cosy two-way apple-cart, the resurgent Turks loomed in the background.

What all this meant was that in order to play the Imperial game with the best hopes of success, some troops were needed to remain on station as long as possible. Alan's regiment was one of these. As the first years after the armistice went by, the artificial, fundamentally unstable, state of Iraq was fashioned out of the three logically separate provinces of Ottoman Mesopotamia. Faisal, the Hashemite Prince, immortalised and romanticised by Lawrence, one of the eager young men of the Arab Bureau, was driven out of Damascus by the French. He was then reinstated in Baghdad by the British, as the Anglo-French imperial rivalry swung back and forth creating many of the problems in the area which still plague the world a hundred years later.

In the end, Alan's demobilisation was delayed for over a year and he did not get back to his normal life in India until 1921. Once back, he wooed and married his childhood sweetheart – Tessa - the daughter of yet another Indigo planter who had a plantation only some miles away from his grandfather's near their home town of Darabad.

Alan's stint during his five years in the army, stationed in the malarial swamps of the two rivers of Iraq, had left his health fatally weakened. He found it difficult to settle down. His father's business, importing Lancashire cotton goods into India, was still fairly healthy, but Alan was unable to garner much enthusiasm for the work, whilst his father had become pessimistic about the future for Lancashire goods. Alan's daughter Harriet was born in 1929, and later in the same year his father died. Alan did not hesitate for a moment. He sold the family business to a local trader and within a year the whole family – Alan, his wife Tessa, together with his widowed mother Chloe and the baby Harriet, all left India and arrived in Liverpool. A month or so after their arrival in England, Alan had confirmed the job he had negotiated before leaving India. This was in Manchester with the textile company of Calico Printers – a company which had been dealing with his father's firm in India for many years.

Harriet Tate was not going to grow into a classic beauty. She had beautiful, long dark brown hair which swept down her back, but as she was rather short this seemed a little inappropriate whilst she was still young. Her eyes were of a deep and piercing blue. When she smiled they lit up her face. However, when she lost her temper, or was angry for some other reason, the blue became so dark as to become almost black. Tessa gave birth to another child – a boy – a year after the family arrived in England, but this infant was weak and did not survive more than a few months, and Tessa was told she would not be able to have another. Accordingly, Harriet remained an only child, daughter of parents who were themselves each single children.

Life in Manchester in the thirties was not easy for this British Indian family. They were used to the many servants and easy life-style of Imperial India in the early twentieth century. Here in Manchester, instead of an army of cooks and cleaners, there was only one young Irish maid who tried unsuccessfully to do everything. Tessa had had to learn to cook and manage a home.

Meanwhile, Calico Printers was not doing well. The whole Lancashire cotton industry was tottering as more and more Asian countries began developing their own textile industry. The complete collapse of the mills did not take place for another twenty years, but the future was already looked bleak. Textiles were almost always the first commercial activity to be industrialised in developing countries. As Alan had entered the firm later than most of his colleagues, he became apprehensive about his position, and this heightened the sense of insecurity he had experienced ever since returning from the war. This increasing lack of confidence affected the whole family atmosphere, and as a result his relationship with Tessa began to deteriorate.

Both parents doted excessively on their only child. Alan's feelings of insecurity, exacerbated by his poor health, amounted almost to despair as he brooded on the difference between his previous life in India and his current circumstances in a dingy Manchester suburb. This had the effect of further souring his relations with Tessa who was also struggling to adjust to their new circumstances. She too experienced the anxiety of an insecurity which had become more acute ever since the death of their little boy. Had the infant died at birth, it was likely that she would have endured the trauma without too much long-term effect. But surviving for six months meant that the death left both parents devastated, increasing the tension and lack of feeling between them. The result was that, beginning to ignore each other, they drifted into the deadly process of competition for their child's affections.

Harriet was already temperamentally disposed to having her own way. As the relations between her parents deteriorated, it became even easier for the child to get whatever she wanted. Inevitably, school and the necessity to socialise with other children, at last taught her that outside the family, getting her own way required some manipulation. She learnt quickly. She had a naturally generous and passionate nature which resonated well with people whom she was anxious to placate or influence. Once her eyes lit up with that piercing blue gaze, she usually managed to get what she wanted. On the other hand, if that failed, and she could not have her way, her anger was uncontrollable.

The depression of the early thirties hit the Lancashire textile industry particularly hard. As the total amount of work available decreased, people in all branches of the trade were continually being laid off, not only in the mills themselves but also in the back offices. In 1934, Alan and Tessa, now scarcely on speaking terms, decided to move to Southport in the hope that the sea air would improve Alan's deteriorating health. He now commuted daily to the Manchester offices of the company. In a continual state of fear that he would shortly be dismissed, his depression refused to lift despite the bracing sea air. There was clearly something more to his state of nerves as in fact his situation was not really as bad as he imagined. He had arrived from India with a capital sum, which although not large, was nevertheless a good deal more than most people in his position had. His purchase of the house in Whalley Range in Manchester had been a good investment, and when he moved to Southport he was able to purchase a substantial house and still have some capital left over. Nevertheless his health and his state of anxiety continued to deteriorate.

Harriet was nine years old when Alan died. That morning there had been a particularly unpleasant scene at home throughout which the despairing little girl had been present. Alan had had to leave for work with the

cruel and vicious epithets of an exasperated Tessa ring-
ing in his ears. The same biting words rang in the ears
of Harriet, as she ran to school at the same time that her
father left for work. Though only nine years old, Harriet felt deeply the injustice in her mother's cruel and
hurtful words, hurled at her father, who had remained
silent throughout, save for a feeble attempt to stem their
flow. At that age, Harriet could see the hurt in her father's dejected eyes and could understand the meaning
of the words her mother flung at him, though not able
to appreciate the frustrations her mother also faced in
the new life that had been thrust upon her.

That day there had been a lot of talk in the office
about redundancies. It was clear that the deteriorating
trade position of the company was going to result in
some cutbacks somewhere. According to all the later
witnesses, Alan had not said a word or made any comment during these discussions. At his usual time in the
afternoon, Alan had left the office and walked down to
Victoria station to catch his train back home. He had
said goodbye to all his colleagues in the usual way and
there had been no sign whatsoever of anything untoward in his behaviour. No one ever knew for certain
what happened – it was surely only an accident – but in
the crush of a particularly full platform Alan had fallen
onto the line right in front of the oncoming commuter
train. He had died instantly.

Both the coroner and, above all, Alan's employers accepted that this had been a tragic accident. The word
'suicide' was never mentioned. Harriet herself never
shed a single tear in public, but young though she was,
as time went on, she never forgave her mother. Never.

Chapter 2

Conrad

Conrad Bridgeman's mother – Olga – was Armenian, born Olga Avakian in Constantinople before the Great War, and hence an Ottoman citizen. She was the second of four lively and well-educated daughters of Karekin Avakian, a highly respected merchant of the city who professed advanced liberal views as to the education of girls. Karekin had been one of the four hundred or so prominent Armenians arrested and deported by the Ittihad government in April 1915 on the day before the landing of the Allied forces in Gallipoli.

Olga had been working as a nurse in the Imperial Ottoman Hospital in Smyrna after the end of the Great War. It was there, in 1922, that she met Harry Bridgeman, a British naval officer, during the terrible and deliberate burning of the Christian quarters of that city by the triumphant Turkish army, as it poured into the city after the defeat of the Greeks. Harry had been in command of one of the British destroyers anchored in the Bay opposite the burning city on that dramatic occasion. Frustrated in his attempt to save some of the burning and drowning citizens, he had returned to the stricken city as a civilian a few days after the British Fleet had returned to Constantinople. He had then personally helped in the evacuation of the quarter million or so largely Greek survivors still lying exhausted and starving on the abandoned quaysides.

Conrad was born to Harry and Olga in 1923 in London shortly after his parents returned to England. His father had been relieved of command of his ship following a court-martial, held to review his actions during the great fire of Smyrna, and had been transfered to work as an Intelligence officer at the Admiralty after his marriage. Unlike his sister Natalie or his young brother Billy, Conrad had straight black hair, very dark – almost black – eyes, and a round face with high cheekbones. He had brooding good looks and had been easily taken as an Italian during his war years, interrogating Italian prisoners-of-war or in Rome working as an Intelligence officer behind enemy lines. This was in contrast to the rest of his family. Olga had the long face, brown eyes and fairish complexion of most Armenians, whilst both Billy and Natalie had their father's blue eyes and fair hair.

Despite his darkly handsome looks, Conrad had a gentle temperment with an enormous capacity for empathy towards the feelings of others. He had a natural ability, often shown by the eldest child, to understand and feel responsibility for those younger and more vulnerable than himself. This character trait was so developed in him, as to sometimes prevent him from taking the firm and decisive action that may have been called for in some situations. His younger brother Billy was always getting into mischief and scrapes of his own making. Conrad was always there to help him out, pick up the pieces and wipe away the inevitable tears that arose in the little boy up to the age of seven and even beyond.

On one occasion Conrad was involved in a situation in which Billy, then well over six, had been caught by an irate stallholder stealing a large and juicy red apple from his cart. The fact that the little boy had been talked into this particular piece of mischief by two other boys older than himself was, of course, no excuse. Conrad, who was around sixteen years-old at the time, had come onto the scene just as Billy was about to be cuffed and possibly even reported to the police. He jumped into the affair without any hesitation, offered the man money and himself took the insults and even two sharp blows after he had stopped the man from striking his little brother. By then Billy, white-faced with fear, but silent until his brother turned up, was now in full flood of tears, clinging onto Conrad's legs as the small crowd that had gathered around argued about the incident. Eventually the situation had calmed down. The stall-holder let go of Billy, took the money Conrad had offered, but insisted on Conrad taking the apple Billy had stolen. His last words, accompanied by a chorus of nods from the small crowd that had gathered, were –

"His father must be told so that he can be properly punished."

Conrad was understandably angry, and had refused to take Billy's hand as they walked away. When Billy eventually stopped crying, and asked tremulously if Conrad was indeed going to tell their father, Conrad relented and said of course not. Throwing the apple away, he finally took Billy's hand as they walked home. One would have thought that the little boy would have been happy to have escaped punishment, but oddly enough he wasn't. He felt his guilt keenly and was actually desperate to be punished, punished physically, and only then forgiven. But Conrad was incapable of taking that course of action.

Conrad had been called up in 1941, immediately after his eighteenth birthday. His father, a professional military man and a Naval Intelligence Officer, had been serving in the Navy since before the first World War. Despite his every effort, he had been unable to persuade his son to join the Senior Service, and Conrad had instead followed in his grandfather's footsteps and chosen the Army. Inevitably, the services still reflected the class-dominated nature of English society, and he had quickly become an officer and had himself chosen the Intelligence service. Already fully fluent in French and Italian due to his family connections, he had had a distinguished military career. He had moved with the Eighth Army through the North African Campaign, successfully interviewing and interrogating captured Italian officers and men, right through the advance up the Italian peninsula. He had been dropped behind enemy lines twice, and had been in Rome throughout the German occupation of that city and until the Allied armies arrived in June 1944. Conrad had by then also acquired a good working knowledge of Arabic.

Conrad had taken the university entrance exams when he was still seventeen, and had secured his place at Oxford before being called up. He had opted to read French and Italian literature and had been accepted at Worcester College. Of course like so many of his generation, his entry as a student had had to be deferred until the end of the war. But he was not destined to be one of the hordes of young, and by now not so young men, ex-soldiers, who poured into the University in 1946 and 1947. He was far too useful to the army in Italy to be demobilised quickly. Stationed in the town of Trieste after the war ended, he was caught up in the earliest stirrings of the Cold War as that city became a bone of contention between the Anglo-Americans, on the one hand, and on the other, Tito's Yugoslav partisans, hovering on the outskirts. At this stage of the confrontation, the defeated Italians had no political clout at all, but as the contours of the Cold War began to take shape, Trieste became an important symbol of the conflict and Italian political influence grew accordingly. Conrad's fluency and natural empathy for ordinary Italians made him very useful to the British administration and he was helpful in dealing with the turbulent conditions that existed in the city.

Meanwhile, as 1946 began to come to an end, the whole British position in the world began to falter. The problems facing the new government in London reached a critical point. India – the ultimate bedrock of British power and influence – was seething and clearly was on the cusp of Independence; the Cold War was becoming more intense and beyond the capacity of the British to deal with it; and then the Palestine mandate erupted. The British Army was stretched to breaking point.

The government had to make a priority somewhere, and, in the event, it had to be Palestine. Indian Independence was assured in any case and the Cold War had to be left to the Americans. Trieste would also have to be resolved between the Americans and the emergent Italians, and so the British pulled out. But what was now vitally needed was a greater Intelligence effort in the escalating situation in Mandate Palestine. Conrad, now a full Captain, was raised in rank to acting Major and told that his demobilisation would have to be deferred for a year once again. Oxford was informed and his entry to the university put back to the Michaelmas term of 1948 – his demobilisation now being fixed for April 1948

Conrad had not been back home or indeed even set foot in England since that moment when he first went to Egypt to join the Intelligence section of the Eighth Army. His contacts with his family had been limited to the exchange of letters. But before leaving Italy to go to the Middle East Conrad arranged a meeting with his father – Harry. Harry had managed to wangle himself a trip to Rome about a year after the end of the war on a low level Naval Intelligence mission. Conrad went to meet him in Rome. Father and son had a memorable four days during which Harry later reckoned he had spent more money in those four days than in a month anywhere else and with anyone else. The Black Market was rife, and, if you had the money, you could certainly live better in Rome or Paris in that winter of 1946/47 than you could in London. It was one of those ironies of life that the restaurants and night spots in the defeated capitals of Rome and Paris were thriving at a level far higher than in the victorious but rationed capital of London.

Of course for those without money, the terrible shortages of food and fuel were much worse in Italy than in England. But Harry took Conrad to all the top restaurants in Rome, paying through the nose for the good food eaten and the excellent wine consumed. For both of them, however, it was not just the good food. Both Harry and Conrad recalled with nostalgia those meals that they had had together before the War at the Art Deco restaurant of the Gare de Lyon on those summer trips to Istanbul. They would leave the train at the Gare du Nord while wife, sister and younger son, wound their weary way on the carriage from Victoria round the 'ceinture' to join the Simplon-Orient Express and Conrad and Harry at the Gare de Lyon. It was a bond with his father that his younger brother Billy had never had.

It was only a week after those memorable four days in Rome that Conrad left Trieste and flew to Cairo to join SIME (Security Intelligence Middle East). This was the title of the department of MI5 currently directing Intelligence work throughout the whole region, including Palestine.

Chapter 3

Billy

Conrad's younger brother, known to everyone as Billy, was born towards the end of 1932. He had blue eyes and fair though not exactly blond hair. He seemed to be perpetually staring with a joyful and naïve wonder at the world around him. His father, Harry, was always very strict with him, and as he often got into trouble of one kind or another, there was frequent punishment involving smacks and the occasional slipper. Administered, as it was, with the certainty of complete love, it was never resented. There would always be tears, of course, even though the smacks given by both parents, were largely nominal. Billy would always run off to Conrad if he could find him. Conrad would always take time off to cuddle him and wipe away his tears and then let him play with anything he wanted in his room. In stark contrast, Harry never once raised his hand to Conrad for deep-seated reasons that only Olga ever understood. However, as a young boy, Conrad was in any case never really in any serious trouble.

Billy took his relationship with Conrad totally for granted. In a sense, it was not just selfishness – after all there had never been a moment in his life when Conrad had not been there. In many ways siblings often have more influence on each other than their parents. So for Billy, Conrad was as much a fixture of his short life as his mother and father. Just as one does not condemn a child for taking his parents for granted – it would not be appropriate to condemn Billy for thinking of his elder brother in the same way. Nevertheless there was a self-centred, if not actually selfish, aspect to Billy's character. He loved his family and like most children he had a possessive love for his mother and wanted her full attention. Where Conrad was cool and clear-thinking from an early age, Billy was all passion and emotional commitment.

Olga tried to cope with his volatile emotions, but no parent can ever always get it quite right. On one occasion, in the late afternoon, curled up on the sofa in the sitting room, she was reading to Billy while he cuddled up to her, snuggling up against her shoulder and looking at the pictures as she read to him. Bliss! Then Conrad bounced in from school – he was fourteen or perhaps fifteen. Some enormous triumph had taken place for him that day – a try scored – a race won – a prize attained –some peer group victory – it didn't matter what it was, and neither Billy nor Olga ever recalled afterwards what it was all about.

Olga, who had already been reading to Billy for over half an hour, immediately put the book aside and got up to admire and share the triumph of her eldest son. On reflection later, she felt she might perhaps have done so a little less abruptly, but in the moment, these things are hard to judge. Billy stared at his mother as she gave his brother a hug – his beloved mother and his beloved brother sharing a love and mutual understanding from which he felt excluded. An entirely irrational and powerful emotion swept over him – abandoned, with the book set aside - still sitting alone on the sofa. At the age of six he simply could not cope with the feelings. Neither Olga nor Conrad, chatting together about whatever the event at school had been, became aware of Billy, fighting back the tears which came to him so easily at that age, as he got up and wandered out of the room.

He ended up in the family's dining-room. As the room was not required for any formal meal that evening, the large Turkish carpet still had all his soldiers lined up for a major battle. In a complete rage, swept by an emotion he neither understood nor could control, he kicked over a whole cohort of blue-trousered zouaves about to charge a line of red-coated infantry. He saw a bowl of oranges on the table, an expensive fruit in those days. There were five in the fine pottery bowl, bright orange and very soft and ripe. One by one he picked them up and, with all the strength he could muster, threw them at the dining-room wall. There they splattered, broke up, and the bright orange juices trickled down the wall.

As the fourth orange crashed against the wall the anger which had overwhelmed him suddenly disappeared. He stood there appalled at the havoc he had created. He began sobbing for the first time and stood with the last orange still in his hand. Hearing the clamour coming from the dining room, Olga and Conrad went there, where Billy was often to be found playing with his armies. For a moment they both stared at the sobbing boy, the stained wall and the flattened oranges. Then, with a bound, Conrad was at Billy's side hugging him, and unconsciously protecting him from what both he and Billy assumed would be Olga's corrective chastisement.

But Olga, though not perhaps the cleverest of women, knew instinctively what had overtaken her younger son. She realised that the 'green-eyed monster' had caught her young son – and that she herself had perhaps been at fault. She waved Conrad away and enveloped the boy in a warm embrace –

"It's all right – it's all right Billy. Don't cry, we all have these strong feelings sometimes – and we all just have to learn to control them."

Great parenting, one would quite correctly say, but oddly enough in the long run it turned out she was mistaken. By this time Billy was feeling deeply guilty. He felt guilty on two counts – on the one hand for the relatively minor matter of his naughtiness in throwing the oranges and staining the wall; on the other, the more serious offence in his eyes, of the terrible feelings he had experienced on seeing his mother and brother in such a close and exclusive relationship. He did not know, nor could he have then understood, the meaning of the word 'jealousy'. All he knew was that this feeling was wrong and that he should be punished for it. He craved punishment, and the punishment he wanted was to be smacked by his mother or slippered by his father later.

Olga did not of course let Billy off entirely. He was made to go and fetch the necessary bits and pieces from the kitchen and required to wash down the wall. Despite Olga's stern reprimand that Billy was to be left on his own to accomplish this task, Conrad came back after she had gone and helped his brother. Within minutes, Billy was his usual cheeky and irrepressible self. But the craving for punishment, whenever he felt that he had done something wrong, remained with him as he grew up.

Chapter 4

Cairo

At the time that Conrad arrived in Cairo, finding accommodation was difficult. Fortunately he found that the personnel staff at SIME had already arranged lodgings for him in a large flat in Heliopolis owned by an Armenian widow of fairly advanced years, though she was loathe to admit it. Conrad wondered whether somewhere in his files there was a reference to his being half Armenian, which had been behind this choice. However, he quickly came to the conclusion that it was simply coincidence – after all there was a large middle class and property owning Armenian community in Cairo, which tended to be concentrated in Heliopolis.

Also living in the flat was the woman's son – a 17-year old young man who had just won a scholarship to go to the United States to study electrical engineering. His place in college was going to be available as soon as he passed his 18th birthday in September 1948. His name was Mardik Levonian, and his mother's name was Sira – short for Siranoush - Levonian.

Mardik's parents, his father Sarkis and his mother Sira, were refugees from Ottoman Anatolia, having survived the horrendous massacres of 1915 as teenagers. During that year, they had been driven out of their respective home towns as a result of the deportation decrees emanating from the Ministry of the Interior in Constantinople. They had drifted into Syria, with countless others in the notorious death marches, where they only just managed to survive the starvation and terrible conditions that caused the death of so many. They had both ended up in Alexandria where they

24

had met and were married. Mardik's father had in due course prospered in the small business he had started and when the war ended, the family had moved out of that city and gone to Cairo. There he had purchased a large flat in Heliopolis. This turned out to have been a good investment. Sarkis had never had good health since living through the privations of deportation as a child. Within a year of the move, Sarkis had died. In order to supplement the family income, Sira had taken to letting a room in the flat.

As a result of the circumstances surrounding his life, Mardik had acquired an amazing number of languages. His parents conversed together in Turkish, which was his father's first language, rather than Armenian – so he spoke Turkish. Educated at the English High School in Alexandria he spoke English fluently; and because French was the language of the elite both in Cairo and Alexandria, he also spoke French. Having been brought up as a child in Alexandria, he could also speak Greek well and Italian indifferently. Finally he spoke Arabic fluently

Conrad was only five years older than Mardik. Nevertheless, due to the war years, he both felt and was considerably more mature. A relationship developed between them in which Conrad took the role of an elder brother. Mardik was full of enthusiasm, his personality bubbling over with joy and energy, keen to learn all about Conrad and his experiences, and to show him in return all the interesting facets of life in Cairo. Conrad had been in Cairo before, when he had first arrived in North Africa as a young lieutenant during the war, but the Cairo of a green young British officer on his first posting in 1941 was quite different to the sophisticated Cairo of the westernised Egyptians, together with the European and Jewish elite, in 1947, six years later.

Mardik learned a lot from his close companionship with Conrad, however it was not a one-way relationship. Conrad too gained much from the friendship.

Sira Levonian was a pious and practising Christian who regularly attended the Armenian church in Heliopolis. Mardik usually accompanied her. Although his belief in Christianity was not as strong as that of his mother, nothing in his education led him to harbour any doubts as to the religious beliefs of his parents and his peers. He attended church services at school, or with his mother, without any great interest in the doctrines and subtleties of the different Christian faiths. So, for instance, during his time as a pupil in the English High School in Alexandria, he would happily attend the Protestant service in the Chapel, routinely ending the Lord's Prayer mouthing the words "for thine is the kingdom the power and the glory for ever and ever amen." It never bothered him, even if he noticed, that when attending with his mother at the Armenian church he ended the same prayer in Armenian with the words "for thine is the kingdom the power and the glory for ever and always, amen".

It was not a question of different translations of the Greek or Aramaic originals. It actually went to the heart of different interpretations of the Trinity – and in the past riots had erupted over and over again in Alexandria on the issue. His mother Sira, though not well educated, would have understood the issue very well, if she had ever thought about it. For her the Trinity had existed 'always' – the Son always being a part of the Father. She could not understand those who believed – or so it seemed – that the Trinity came into existence only after the birth of Christ. Hence the different endings: – on the one hand "for ever and ever (after)", and on the other "for ever and always (i.e. also before)". She was totally unaware of all the other sophisticated arguments that swirled round these and other interpretations of the nature of Christ; nor did she care.

Sira had persuaded Mardik to go with her on a pilgrimage to Jerusalem which she would be undertaking shortly. This was not so much a pilgrimage in the strict meaning of the word as an early version of a 'package tour', but organised by a local church rather than a 'tour operator'. Travel for such a purpose between Egypt and Palestine was still easy.

Conrad was more uncertain than Mardik about his religious beliefs, despite being five years older and having experienced six years of war and turmoil. Unlike his younger brother, Billy, or his mother, he had a natural instinct to do the accepted thing and conform to the mores and beliefs of those around him. On the other hand, he was old enough at the time to remember well the aggressively 'secular' attitude of his Armenian grandfather – Karekin. This was a man who had continually thrown questions and doubts at him, even when he was quite young, during those summer visits Conrad had made with the family before the war to his grandfather's home in Istanbul, insisting he think for himself on these matters. Nor had Conrad had any help or guidance from his own parents. His mother, Olga, had also been heavily influenced by her father, Karekin, but in any case never gave these issues much thought. As a matter of cultural propriety she would attend the beautiful gem of an Armenian church, built in the thirties by Calouste Gulbenkian, situated in a little square behind Derry and Toms in Kensington. She would go there at least once at Christmas, taking Harry and all three children with her, and once at Easter when she took only Billy. But that was all it amounted to.

Harry was no help to his son in this regard either.

He had a simple military attitude to his Maker. He attended Church of England services regularly whilst on active service as a matter of duty and to keep up morale. When back at the Admiralty in a desk job where such attendance was no longer so necessary, he would still go to church with colleagues at Easter and for the occasional commemorative services, but only because he viewed God in much the same way as a commanding officer, who had to be saluted from time to time. He attended the occasional Armenian service with Olga, largely because he loved the music and the Kensington church choir was excellent. However, he had little idea what were the doctrinal differences that separated the two churches, nor could he care less.

Harry was not simply a philistine on these issues, and this description should not imply a cynical belittlement of his character; he simply had a lack of interest in religious matters. He had never been required to question the way he had been brought up. Like Conrad, and unlike Billy and Olga, he too always tended to want to conform with his peer group – subject however always to his strong sense of what was morally right or wrong. So at school – if everyone in his year became confirmed and went to communion, he did too. But if everyone in his year accepted the bullying of the younger boys, he did not, and on such matters he was willing to stand out from the crowd, even to the point of a fight. Harry saluted the God that all of his peers seemed to accept, but was clear in his own mind that he would not press his beliefs on to his sons or anyone else.

So it was that Conrad had been left to work these things out for himself. Despite all his instincts to conform, the memory of Karekin's forceful logical positivism always interfered. It was interesting that even though both he and Mardik were seeking to work out their respective attitudes to the religious debates swirling around them, this was the one subject which they only hardly touched on in their long conversations together despite dissecting everything else. Conrad had enough of his mother's talkative family background to make questioning discussions and argument a principal part of his character, whilst Mardik, already full of enthusiasm, was at an age where he was quite capable of going on about anything.

Talking together one day after he had returned from another day's work at the department, Conrad said –

"How wonderful Mardik to have such a fluency in so many languages."

"Oh no – oh no – I'm not like you. You not only speak French, Italian and English like a native, but you read in those languages and have a complete command. Me – I have no mother tongue at all. Turkish? I've almost forgotten it. English is I suppose the nearest, but I didn't speak it at all before I was ten year's old."

"What language do you think in?"

"Think in – think in. God, now you ask me I don't know. I add up and do all my arithmetical calculations in Turkish – I know that for sure. Apart from that I think that I think in English....Hey that's funny ... I think that I think ... Conrad, isn't that like Descartes or something?"

"Mardik concentrate! It's actually quite interesting. Tell me what nationality – no what identity – do you consider you have?"

"Identity, what are you talking about Conrad? I am an Egyptian citizen – I have an Egyptian passport – is that what you mean? Perhaps you are referring to cultural identity. If so, then having been brought up in an English High School that might make me English. Or are you talking about 'race'. That makes me an Armenian I suppose, though Armenian is the language I know the least – just a few childish words imbibed from my mother. I still remember – "lumentsa, lumentsa" – meaning "I'm finished. I'm finished", which I would shout out to my mother when I was two years old after sitting on the potty. Furthermore, I would like to add that …."

"Stop talking just for a minute Mardik and calm down. Look I take the question back – you are uniquely you and that is your identity. Who cares about anything else"

Conrad and Mardik had conversations like this about language and race and identity over many weeks of intense and satisfactory companionship in the evenings after Conrad returned from work. In almost every case Conrad would end up taking the view that it didn't matter – everyone had a unique identity and no one facet was more important than any other, so in the end it was of little importance. Mardik was uniquely Mardik and it was unnecessary, immaterial, indeed even positively dangerous, to insist on categorising him in some group – racial – national – or religious.

But Conrad was about to move to his new posting in Palestine, where he would find that a man's identity would be reduced to its most basic single factor – and that factor would be so important as to be a matter of life or death.

Chapter 5

Palestine – the British administration

Conrad arrived in Haifa early in July 1947 and reported for duty with the Army Intelligence unit. He was one of the most senior officers operating directly in the field and was given a roving commission, with the major task of keeping watch on the activities of the three Jewish military organisations currently operating in Palestine. He was to report directly to Sir Henry Gurney, who as the Chief Secretary was, in effect, the head of the British Administration in the country. He was given a permanent base in Jerusalem, messing with one or another of the two regular army regiments currently posted there, although it was understood that he would be free to roam the whole country as he thought necessary. For that purpose, he had the use of a jeep with all British markings removed, together with a local Palestinian driver. At the time of his arrival, the British administration indiscriminately utilised the services of all the communities living in Palestine.

The situation he faced was that the Zionist movement had, by then, thrown up three military organisations in Palestine. The Haganah, by far the largest, was the main Jewish military force. They operated throughout the whole country, and, as an established force, were close to, and cooperated intimately with, the Jewish Agency leaders in Tel Aviv. The Haganah, highly motivated and superbly well led, dedicated to the protection of all Jews in the country, became in due course the army of the new Jewish state, to be known as the IDF – the Israeli Defence Force.

There were however two further organisations – the

Irgun Zvai Leumi, which was a classic terrorist organisation numbering at this time little more than three thousand members – and a small even more fanatical off-
shoot of the Irgun known as the Stern Gang, amounting
to scarcely more than three hundred. These two groups,
with an influence far in excess of their numbers, were
impatient with what appeared to them to be the slow
progress towards 'Eretz Israel'. They both wanted more
direct action against the British authority, though only
as soon as that authority had won the war against Germany.

Up to that time, the most notorious exploit of the
Irgun had been the bombing of the King David Hotel
in Jerusalem, which was the headquarters of the British
administration. Ninety-one people – Britons, Arabs and
Jews – had been murdered and dozens more wounded. Body parts were splattered all over the surrounding
streets. Many in the Yishuv (the Jewish community in
Palestine) condemned this terrorist outrage, but then,
as now, one man's 'terrorist' was another man's 'freedom fighter'. What the action did do, however, was to
force London's attention onto the growing crisis in the
Mandate, where almost 100,000 British troops and personnel were involved. Mountbatten was already in India preparing for independence, and it was clear that
some of the British troops there were going to have to
remain for some time as partition loomed. At the same
time the Cold War was intensifying and that too needed
the military's attention. But it was not just a matter of
being physically and financially unable to keep up the
inherited power of Empire. The public will of the British people for imperial grandeur had also gone. The
new Labour government was not interested in expend-
ing yet more working-class lives in what both it, and
now the British public thought of as unnecessary Impe-

rial prestige projects. There had to be some reduction of British commitments around the globe.

By the time Conrad had arrived in Haifa and then moved on to Jerusalem, British Foreign Secretary Bevin and Prime Minister Attlee had already decided that the Mandate issue was no longer a British priority and should be wound up. Bevin, brought up in the hard-headed atmosphere of trade union negotiations, took a clear and unbiased look at the situation in Palestine. He was not concerned with romantic notions of history, only with what was the best interests of Great Britain. He was quite clear that Great Britain had to extricate itself from the contradictory promises lavishly offered to all and sundry during the Great War. Palestine had become only one of many problems that were pressing on a country enduring a particularly impoverished and miserable winter. The government made one final attempt to suggest a solution to the Palestine dilemma, but once this was soundly rejected by both sides, they decided that the whole problem should be put back into the lap of the new United Nations, as the successor organisation to the League of Nations, which had created the Mandate in the first place.

However, even on the brink of winding up their Empire, Great Britain was not a Belgium. There would be nothing like the undignified rush out of the Congo. There was to be no question of scuttling and departing overnight from their responsibility. Palestine was a potential humanitarian calamity in the making and the British Empire had to do its best to minimise the impending tragedy. The Administration had to continue functioning as best it could in order to minimise the cost to the ordinary people. So it was in this context that Conrad did his job, traveling the country, sending back his reports and watching and reporting as the

Haganah became stronger and stronger. He also documented how the Palestinians, abominably badly led by the grand Mufti of Jerusalem – Haj Amin al Husseini, a British creation of the thirties – became weaker and weaker despite their numbers. It was Conrad's reports, and those of his few colleagues, which soon showed the British that in any future conflict the IDF were certain to prevail over the hopelessly ill-prepared and disunited Palestinians.

Bevin may have been right in his clinical analysis of the situation in which he considered the Balfour Declaration to have been the single biggest mistake of any British Foreign Secretary in the last hundred years, as did his officials in the Foreign Office, but this analysis did not necessarily apply to the men on the spot in Palestine. As the United Nations deliberated, London and Jerusalem drifted slowly apart. Sir Henry Gurney, the Chief Secretary, the official head of the Jerusalem Administration, trying hard to keep the two warring communities apart, was convinced that the UN would do nothing but talk and would be quite unable to impose any solution on the country. His argument was straightforward; that if the British with all their experience and with 100,000 troops available were unable to impose their will on the two communities, how could a few well meaning negotiators from UN succeed. But it was not only the hard-working administrators; the political appointees too could not agree with London's view. Sir Alan Cunningham, the High Commissioner, was sympathetic to the Jewish ideal of a sovereign state, and he and others like him could not understand the increasingly pro-Arab stance of Bevin and the London Foreign Office.

What about Conrad?

Well Conrad, like so many British officers caught up

in the whole Mandate situation, simply wanted to do his job well. As he saw it – and as most of his colleagues saw it – the job was to make sure that the lives of as many of the ordinary people of both communities was as safe as possible. By patrolling, by intervening between the two sides, sometimes dangerously, their aim was to keep the military wings of the two communities as far apart as possible. Conrad's natural instincts, when he first arrived, was to favour the Jewish position. The ghastly revelations about the Holocaust were just coming out, and, in his family, his own Aunt, together with her adopted Jewish son, had disappeared in the maelstrom of Auschwitz during the war. How could he not be sympathetic? But this had to be moderated as he met and intervened to protect Palestinians in villages targeted for strategic reasons by the Haganah.

Conrad was not directly involved in the army patrols regularly sent out from the British camps to protect one community or the other from raids or reprisals. As Jerusalem itself progressively became the focus of the conflict between the two communities, the Palestinian leaders began trying to close down the road between Jerusalem and Tel Aviv. As a reaction to this, the Haganah took to mounting large protected convoys to force their way through to the beleaguered city. Increasingly, they called on the British authorities to honour their obligation to keep the roads of Palestine open to all legitimate movement. So it was that Army patrols regularly had to go out to rescue Jewish Agency convoys ambushed in the hills around Latrun as they slowly wound their way up from the coastal plain. Many British soldiers lost their lives in the struggle to keep the road open. They were of course condemned by both sides – the Arabs because they had at last hit on a workable strategy for isolating Jerusalem and resented the British attempts to prevent this – the Jews because they would not accept that the Mandate administration was trying to do its best to help the convoys get through.

This is not to suggest that as the Empire tottered to its inevitable end, the British in Palestine were squeaky clean. In an essay published only the year before, George Orwell wrote, "The nationalist not only does not disapprove of atrocities committed by his own side, but he has a quite remarkable capacity for not even hearing about them."

There were of course several instances of rogue sergeants and bent officers in the British army selling off military equipment on the side to both communities. No doubt there might well also have been some heavy-handedness at police stations affecting and harming over-enthusiastic young men on both sides. But on the whole, the senior officials of the administration, both civil and military, were doing their best to maintain a balance in an impossibly difficult situation.

Then, in the midst of all the growing turmoil and violence, about four months after Conrad's arrival, the General Assembly of the UN voted on the 29th November 1947 to endorse the Partition Plan.

The British abstained in the final vote. London considered that the plan was completely unworkable in its first state and made it clear that British armed forces on the spot would not be used to impose the UN plan by force. Almost no one in the United Nations believed or wanted to believe the constant British assertions that British troops would not be available to enforce the partition plan. The Attlee government, despairing of ever persuading the organisation to face reality, then dropped its bombshell, declaring that the British Mandate would end and all British forces would be evacuated by the 14th May of the next year.

Chapter 6

Easter 1948

Early in March, three months before the date of the proposed British evacuation, Sira and Mardik arrived in Jerusalem with a group of Christians on a tour sponsored by their local church in Cairo. They stayed in the great Armenian monastery in the Armenian quarter of the old city. Conrad was in Jerusalem messing with the Highland Light Infantry, and Mardik had no difficulty in getting in touch with him. By now, all the British officials remaining in Jerusalem, and indeed throughout the country, were in an increasingly impossible situation. The fighting, the daily gunfire and the violence in and around Jerusalem became more and more fierce, and the British officials were living more or less under 'siege'. The problem was that as the date for the end of the Mandate approached, and the evacuation of soldiers and civilian administrators continued, there were fewer troops left to maintain law and order.

Conrad renewed his contact with the Levonians with great eagerness. Mardik was not interested in attending at all the interminable Church services over Easter with his mother and suggested to Conrad that they take a trip together somewhere. Conrad was enthusiastic and approached the Chief Secretary – mentioning that he had had no leave since his arrival. He was given three full days over Easter on condition that he did not take his holiday in Palestine itself.

It might appear odd for Conrad to have been granted leave, however short, considering the prevailing turmoil. However, amidst all the violence and insecurity, the British administration had managed to continue to provide a modicum of reassurance to ordinary people only through the exercise of enormous self-control and restraint. This attitude was typified by the Chief Secretary, Sir Henry Gurney. He felt that everything had to be continued – golf played – tennis enjoyed – afternoon tea served – in a cool and calm manner; otherwise nothing would have been done at all. In hindsight, this was indeed probably the only way that ordinary law and order could have existed at all. But to all the combatants, it looked like typical British arrogance. It was this attempt to maintain as calm an external atmosphere as possible that allowed Gurney to give Conrad a few days off. His unshakeable equanimity, in the face of the most terrible incidents, occuring all around him, infuriated both sides. Mrs Golda Meir of the Jewish Agency remarked when referring to Gurney that his very composure was the reason she hated him so much. No one in that position had any right to remain so unruffled, she said. On the other side of the community divide, the Grand Mufti had even ruder comments. Yet Gurney was not unfeeling – he was simply not prepared to 'flap' or to allow his subordinates to panic. When some particularly bloody incident in Jerusalem was reported to him, his first comment was to thank the reporter for keeping him informed; his next was to express sorrow at the loss of life; his final question was to ask if there was anything that he himself could usefully do right away. If there was he would do it – but if not he would immediately turn his attention to something else, even if that was only to write an encouraging letter to an injured subordinate who had been sent to hospital.

Conrad took his three days leave and went off with Mardik to Transjordan. He took his own jeep, which had no military markings and which he had been using for the past seven months. The weather in Jerusalem had been wet and cheerless and, indeed, on the 16th March, it had snowed heavily. However by the 26th, ten days later, the snow had cleared and the weather was glorious. Unfortunately, the improvement in the weather meant that all the snipers and 'freedom fighters' on both sides came out of their cosy homes and night after night started taking pot-shots at each other.

Driving down past Jericho, Conrad and Mardik crossed the Allenby bridge and then drove off the road to take the traditional swim in the Dead Sea, though without the customary newspaper to read while floating on your back. Ten miles before reaching Amman they turned off and drove to have a look at the ruins of Jerash. They wandered down the main paved street with the colonnades in ruins on either side. This led to two theatres where even the numbers on the stone seats were still visible. Mardik ran down and, standing in the centre of the stage, declaimed Mark Antony's speech from 'Julius Caesar' without faltering once through the first ten lines – but then Conrad called out –

"Stop shouting Mardik – let's test the acoustics properly – just whisper."

But Mardik who had now remembered the rest of the lines went on declaiming. The two of them wandered on. There was a quiet sense of historical continuity in the calm and peace of the afternoon. The Ottoman Empire had ruled over these lands for five hundred years and it looked as if nothing had changed in all that time.

They stretched out on the warm stones of the empty ruins and began a desultory and lazy conversation. As it was Easter, their discourse turned at last to their religious inheritance. Both of them were, by their cultural backgrounds, Christians, and this holiday was a reflection of that fact. Mardik was Armenian and Conrad half Armenian, so their first thought, once they had ascertained that they did both believe in God, was to try to decide what they each thought or had been taught to them about the nature of Jesus Christ, whose death and resurrection was being celebrated here at the same spot where it had occurred two thousand years ago.

This was a subject on which Mardik was a good deal more knowledgeable than Conrad, and as the evening shadows lengthened, he started lecturing his friend –

"The question my dear Conrad is this. If Christ was the son of God by a human woman – was he human or divine – or in some way a mixture of both. In Greek mythology and in the Norse Sagas the children of Zeus and Wotan from human women were always clearly human. There was a lot of dispute about this, from the Nestorians, on the one side, who stressed Christ's human nature, to the Monophysites, on the other, who believed that Christ had only one nature, and that nature was essentially divine."

"Well that is all very interesting, Mardik, but does anyone care today – and anyway how was the issue decided?"

"Two questions! The answer to the first is that to be a Christian, even today, you cannot just live a good life and do good works, you must believe that Christ was – is – the son of God. The issue was decided or they attempted to decide it by a great Church Council held under the auspices of the Byzantine Emperor in Chalcedon in – oh I can't remember – four hundred and something. There it was decided that Christ had two natures, one divine and one human, both perfect God and perfect Man – but all in one single nature. The Armenian Church did not accept this entirely in the way the formula was put and ended up somewhere in between – denying always as they did so, and as they still do – that they were in any way Monophysite."

"You know Mardik, I vaguely remember all this stuff. My Grandpa used to say that due to brigands on the road, or some other equally unlikely excuse, the Armenian delegation to the council arrived late, after the Council had already decided and produced it's formula. The Armenian priests, annoyed that the Council had not waited for them, sulked and refused to accept the formula agreed by all but the incorrigible Mono-whatevers, though they did agree to condemn the pure Mono point of view. But then my Grandpa was a complete cynic when it came to clerics and religion – always trying to prevent me from meekly accepting any beliefs without first…"

"What do you mean?"

"Well, if I ever made even the mildest statement of any faith or belief, he would jump on me and insist on my stating exactly what I meant. As a result, I would often end up confused. Billy was only seven and he never got quite the same treatment. But that was not simply because of his age – Grandpa never took the slightest notice of how old children were once he was holding forth. No – it was because Billy never came out with conforming ideas like I did. Grandpa only jumped on people who repeated things without thinking them out for themselves."

By now, Mardik was already losing interest. It was still warm and the conversation – or more to the point, their individual monologues – were slowly petering out. He asked –

"Is your grandfather still alive?"

"No he died during the war," said Conrad as they dozed and said nothing more.

After a night in a somewhat decrepit hotel in Amman, they took a track down south along the top of the undulating plateau known as the Mountains of Moab.

Every square inch of the land of Palestine was contested and a source of permanent friction between two peoples – but here, the countryside, though covered with green crops, was virtually uninhabited. Skirting Madaba, they took a rough track and eventually halted on Mount Nabo. They had a picnic and spent the rest of the afternoon lying on the ground, dreaming and chatting in the hot sun, as they looked at the fine view across the other side of the Dead Sea to the mountains of Judaea. This was the spot where Moses was supposed to have stood and beheld his only sight of the 'Promised Land'.

The only disturbance was the arrival of two little Arab boys – God knows where they came from as there appeared to be no village for miles. They stood and stared at the strangers and were much taken aback when both Mardik and Conrad greeted them – Mardik in excellent upper-class Egyptian Arabic and Conrad in the much rougher Palestinian vernacular.

"For heaven's sake, Conrad, look at those blue eyes and fair hair – how come?"

"This is a part of the world into which came the Greeks, the Romans, Crusaders, Desert Arabs, the Turks – just about everybody, even Australians and Cockneys."

The two little boys gave no answer to the attempts by the two young men to be friendly, but simply squatted down beside them, played with some stones and started chatting amiably to each other, as if they all formed a group of four male friends. It was neither disconcerting nor embarrassing, and in the midst of the quiet and desolate splendour, as all four stared at the Judaean hills in the distance, it seemed completely natural. Mardik and Conrad continued their interminable discussions about identity, adding speculation about the identity of the two boys to their conversation. Did it matter whether they were Moslem or Christian? Did it really even matter whether they were Arabs at all?

Unfortunately this was Palestine in 1948 and it mattered a lot. They dozed and were not even aware when the two boys quietly left them.

After another night in Amman they returned driving slowly back across the Allenby bridge and arrived back in Jerusalem in the early evening. Shooting had already commenced and although both Jews and Arabs tended to avoid British vehicles, an unmarked jeep with two civilians attracted some shots, which came perilously near, as Conrad dropped Mardik at the entrance to the great Armenian monastery on the edge of the Armenian quarter. Conrad drove on alone to Bevingrad – the ironic name given to the main Security Zone of the British in Jerusalem, where the whole administration was now centred.

Chapter 7

Zipora

South of Jerusalem, close to the main road between Hebron and the City, lay a Jewish settlement called Kfar Etzion. This had been growing since the end of the war in 1945 and had become a thriving kibbutz. It was manned by a mixture of hardy young settlers who had come from a large kibbutz near Galilee at the request of the Jewish Agency leaders, together with some emaciated survivors from the Nazi death camps. The settlers had worked hard at the back-breaking task of clearing the poor soil, stone by stone, and planting fruit trees and vines. Water was scarce and they would often go short themselves in order to help their precious crops thrive.

The position of the settlement was of strategic value to the Jewish leaders in Tel Aviv as it formed a sort of bastion for the southern part of Jerusalem, preventing any direct assault from the south. Since the massacre of some helpless religious scholars during the Arab uprising of 1929, the last few remaining Jews in Hebron had finally left, and Hebron was now firmly within the Arab sector. Nevertheless, the Jewish Agency was anxious to keep Kfar Etzion alive as a Jewish enclave, even though it was surrounded by a sea of Arabs.

In the developing drama of keeping the roads of Palestine open for all legitimate traffic, Gurney was particularly concerned about this settlement. In the UN partition plan the whole of this area had been designated as part of the Arab sector. So, while the rest of the Yishuv celebrated in a riot of joy on that 29th November 1947, the settlers at Kfar Etzion were gloomy. The high command of the Haganah in Jerusalem advised the leaders in Tel Aviv that this settlement should be abandoned, as supplying it would be enormously difficult and costly. But Ben-Gurion insisted on sticking closely to his basic policy – that no Jews should voluntarily give up anything which they already actually held in Palestine. He was particularly adamant that this should apply to all the Jews in and around Jerusalem – both those in the new city and those who lived in the Jewish Quarter of the old city.

In the four months immediately following the UN declaration, Gurney had asked Conrad, who was now stationed permanently in Jerusalem, to keep a special eye on what he considered were the two danger spots. One of these included the Palestinian villages in and around the Bab el Wad defile on the road leading up to Jerusalem from Tel Aviv. The other was the situation in and around Kfar Etzion on the road leading from Hebron to the city. Conrad agreed with the Chief Secretary's assessment and now spent most of his time patrolling back and forth in these areas.

Conrad never used a disguise, but on most trips his jeep remained unmarked and was driven by a Palestinian. He himself wore a khaki shirt and shorts, but with no indication of rank. He never denied that he was a British officer in the service of the Mandate administration, neither in the Palestinian villages nor in Kfar Etzion. He managed to make and develop good relations with many families and their elders in the Palestinian villages that he visited on the road between Tel Aviv and Jerusalem. He was thus able to send back valuable information about general plans and pervading atmosphere, which was of great value to the British patrols in their attempt to keep the road open.

Trying the same 'charm' tactics amongst the settlers

of Kfar Etzion did not work quite so well. The original settlers, leavened by survivors from the European holocaust, struggled hard in very difficult conditions. The settlement was fairly bleak and during the winter of 1947/48, whenever Conrad arrived in his jeep, there was always a cutting wind that howled round the three settlements, and on a couple of occasions, even snow. Even though the majority of the settlers were orthodox, the Irgun had been active and had managed to convert at least two of the young settlers as active members. They kept a low profile but reported back to their leaders. Conrad had no idea of this, which was not surprising, as most of the settlers had no knowledge of this either.

The whole settlement was aware of Conrad's interest and of his position in the administration, but as his task clearly was to make sure that any threats to close the road were immediately reported back to Jerusalem, they contrived not to antagonise him, and to give him as much information as they thought appropriate. Just as they knew that he was a British officer working for the Mandate administration, this was also well known to the Irgun, who instructed one of their committed operatives to try and get as much information as possible about this officer and his orders.

Conrad had a deep admiration for the dedication and hard work of these settlers. The young men and women drove themselves hard, and the old men, the recently arrived survivors of the European holocaust, did their best. But he never experienced quite the same friendliness and hospitality that he found in the Palestinian villages. It was therefore with some surprise that one day, whilst he was enjoying a coffee outside the house of one of the leaders of the kibbutz, he was approached by a long-legged girl, who was introduced by Conrad's host as Zipora and, without any show of formality, sat down next to the two men. Despite the cold weather, she was dressed simply in a shirt and shorts. It was early in the afternoon and, out of the blue, she invited Conrad to come to the house she shared with her brother. Conrad, always seeking to make personal contacts with citizens on both sides, finished his coffee, thanked his host, rose and strolled down with Zipora to her house. This settlement was not the sophisticated socialist kibbutzim of a later generation; there were no communal buildings; the settlers lived in small one or two-room stone houses. Short of money while their crops were still developing, they would often let their houses in the summer to Jerusalemites seeking a week or two in the countryside, when they would repair to tents alongside their fields.

Zipora was twenty-three, a few years younger than Conrad. She had long black hair always tied up in a bun whenever she was out of the house. Her features were sharp with an aquiline nose and dark black smouldering eyes which matched Conrad's. On this first occasion, her brother, two years younger than her, was present. Surprisingly, he had fairish hair and his eyes were grey, but he had a pleasant, gentle, rather shy smile. Conrad warmed to him immediately and exercised all the charm he could muster, pleased that at last he had broken through to a Jewish family. He promised to return the next time he was in Kfar Etzion and in fact he returned two days later, and visits then became regular. Zipora had a fierce certainty of the righteousness of the Jewish cause and argued passionately with Conrad on each occasion during his increasingly frequent visits. On all his excursions, both to the Palestinian villages along the Bab El Wad defile or to Jewish settlements, Conrad took care to bring a little something with him from the city – a bottle of brandy or arak – some fresh fruit – chocolate. But now, as the days passed, he began bringing presents directly for Zipora as well – stockings – a book – some fresh flowers.

As their friendship developed, Conrad suspected that her original motivation in approaching him was the result of some sort of direction, but he assumed that this would have emanated directly from the Jewish Agency in Tel Aviv, or that she was attached in some way to the Haganah, or even that she was just acting for the settlement leaders directly. He did not know, and never tried to find out, what might have given rise to that first meeting. In fact Zipora had indeed been approached by an operative of the group known as the Irgun, whose request she could not refuse. Conrad never found out who that Irgun member was until many weeks later on the fateful 9th April. In any event, it almost certainly would have made no difference to their developing relationship even if he had known. At the time, for the average British officer, the Irgun was simply a terrorist organisation and nothing more. But in Conrad's case, his professional instincts as an intelligence officer would have been aroused. Zipora was not herself a member of the Irgun, nor did she know that the person who had approached her, asking her to make a friend of the British officer, had any connection with that group.

Neither Conrad nor Zipora were ever in love. But while it was true that Zipora had indeed been asked to cultivate the friendship of this officer, there was nothing sinister behind the request. She had not been asked or required to seduce him, just to befriend him and seek his confidence in case it might be useful in the future. On the other side, Conrad, physically attracted to the young girl in a perfectly normal way, simply wanted to get closer to a Jewish family for purely professional reasons.

But what started as a mutually convenient friendship very quickly developed into something more. Conrad was good-looking and had an abundance of natural charm, whilst Zipora with her shapely long legs and revealing shorts was a sexual bombshell.

Conrad was not a virgin, having had sex with women during his years in the army, both in North Africa and in Italy. But until now, he had not had any long-term relationship with a girl of any significant duration. He had a natural reserve which prevented him from having anything approaching an 'affair' with any girl of his own class and educational background. As soon as serious discussion arose between him and any girlfriend, his highly developed empathy for her feelings and insecurities prevented him from making any decisive advances. But Zipora turned out to be different. Uninhibited, practical and strong-willed, she had no patience with Conrad's initial diffidence and reserve. Requested to develop a friendship, her own sexuality was soon aroused on an entirely physical plane by Conrad's body as well as his charm.

Within two weeks of their first meeting, they were in bed together at every subsequent visit. Conrad was overwhelmed with the sheer exuberance of his first sexual encounter which was more than just a one-night stand. He noted that the girl's younger brother, whom he had liked on their first encounter, never seemed to be around when he and Zipora took off each other's clothes. There was never any interruption during those afternoons when they were together, and this lodged in that part of his mind which remained a professional intelligence officer. Zipora made no attempt to chat about the British dispositions in Jerusalem or about the plans for the coming evacuation. The whole relationship was lightweight with neither party displaying any desire to make more of it than a shared sympathy and a mutual wish for physical release. With six years experience of discretion, Conrad had no difficulty in avoiding anything controversial.

Their coupling was mutually satisfying and convenient, but neither of them were in love. Their mating was more like a battle. Zipora liked unusual positions and more often than not wanted to be on top, which Conrad felt was his prerogative. Coupled together, they often struggled and panted at each other, sometimes falling off the bed in their exertions. Meanwhile, as the days passed, all Conrad's trips, not only those to Kfar Etzion, became more and more subject to sniper fire – inaccurate but sometimes close. Eventually, by the end of January, Conrad had to start sporting the British flag on the jeep, and he himself began wearing the regulation cap with his rank on his sleeve.

Zipora had lost both her parents in her early teens. At just 16, she had been left on her own to look after her younger brother Benjamin, who was only just over twelve. The genetic make-up of brother and sister seemed to have become mixed up. Zipora was strong, forceful, sure of herself and her opinions. Benjamin on the other hand was much frailer physically, devastated by the death of his parents at such a tender age in a pointless motoring accident, and highly dependent on his sister. He was now 21 and appeared to be still dominated by her. If anyone in this triangle was in love, it was Benjamin, and the love that he felt for his sister was both immoral and illegal, and he knew it. He carefully kept away whenever Conrad came visiting, but he was jealous – furthermore it was straight sexual jealousy. If he had decided to meet Conrad on equal terms, both of them could have gained by it. Conrad's strongest attribute – empathy – would have ensured he understood and warmed to Benjamin's vulnerability. He might have been able to give him the support and male camaraderie, which perhaps could have dissuaded him from continuing on the unfortunate course he was taking. But one way or another it was not to be. Zipora, for all her sexual passion, had never had more than maternal feelings for her younger brother, and was quite unaware of his sexual fantasies in which she figured so prominently.

Aware that Kfar Etzion had a military value to the Jewish Agency, the local Arabs began attacking it. Not being successful in direct assaults, they began ambushing vehicles travelling along the road to the colony, with a view to disrupting supplies to the settlement. As January turned to February, Conrad reported back to Gurney that the settlement was now virtually in a state of siege and that civilians living there were in real danger. Gurney arranged for the High Commissioner to contact the Haganah commander in Jerusalem – David Shaltiel – with this assessment. Shaltiel had already reported to Tel Aviv that he wanted to evacuate the entire colony, but Tel Aviv remained adamant that there were to be no evacuations. They did, however, agree that under British protection women and young children could leave. When Shaltiel contacted the British in respect of this suggestion, Gurney approached Conrad for his advice and Conrad reported that, on condition it was clearly a British operation and not a Jewish one, there would be no danger in bringing them out.

It was the Suffolks who mounted the operation with Conrad going along with them. The British flag was much in evidence and Conrad had already passed his assurances to his contacts amongst the Palestinians that there would be no reinforcement of arms or munitions in this convoy. On arrival at the settlement, as the British convoy slowly filled up with women and children under the age of fourteen, Conrad strolled down to see Zipora and tried to persuade her to leave with the others. They then had a conversation which they should perhaps have had long ago in their relationship. Conrad started by saying –

"My dear Zipora almost all the women are leaving. This may be your last chance to get out safely. After all if the Partition plan is implemented after we leave, this area is going to be part of an Arab state."

"Look Conrad, there is no way Benjamin can or should leave, and I am not going to abandon him."

"Where is he by the way – I only rarely see him these days?"

"I don't…."

"Zip., my love, you are going to have to let him make his own way in life sooner or later, and this must surely be a good moment to do so."

"You don't know what you are talking about. He is much tougher than he appears, but nevertheless I won't leave him…."

"My dear I understand that you feel 'parental' towards him – but even a parent learns to let go, particularly in respect of a boy."

"Rubbish – that's so old-fashioned and sexist. Why should a boy need to be 'let go' as you put it whilst a girl doesn't."

"Fine, fine, calm down. I take back the gender part of what I just said – but boy or girl they both have to be allowed their wings to flee the nest. Ah well, never mind, you obviously know him best. But just listen Zipora, you must understand that with all the sniping and ambushes getting worse every day, this is likely to be the last visit I can make. I understand your decision to remain, but I will miss you – I mean it – I really mean it."

"Oh Conrad – I know – I know – but neither of us

have come to be dependent on the other have we? So see – no harm has been done and we can still part friends, can't we?"

As she said this she leant forward, as the convoy cars began hooting to signal their imminent departure, and Conrad clambered in to his jeep. Then with a wry smile Zipora nodded and looking straight into Conrad's eyes, as black as hers, they kissed and parted, both knowing that it was unlikely they would ever meet again.

Chapter 8

Supplying Kfar Etzion

As the month of February gave way to a rather cold and cheerless March, the supply situation in Kfar Etzion became critical. There was constant sniper fire and haphazard assaults from the surrounding Arab fighters, all of which were fairly easily beaten off. But if supplies could not get through, the settlement was ultimately doomed. Tel Aviv was bullish and decreed that the settlement had to be supplied. The argument was that they only needed three months supplies as once the mandate ended on the 15th May, everything was in the melting pot – anything could happen – and having this military outpost in the hills south of Jerusalem would be of inestimable value. The leaders of the Jerusalem Haganah were not so sure. It would take all the transport that they had available to move the 200 tons of supplies that were needed. It would require at least 60 large trucks in convoy, protected by over 20 armoured cars. Shaltiel reported that it was too much. The Haganah would be left with virtually no transport at all if things went wrong. After speaking to Gurney's aide, he got in touch with Tel Aviv again reiterating that the settlement could be evacuated under British protection. He pointed out that this would also have the effect of reinforcing the Jewish force available in Jerusalem itself. But Tel Aviv refused. A supply convoy had to be attempted by the Jerusalem Haganah and the British were not to be informed, or involved in any way.

The convoy, now consisting of 65 trucks and 25 armoured cars, gathered in the morning of Saturday the 27th March – Easter Saturday. The idea was to leave at 6.00am in the morning in the hope that this being on a Saturday – the Sabbath – the Arabs would not be expecting any action and would not be prepared to oppose the expedition. But as the motors revved up, there were still several trucks to be loaded and the enormous long convoy did not get started until past eight. Meanwhile the noise of the revving engines woke up half the city – but did not alert the British in Bevingrad, who remained unaware of what was happening. Conrad would undoubtedly have learnt what was being proposed through his contacts and would have warned Gurney, but he was still holidaying in the mountains of Moab, so was not involved in any of what occurred.

The idea was to take the convoy down the road as fast as possible; unload all the supplies and race back, all before the locals could react. Clearly speed was of the essence. The convoy did safely reach the settlement within the two hours allotted, but then, instead of taking the half hour prearranged to unload and begin the return journey, it took over two hours. By that time, the local Palestinian villagers had been fully alerted and were converging onto the road in their hundreds, indeed almost thousands. Fathers fought with their sons to grab the old family rifle to have the honour of going down to the coming battle. Acting instinctively and without leadership, they all ran to the narrower and more vulnerable parts of the road leading back to Jerusalem from the settlement. Rocks and stones were thrown onto the road in several places. By now, the British authorities were also alerted and after getting the full information of what was going on, Gurney warned the Haganah commander that the convoy should now remain in the settlement until the Administration could do something about getting it back. Shaltiel, knowing what Tel Aviv would say, refused the offer and frantically continued urging the convoy over the radio to get moving.

There were two reasons why the convoy was taking so long to set out on its way back to Jerusalem. The first was that the leaders of the settlement had decided, regardless of what Tel Aviv thought, that one way or another, the settlement was probably doomed in the long run. That being so, they were determined that their prize bull – famed throughout Southern Palestine - should be saved and should be evacuated. The bull was already waiting patiently by the side of the road as the long convoy came in. The unloading was completed in the half hour allotted in the plan. But then disaster struck – the bull refused to clamber up the wooden ramp and onto the lorry chosen for his departure. Pushing and pulling, swearing and kicking at the stubborn animal, the settlers could not get it to budge. They tried advancing a willing cow to go ahead but the bull would not follow, they tried shouting, they tried prods - and whips – and even prayers, but the bull stayed put.

Meanwhile to make matters worse, the same leaders of the settlement had also decided that every woman left in the camp should also now leave and return to Jerusalem. However as stubborn as the bull, the four women left in Kfar Etzion, one of whom was Zipora, also refused to budge. The cacaphony was as bad on their side of the road as with the obdurate animal on the other.

Meanwhile Shaltiel in Jerusalem was frantically shouting down the radio, demanding to know why the convoy was not moving. The drivers now joined in with a wonderful, but ultimately dangerous, expression of feelings. Then, all of a sudden, as if on a film director's cue, the great prize male on the one side, and the four stubborn females on the other, gave in simultaneously. The great bull with a triumphant bellow finally clambered up the ramp and onto the lorry; while to enormous cheers from the men, the four women signalled for their small cases to be brought as they too stepped up into the armoured cars.

At last the convoy turned and began the drive back to Jerusalem. It passed the first two road blocks, brushing aside the stones with their forward tractor. But they were then permanently held up at the third point where the rocks and stone barricade was too large to be moved. With a second barrier now being constructed behind them, the convoy was trapped. Nearby was a large abandoned Palestinian stone house. The old house was occupied by the drivers of the trucks and the soldiers from the armoured cars, and a sort of laager round the building was formed by those vehicles that could get there. The position was now desperate, and there was nothing the Haganah could do about it, having put almost all their transport capacity into the convoy at the insistence of the leaders in Tel Aviv.

Frantic calls for help were now made to Gurney and Cunningham, who passed them on to the military. As it happened, both of the senior British commanders were away and the Colonel left in charge – one Colonel Harper – found himself with a dilemma. The convoy had been mounted without going through the regulations requiring that the British be informed of all such road movements. Furthermore, it had then started the return journey against the express orders of the Chief Secretary himself. If the lives of British soldiers were lost to save a convoy that had so blatantly refused to accept British procedures, he would be in serious trouble. However the British Empire was still ready to flex its muscles, unlike the situation that arose a few weeks later.

Harper took a detachment of Suffolks and moved

out to face the Arabs surrounding and shooting at the
trapped convoy. He needed to avoid a battle if he could,
and tried to arrange terms that would enable him to get
through to the besieged convoy defending the decrepit
stone building before which they had mounted their
defense. But now the Arabs were no longer an aimless
mob of villagers, but had thrown up some leaders who
were in touch, by radio, with the Mufti in Cairo. True
to the intransigent and hopelessly outclassed leadership
that he had shown throughout the whole crisis, he persuaded the villagers to demand the complete surrender
of all the trapped men as prisoners of war. Despite the
pressure on the hapless Colonel not to risk the lives of
his men, there was no way that he was going to accept
such a proposal. He knew perfectly well what the miserable Mufti was likely to mean by 'prisoners of war'. Accordingly, he ostentatiously ordered his men to form in
line and prepare to move forward, flanked by their armoured cars, in an advance against the besieging Arabs.
No shots had as yet been exchanged between the British
and the Palestinian villagers, although shooting was still
continuing against the makeshift Jewish fort.

As the British force slowly advanced, there were
more frantic calls to Cairo. Then one of the Palestinians
walked down the road towards the advancing armoured
cars waving a white flag. Harper immediately ordered
a halt and went forward to parley. The Arabs had now
changed their terms and agreed to an evacuation of the
besieged convoy, demanding only that all the vehicles
and any arms be handed over – but they accepted that
all the trapped men could leave with the British. The
Colonel agreed to this and his detachment moved forward and finally arrived at the beleaguered convoy. The
200 exhausted men inside the old Arab building, with
their ammunition almost entirely gone, were informed

of the terms and began coming out piling up their arms in front of the almost one thousand local villagers who looked on silently. All the wounded were also loaded on to the special trucks brought by the Colonel. With the men were the women from the threatened Kfar Etzion settlement, who had been ordered to leave with the convoy. Under the protection of Colonel Harper and the Suffolks they all finally arrived safely back in Jerusalem.

There was, of course, no way that Tel Aviv was ever going to acknowledge, either then or later, that the Imperial Mandate authority, in its last dying days, had saved at least 200 Jewish lives. One of those lives saved was that of Zipora, who, under deep protest, had been forced to leave the settlement and to leave her young brother to make his own way in life, which he had, in fact, been doing for some time.

Chapter 9

Uncle Benjamin

It was now early April and less than six weeks remained before the scheduled departure, once and for all, of the unlamented British administration. As the certainty of this exodus, sank deeper into the minds of the two communities, the atmosphere of crisis and the deepening violence increased. The United Nations remained in complete denial right up to the last minute.

At the urgent plea of one of the leaders of the settlement who had returned with the Kfar Etzion convoy, Colonel Harper was able to negotiate the safe transit of the bull with the Arabs, together with two of the armoured cars. Accordingly, one irritated and bad-tempered prize bull, together with four equally angry but traumatised women, finally arrived in Jerusalem. Zipora, after reporting to her superior, went to live with her only relative in the town, her father's older brother, an elderly uncle, whose father had come to live in Jerusalem as long ago as the calm and placid days of the Ottoman Empire in the late nineteenth century. Her uncle's name was Benjamin, and Zipora's young brother had been named after him. He was in his eighties and had lived in Jerusalem all his life. He had a full head of white hair over a lined, weather-beaten face and shuffled a bit when he walked. His eyes were sharp, but he had an old-fashioned gentleness coupled to a tolerance for all the different races and creeds of Jerusalem, a tolerance which seemed to emanate from him at all times.

Conrad had come to believe, at some point during the last days of his relationship with Zipora in Kfar Etzion, that she either worked for the Haganah, or even possibly the Irgun. It had not worried him in the slightest. He had never, for one moment, considered, as perhaps Billy might have done, that either he was in love with Zipora or that she was in love with him. Furthermore, he did feel that, even if she had initially been instructed to make friends with him, that friendship had developed into something greater than she had anticipated; and she had pursued it for her own satisfaction, not because she had been required to do so.

He was wrong. Zipora had never belonged to the Irgun or any other organisation. She had simply been asked by someone she could not refuse to befriend the young British officer and to pass on any useful information she might glean. She never questioned why – it was just part of the atmosphere in which they were all living.

Within days of settling in to her Uncle Benjamin's house, the day after Conrad returned from his short holiday in Jordan, Zipora got in touch with him. She had not been asked to do so, and indeed the attempt to keep tabs on significant British intelligence officers was ceasing to be of any importance as the Mandate authority's power began to dwindle. She contacted him simply because she realised she missed his company – and also his body. But she too had no illusions about their relationship. In the midst of the conflict and violent passions on both sides of the community, their easygoing friendship gave them both comfort and consolation.

For four passionate days at the beginning of April, Conrad visited every evening, and most of the night, with Zipora. Old Benjamin's equally old housekeeper cooked wonderful Jewish dishes, which Conrad adored, and would then disappear. The old man, Conrad and Zipora would then sit over several cups of Turkish coffee, carefully prepared by Uncle Benjamin, and conversation would continue quietly, in deference to Benjamin, until quite late. Conrad would leave at first light the next morning, once curfew allowed, in order to get back to Bevingrad before he was missed.

On their third night, Conrad and Zipora sat on after Uncle Benjamin had gone to bed. The quietly persuasive and tolerant views of the old man had had their effect on the ardent young girl. As they both sat staring at the flickering fire, still required in the cold evenings, revelations which had not been possible to discuss previously, came out in the open now.

Conrad had been sure that the young girl had been asked by someone to cultivate his friendship. He had not been an Intelligence Officer with the British Army for nearly seven years without developing a sixth sense about such things, an important part of his professional training. But for once, his instinct had misled him as to the true situation.

Like everyone of her generation living in Palestine in 1947/8, Zipora was of course totally engaged in the coming birth of some sort of Jewish state. Whether it was to be a small sovereign nation-state, or an autonomous part of a larger federal state, or something in-between, remained uncertain; but she was inevitably caught up in the excitement and uncertainty of the situation. However she belonged to no specific group or organisation. Her naïve individuality was intact, and she had no need to shelter behind any formal organising group. Her affection for and sexual need of Conrad was entirely her own affair; and she was becoming less and less certain whether or not she was in 'love' or not. She hesitated on the brink of a deeper connection beyond affection, while Conrad had no such uncertainty.

So it was that Zipora replied to Conrad's gentle queries, confirming what was the truth – namely that she belonged to no group, terrorist or otherwise. Conrad would not have been shocked, even if she had belonged to the Irgun, a thought he had entertained. But, like all his colleagues, as a British officer he could not see that organisation as 'freedom fighters'. For him and his peers this was a terrorist organisation pure and simple. But then what did it matter. His girlfriend had always acted reasonably and her enthusiasms were sincere and genuine. She had never made any hateful or racist comments. He turned and smiled at her to reassure her, as she anxiously watched for his reaction to her denials of any connection –

"I'm not sure that I can ever come to approve of the Irgun. Whilst I accept completely the necessity for the Haganah, I am really not happy with the idea of 'terror' as a means."

"But Conrad, I am not a terrorist. I hate no one. I do believe we can live with the Arabs side by side. But we are fighting for freedom and we need to show that we mean business."

"I believe you, my love. Terror often only consists of useless cruelties, perpetrated by frightened people, largely to reassure themselves of the rightness of their cause. It's not your style. Enough chitchat – let's go to bed."

On their last evening together, the conversation between them turned to the current situation and the way in which the Zionist ideal was turning out. It was still chilly and a fire was again burning in the hearth. This had a soporific effect on them, and the conversation did not flow as easily as it may appear in the recounting. Instead, they continued in fits and starts, with great gaps and silent stares at the crackling flames. On this last evening, Uncle Benjamin initiated almost every aspect of the conversation, and it was clear that in his quiet and old-worldly way he had as strong views as Zipora.

"It's really very difficult, children. You have to face up to the fact, both of you, that however the partition is finally settled, the resulting Jewish state will have if not a majority of Arabs, certainly a very significant minority."

"Perhaps so Uncle, but we represent a very dynamic and well-educated community; we can give so much to any Arab minority living alongside us. If only they could have accepted the situation wholeheartedly, it could have worked out, even in a united unpartitioned Palestine. Eretz Israel. Forget how it might have come about – forget about the details of who could or could not vote or whatever, we could have created a truly amazing state."

"But the devil is always in the detail in these matters. Is your new state to be a Jewish state or in some way a multi-cultural one. I mean, is the state religion to be Judaism, making other faiths second-class citizens," said Benjamin softly, much to Conrad's great surprise.

"Uncle I don't know what you mean by second-class citizens, but yes certainly there is no point in setting up a new state unless it is primarily a Jewish state. However in accordance with our principles, I'm sure other faiths will be tolerated."

"What I fear my dear," said Benjamin settling further into the sofa, "is that your Zionist ideal ultimately involves displacing a population that has lived in this land for almost two thousand years. That's a very long time. The worry I have is that neither the Palestinian locals nor the wider Moslem world could ever accept your new state. Accordingly, any State of Israel would be likely to be in a perpetual state of war."

"Well, firstly Uncle, most nation-states have been in a continuous state of war with their neighbours over centuries, and yet they have thrived. Secondly, once we set up the new state, the locals and the rest of the Arab world will come to terms with us after everything settles down, and that will be within years not decades."

Here Conrad intervened for the first time

"I'm not sure that you are right there, sweetheart. I have seen the depth of feeling of the Palestinian villagers. They think of it as their land and they will always resent the second-class status to which they will be relegated in any new state."

"Nonsense both of you. The new State will galvanise and regenerate an area which the Ottomans neglected and left alone for centuries. That new dynamism will drag the Palestinians out of their current sleepy poverty into a pulsating twentieth century and take them to a new prosperity."

"Your enthusiasm is infectious," said Conrad. "I really think you could be right and it might be possible. If it were to succeed, it would be the first nation-state to integrate a substantial minority satisfactorily."

But old Uncle Benjamin shook his head sadly.

"There are several objections, children, but I will mention only two. Firstly, a State of Israel will raise concerns for all those remaining in the diaspora. An issue of divided loyalties is likely to arise. This would mirror, Conrad, the position of your Armenians thirty years ago, who wanted to remain loyal to the Ottoman Empire, but who were viewed by the Young Turk government as constituting a fifth column when the Russian army, with many Armenian units, invaded in 1915. ... Well I know, I know – not exactly the same, but the principle is similar."

"I don't think, sir, that...."

"But secondly and above all, the basic principle is that you are displacing another people. The new state will be in a permanent state of war. Zipora my dear, your reply is not sufficient. Nation-states do indeed get into wars all the time of course, but not with this element of permanence. This awareness of a permanent enemy will have the effect of subtly turning a democratic state into a military one."

"No, no," said Zipora and Conrad together. "Those same ridiculous religious sects you were complaining about yesterday, sir, added to the generally bolshie argumentative side of the Jewish character would prevent that surely," continued Conrad with a smile.

Benjamin too smiled and stiffly got up from the sofa, with a sigh of contentment at his niece's enthusiasm and by the fact that the two young people were going to sleep together in his house. Zipora jumped up as he shuffled out of the room, kissing her uncle and crying out –

"Dear, dear Uncle Benjamin – I do love you so."

For his part, Conrad too felt a warm contentment at the humanity of the old man. He also thought to himself that his influence on his young niece was likely to be very profound and would hopefully turn the girl's enthusiasm away from the possibility of 'terror', while retaining her Zionist ideals.

* * *

Conrad left as usual the next morning at the crack of dawn, quietly slipping out without waking anybody. He was not too far from the repaired King David Hotel and Bevingrad. Conrad walked quickly back in the quiet early morning. The sniping and violence was usually less in the early mornings. The zealous young men on both sides tended to shoot all night, but then slept during the early morning like teenagers. This was when the women came out to do their daily shopping, and for the moment the women and their families were not being targeted by either side.

But there was always danger now in walking the streets. This was especially true if one was moving along a community boundary or moving from one community area to another. Civilians going about their legitimate daily business could be injured in the crossfire when there were shoot-outs between the fervent young men on both sides. Furthermore, ever since Easter, the violence had got worse, as there was less and less police or British troop presence on the streets.

For many years, every morning without fail, Benjamin had made his way to the same Palestinian bakery, not three blocks away at the beginning of what had always been an Arab quarter. There he bought his supply of bread and other goods, chatted with the baker, who had become a good friend over the years, and slowly walked back home. It never crossed his mind for a moment that this daily routine was becoming dangerous, or that a time might come when he could not make the journey at all.

It was, in fact, on the very next day after their long conversation in which he had tried to articulate to the two children – for such was how he thought of them – his worries about the coming events, that it all came to an end. The bakery was empty when he arrived. Most of the customers, now almost exclusively Palestinian, aware of the danger as the morning progressed, had already come, bought their bread and gone. This gave Benjamin time to chat with his old friend whom he had known for over twenty years. Accordingly it was quite late, just before the bakery closed for the morning, that Benjamin began to make his way home.

No one ever knew exactly what happened. It was just another statistic. Shooting started and in the midst of all the firing Benjamin was shot and died instantly. Only one thing was clear – the shot that killed the old man was into Benjamin's back as he shuffled down the street on his way home and it must therefore have come from the Arab side. Two local policemen eventually turned up – there was no British presence. The man's home address was found in his wallet and one of the police went to the address to bring the news. The body was whisked away in an ambulance. The shooting had stopped while all this was going on, but soon started up again.

That afternoon Zipora, having wept her way to the morgue, and having wept her way back, now in a red wave of rage, telephoned Conrad to give him the news –

"Oh my God. I'm so sorry Zip. I will...."

"It's not enough. It's not enough. Where were you British. You're supposed to be protecting civilians on the streets aren't you. Isn't that why you are here. Isn't that the excuse for why you are lording it over us."

"But Zipora you must...."

"No, no, there is no must. This confirms, as always, that we have to act for ourselves. We can't rely on anyone else.

"But Zipora...."

"Conrad – I've given you the news. My Uncle is dead and I don't know why. I don't want you to come round anymore. You may be personally blameless but you represent an authority that can no longer even keep the peace on the streets just a few blocks away from their own headquarters. You can go away and good riddance to the whole arrogant bunch of you."

Before Conrad could say another word, she put the phone down and burst into more tears. But she didn't change her mind. Conrad just stood and stared, feeling desperately sorry for the passing away not only of the old man, but of all he represented.

Chapter 10

Palestine – the end of the Mandate

It all happened within the space of five months from the day the UN voted for partition. But during that five months, myths and misunderstandings came to surround the so-called historical truth of what actually took place from all sides; myths that continued to persist for decades, and which over half a century later continue to swing the debate from one side to another.

A listener in Tel Aviv to Radio Armenia during the Soviet period once telephoned their office, whose number was well known throughout the Middle East, and asked "Is it possible to foretell the future?" The network secretary replied at once - "Certainly, certainly sir, there is really no difficulty. We know exactly what the future is likely to be, both ours and yours. Our problem, my dear sir, is with the past – that keeps changing all the time."

What was quickly forgotten, because it suited neither side to remember it, was the manner in which some communities, some villages, some suburban areas, made unspoken arrangements with neighbours of the other community to keep the peace between them. Some schools, encouraged by the Mandate authorities, continued until April to take in boys from both communities. Many undercover officers like Conrad strove to arrange contact between the elders and leaders of both sides – but it was getting rarer all the time. Then early in April – April 9th to be exact, followed four days later on April 13th – two events occurred which changed the whole situation for ever.

Just to the north-west of Jerusalem, not more than nine miles away, lay the village of Deir Yassin. It was a great blessing for the inhabitants that their location had absolutely no strategic value to anyone. Sitting in their village, the people could hear the echoes of the continuous fighting along the road from Tel Aviv to Jerusalem, but they were able to ignore it as their own elders had refused to get directly involved. The Haganah commander in Jerusalem – David Shaltiel – had commented in one of his reports sent to the Jewish Agency only a few weeks before, that "this village has been quiet from the start, there have been no reports of any attack on Jews and it is clear that they have refused entry to any foreign Arab bands."

On the evening of the 8th, six or so men from the village – three masons, a stone-cutter, and a truck driver – joined the local baker to mount guard as night watchmen, not expecting any trouble. A single voluntary night-watchman each night was traditional in the village and had been for decades, but in view of all the turmoil around them, having six, rather than one, seemed prudent. They were armed with one old Mauser and three antique Turkish rifles. The rest of the villagers were all sound asleep. They chatted – smoked a common narghileh – and if the truth be told, one or two of them dozed off.

Then, early in the morning, but before the sun had arisen, some shots rang out. Commandos of the Irgun and the Stern Gang, acting for once in close collaboration, had stealthily moved into position, huddled together behind a stone wall waiting to mount an attack on the unsuspecting village. To this day the original motivation behind the attack is a subject of enormous controversy. Conrad, whose report to Gurney on the incident was probably one of those closest to the truth, had no idea why or what had motivated these young men, women and their leaders. They had come with an armoured car equipped with a loudspeaker which was intended, so it was claimed later, to warn the villagers to flee. This vehicle had unfortunately broken down so never arrived in time. The result was a terrible and bloody fiasco.

Arguing amongst themselves about what to do when the loudspeakers failed to arrive, the young group delayed their first rush, and this gave time for the six elderly night-watchmen to load their antiquated weapons and two of them to rush round to their sleeping neighbours' houses warning them of the attack. All Arab males owned guns of one sort or another in the villages, and roused in time, they began tenaciously defending their homes and families. Meanwhile, after the first rush, these terrorists – freedom fighters of course – found themselves floundering. These were not the disciplined Haganah – they had no training or experience in attacking defended villages. It had not crossed their minds, nor that of their older commanders ultimately responsible for the attack, that it was considerably more difficult to attack a village which was resisting, than it was to toss a bomb into an unarmed crowd waiting to board a bus.

It would seem that a kind of collective hysteria overtook the attackers, so that as the old Mausers and decrepit rifles finally began to fall silent, they fell with increasing rage on the now defenceless villagers of Deir Yassin. The atrocities that then took place were reported back to Gurney by the team of policemen sent by the administration to interview the survivors. While Conrad thought there was no doubt exaggeration in these reports, he could not gainsay the evidence of his own eyes when he himself arrived at the village.

Bit by bit the village was overcome by a maelstrom of screams, gunshots, explosions and the smell of blood.

71

The attackers killed and they looted. As the morning advanced, the commandos began to work their way through the houses still left standing, using machine guns and what was left of their grenades, shooting the fleeing women and children.

It took more than five hours before the news of this massacre reached the British in Jerusalem, despite the proximity of the village. Gurney immediately arranged to send out a team of British policemen to investigate what had happened. Conrad was asked to accompany the team to give such assistance as he could, and to help with the interpreting. But it then transpired that the twelve experienced police officers appointed were not in a position to go out for a couple of days, as most of them had to be gathered together from different locations all over the country. Making sure that he was not needed immediately, Conrad slipped out of the town and drove to the village. Fortunately for him, he arrived at the same time as the Swiss representative of the Red Cross – Jacques de Reynier – with a small party of nurses and other medics. The Irgun guards had constructed a road block across the road leading into the village. All vehicles had to be left on the other side. Conrad pulled up his jeep right behind the Red Cross vehicles, and slipped past the guards as if he was part of the Red Cross party.

The village was still being held by the terrorists/ freedom fighters. Conrad could hardly credit what he saw. Young men and women all heavily armed running about haphazardly, rushing in and out of half-demolished houses, still occasionally shooting, although it was blatantly clear that there were no more armed villagers left. Conrad felt that they were in a state of crazed madness. He went round in a daze at the horror of what he was seeing, coming upon the scene of a young woman

– probably still a teenager – stabbing an elderly man cowering on the steps of his tiny one-room house. She ran past Conrad with glazed eyes and with her blood-covered dagger still in her hand. Conrad moved on and went into a house with a great gaping hole in the wall. There were bodies strewn about throughout the house. Everything appeared to have been torn apart and turned upside down.

Conrad was still there, looking with incredulity at all around him, when the Red Cross representative came in on his own. At the same moment, they both saw something moving near the far wall under all the debris. Bending down, de Reynier discovered – as he put it himself later in his own official report – "a little foot still warm to the touch." Motioning to Conrad they both worked carefully to disentangle it from the mess. It belonged to a ten-year old girl still alive, although bleeding profusely. He asked Conrad to take her back to one of his two ambulances waiting on the other side of the road block. Conrad picked her up and carried her back to the road, trying to ignore the screams, cries and delirium all around him.

He stepped carefully and slowly through the rubble, holding on tight to the little girl who was now quietly moaning. The frenzy seemed to be lessening as many of the young men and women, dressed alike in dark shirts and black trousers or shorts, sat on the ground staring listlessly around them with glazed eyes. Conrad walked gingerly on, avoiding eye contact as much as he could, wishing that he had a Red Cross armband like the others. He was not far from the guards at the road block when he could not avoid seeing a young man in shorts and a black shirt squatting by a rock with his eyes focused on him. This time he was unable to avoid direct eye contact.

It was the young Benjamin – Zipora's brother.

His eyes too had that blank, faraway look he had seen in so many of the other boys and girls involved. He never knew whether Benjamin had recognised him or not. In any event, he never spoke a word and Conrad quickly moved on, passing through the guards at the road block, tenderly carrying the little girl to the ambulances on the other side.

As he stumbled forward, his whole relationship with Zipora and his mistaken instinct about her motivation suddenly flashed before his mind. It now seemed obvious that it was the frail ineffectual-looking Benjamin who was the dedicated member of the Irgun. It was Benjamin who had been ordered to ask his sister to befriend him, and it was he whose request Zipora had been unable to refuse. Conrad thought of the charming and shy young man who was so dependent on his sister. What had persuaded him into joining what was, in effect, nothing less than a highly developed terrorist organisation. He could not work it out as he passed the guards and gently left the little girl with the Red Cross nurses.

By this time, the Irgun and Stern leaders were beginning to get nervous at de Reynier's presence, and were jostling him and his few staff encouraging them to leave. Once he had delivered the little girl to one of the ambulances, Conrad realised that the guards were unlikely to let him back through. He felt, in any case, that being in the middle of what seemed to be a crazed mob, placed him in considerable personal danger if anyone discovered or guessed at his true identity as a British officer. Although Benjamin had not said a word, he could not be sure whether he had recognised him or not. He turned the car and drove back into town.

Conrad was never able to work out in his own mind

why young Benjamin had become a terrorist. As the next dramatic and urgent days went by, this dilemma ceased to concern him. But the explanation was not really that much of a mystery. Left without parents, particularly any male role model, the adolescent Benjamin had come to rely more and more on his sister's strong personality. Like all his generation, he was fully involved in the unfolding drama in Palestine created by the resolution of the Balfour Declaration. But lacking the personal self-confidence Zipora possessed, he felt the need of some overriding authority under whose discipline he could subordinate his own weak and indecisive will. All this, coupled as it was, to his guilt-ridden sado-masochistic fantasies about his sister, had left him completely open to the recruiting efforts of the Irgun, who had needed to have a man in Kfar Etzion who was dedicated to their group.

Later in the morning after arriving back in Jerusalem, Conrad reported directly to Sir Henry Gurney, who had already started the process of trying to get together the team of policemen to investigate what had happened.

Later still, Gurney himself reported to the High Commissioner – Sir Alan Cunningham – who had close contacts not only with Ben-Gurion and the Jewish Agency in Tel Aviv, but also with the leaders of the Haganah in Jerusalem. He knew at once that that organisation was incapable of such a messy, pointless exercise. He knew immediately that it was the terrorists, whom he despised and deplored. He immediately picked up the telephone and got through to the General in command of the whole British army in Palestine and explained what had happened – ending with the words –

"At last we can deal with those bastards. We have clear and incontrovertible evidence of pure bloody criminality. For God's sake go up there fast and get them."

It was the moment of truth for the High Commissioner, and indeed by inference for the whole British Empire. Here was an open and shut case, without any political excuse, where the Imperial power could act decisively again – as it had at Kfar Etzion only a few months earlier. But this time his military commander told him that he simply did not have the troops available. This was only partly true. At any other time during the past 200 years, a detachment would somehow have been found and an attempt to enforce Imperial justice made – but Empire was over, the will had gone. Nothing that happened throughout his whole time in Palestine upset the High Commissioner as much as this one moment when the Mandate authority was unable or unwilling to act.

The Haganah itself, appalled as the first reports came in, moved in as fast as it could to take over the village. The first group to reach the area was a Zionist youth organisation led by a veteran of six years with the British army. He left his men and the boys outside the road block and passed through and entered the village alone. De Reynier had already left, and there was now almost silence as the terrorists/freedom fighters now lay about exhausted by their own madness. The Youth organisation leader later reported back to Tel Aviv that "the dead we found were all unjust victims and none of them had died with any weapons on them." In fact, so horrible was the scene – the blood – the continuing wails of the wounded – the dead children – that he returned and ordered his officers still outside not to let the youngsters in, but to remain waiting outside with one of their officers. Meanwhile, he instructed the rest of the officers to come in and help start the clearing up.

Slowly, more men from the Haganah arrived, until

the Irgun and Stern Gang were finally outnumbered. They were then made to help clear up the mess. They ended up carrying the bodies of their victims to the quarry at the end of the village. There they laid them out on the stones, poured gasoline on them and set them alight in a huge funeral pyre. Conrad was back in Jerusalem as the black pillars of smoke, easily visible from the city, rose into the sky. He knew immediately what it meant. In the end, as he was caught up in the next incident which occurred, he never did accompany the British Police group that went to interrogate the survivors, though he did read the reports that were passed on to Gurney and Cunningham. He later reported directly to Gurney, with whom he had now developed an easy and friendly relationship, that in his travels around the country, he was totally satisfied that the overwhelming majority of the Yishuv he had talked to, had been shocked by the actions of these 'freedom fighters', and were prepared to say so. Gurney simply looked at him and said –

"So what, Bridgeman, they are still reaping the benefits aren't they. Only yesterday, you pointed to the misery of the large number of Palestinians packing up and fleeing from their villages."

It was indeed ironic that the action of the Irgun and Stern Gang on April 9th resulted in partly resolving the most problematic difficulty facing the Zionist movement – namely, how to deal with the fact that the new state, however partitioned, would inevitably have a majority of Arabs living within it. Once again the Palestinian leadership, such as it was, ended up making a mess of the situation. They decided to broadcast to the world – particularly in the hope of influencing the wavering governments of the surrounding Arab states – the full horror of what had happened. In the end, the gruesome details of Deir Yassin made not a whit of difference to the vacillating attitudes of those governments. What it did do was to fuel a growing sense of panic among the wretched Palestinian villagers. It was one thing when young men of both sides shot at each other and fought bloody battles in the streets. It was quite another when family homes were demolished and their women and children massacred. Palestinian villagers began to flee in their thousands from the homes they had lived in for centuries.

Only five days after these events Conrad was involved in yet another incident in which the increasingly enfeebled Mandate authority was unable to enforce its will.

* * *

Situated on a hill known as Mount Scopus to the north of Jerusalem were two institutions close to the heart of Ben-Gurion and the Jewish Agency – the Hadassah Hospital and the Hebrew University. Supplying these two institutions had been a problem as the only road up from the centre of the city passed through a well-populated Palestinian suburb. The British had expended a lot of time and effort and the lives of soldiers in keeping this road open. They had succeeded in the main, as unlike the Tel Aviv–Jerusalem road, where despite every effort they had undoubtedly failed, this route was much shorter and easier to patrol. On Tuesday, the 13th April, only four days after the terrible carnage at Deir Yassin, the Haganah ran a protected convoy up to the two institutions. No one anticipated any trouble. The long train of trucks, ambulances and buses approached the last road block before the road entered the Arab quarter. There the Haganah liaison officer made a routine inspection with the duty British police inspector – checking that there were no illicit arms hidden away. A

British armoured car had just finished patrolling the road, and the convoy was waved on.

On this occasion, the convoy did not just contain food, medical supplies and other necessities – but also a distinguished assembly of professors, doctors, research assistants and nurses, all headed for the new modern hospital and the prestigious University. Convoys had been passing through this Arab quarter every three or four days without incident for weeks – though never with such a distinguished passenger list. Furthermore the British were still regularly patrolling the road.

But this time there was a change. Crouched by the side of the road as the convoy came to the end of the row of houses and approached a flat area before the final climb up the hill were some Palestinian 'freedom fighters'. As the lead armoured car appeared round a bend and drove forward, an enormous explosion shook the ground and a large crater appeared in the road, into which the forward armoured car plunged, as the rest of the convoy stopped behind it. Immediately a rain of bullets hammered into the stalled convoy up and down the road. The explosion and gunfire resounded all over Jerusalem. Soon hundreds of Arabs from all over the neighbouring area began pouring towards the stricken ambulances. Why now? What had made the difference to an area which had till now been kept clear by the Mandate authorities?

The smoke pouring up from the burning bodies of Deir Yassin was beginning to take its effect.

Not more than a couple of miles away, Conrad was having an early morning breakfast in the Officer's mess of the Highland Light Infantry – one of the last of the British regiments scheduled to leave. He jumped up, joining the Colonel in command who leapt into an ar-moured car, calling out for a second car to follow. They

set out towards the commotion up the road. Some of
the ambulances and trucks at the rear of the convoy had
managed to turn and were trundling back down. By the
time Conrad and the Colonel arrived, the leading armoured car, two buses and two ambulances were caught
in the crossfire, unable to turn and stuck in the middle
of a fierce fire-fight. Despite the cursory inspection at
the road block earlier in the morning, the convoy was
filled with small arms, and the occupants were firing
back through the slits in the sides of their vehicles. The
Colonel jumped out, calling for a cease-fire, but no one
heard or, if they did, took no notice, though neither side
fired directly at the two British armoured cars. Conrad
yelled at the Colonel, warning him that Arabs had by
now occupied all the houses nearby and down the road,
and as more and more were coming the Jewish convoy
would soon be hopelessly trapped.

The Colonel radioed headquarters requesting the
arrival of a troop of Life Guard armoured cars – and
also requesting that the Arab houses at the side of the
road be shelled. These were the sorts of decisions that
the Mandate authorities were being asked to make on a
daily basis but with only a dwindling force available to
enforce them. The answer came from Army HQ that
they would not authorise any indiscriminate shelling of
the houses, but that a troop of armoured cars would
be on their way as soon as possible. Conrad raced back
with the second armoured car in order to collect a further truck with British markings, to enable the Colonel
to mount a rescue attempt of his own. He returned and
turned the truck round facing back to the city. He and
the Colonel banged on the covered trucks and ambulances carrying the nurses, professors and doctors, urging them to get out and run to the British marked truck
alongside which would take them to safety – but none

dared as the gunfire was increasing all the time – and in fairness, when asked, neither Conrad nor the Colonel were able to guarantee their safety. They were already risking their own lives, but if the ambushers saw the occupants of the convoy escaping, they would certainly turn their guns on to all on the road. "We'll wait for the Haganah," was the cry. Conrad drove away a second time and, on his own phone, joined the Colonel urging speed on the Life Guards support.

It was true that the Life Guards were slow in getting moving – but it should be said that the Haganah, too, had not realised the seriousness of the situation, and failed to react with their usual speed. At about 11.00 o'clock, the first British troops reached the scene, now one of indescribable confusion. More and more Arabs screaming "Deir Yassin. Deir Yassin" surrounded the stricken convoy. A massacre of the distinguished professors and vulnerable nurses seemed in the offing. Eventually, while a detachment of Highland Light Infantry, under the command of their Colonel, provided covering fire, the Life Guards armoured cars arrived and moved up alongside the besieged vehicles. The soldiers used their own car covers to create a sort of corridor between their armoured cars and the trapped trucks and ambulances to get the survivors and the wounded out. There were many already dead, but a substantial number were still alive. Those who survived only did so due to what turned out to be the final effort of the Mandate authority in protecting as many lives of both communities as they could.

The British were due to depart in exactly four weeks. The rapidly dwindling military presence was causing them immense problems, simply trying to carry out their own orderly evacuation plans without further loss of life. This failure to prevent the attack on the convoy to Mount Scopus, following immediately after the failure to act against the terrorist attack on Deir Yassin was the last straw. Needless to say, once again, Tel Aviv never acknowledged the effort and the success of the Mandate authorities, even if a little belatedly, in saving the trapped occupants of the convoy. The Arabs made the opposite complaint; that the perfidious British had yet again acted to pull Jewish chestnuts out of the fire. But the great majority of the British officers on the spot never had any political agenda other than the saving of lives.

However, following on from the events of these two days, the conclusion was that, covertly, and certainly without the knowledge of London, the British military on the spot had become more and more reliant on the Haganah for the remaining logistical support for the final departure from Haifa.

* * *

On the 30th April, two weeks before the final end of the Mandate, Conrad was at last released from the army. That very day, he was driven to Haifa and left for Malta with the first detachment of the Highland Light Infantry to leave.

On the 13th May, two weeks later, the British police in Jerusalem dismissed all their civilian staff, burnt their more sensitive files, locked up all their stores, and brought the keys to the United Nations representative in the city, who refused to accept them. Gurney was told, and he hurried round to point out that in accordance with their own resolution five months previously, the UN was supposed to be responsible for the administration of Jerusalem, which was supposed to become an international city, from the next day. They still refused to accept the keys and so they were left on the doorstep.

The administration packed up early on the morning of the 14th May, when four police cars, and a dozen or so civilians in a bus and two cars, drove out of Bevingrad, the British flag over the King David Hotel was lowered and the Red Cross flag raised. Before leaving in this group Gurney, calm and resolute as usual, took the step of going to see the commanding officers of the Highland Light Infantry and the Suffolks to thank them personally for all their efforts on behalf of the civilian authorities. Neither said a single word, but simply handed him the two final casualty lists of the British soldiers who had died trying, even if failing, to keep the peace.

* * *

Neither side have ever accepted that the vast majority of British officers and soldiers were simply trying to do their duty to keep the peace as long as possible, trying to minimise the bloodshed on both sides.

It has also been claimed that the failure of the two sides in Palestine to co-exist, was in some way the fault of the Mandate authority right from the start. It is certainly true that whilst the Ottoman Empire may have become corrupt and senile, everyone could see at the end of the Great War that all three communities of Jews, Christian Palestinians and Muslim Palestinians, living in the Ottoman administrative unit comprising Palestine, lived together in reasonable amity. They had done so for centuries and were still doing so in 1918. It seemed perfectly reasonable to believe that such amity and the mutual benefit which could have resulted from peaceful coexistence might have continued. It was what the mandate authorities would have wanted but it was not to be.

The power vacuum left by the demise of the multicultural Ottoman Empire had to be filled somehow.

The United States might carp and criticise, but in the end it had refused all the mandate authorities offered. The British might well originally have been motivated by an old-world and increasingly old-fashioned and irrelevant Anglo-French rivalry. But in the end, once settled in to administration, the Empire did its best to try and seek a balance between the communities. The failure was tragic – but there was no conspiracy or any deliberate creation of antipathy between the communities.

The British officials sitting stiffly in their black cars, drove out of Jerusalem on the 14th May 1948. It was not a Belgian scuttle but it was an admission of failure.

The State of Israel was declared the very next day.

Chapter 11

Billy

Once he came out of the army at the end of April 1948, before going up to Oxford at the end of September, Conrad spent the whole of those five months at home. His sister Natalie was now 19 and already at work. She had not been interested in carrying on any further in academia, but had decided that she wanted to follow in her mother's footsteps and become a nurse. Harry and Olga had tried to persuade her to go further and study to become a doctor. However, she chose not to, preferring the caring to the healing.

Throughout the war and after, she had always been surrounded by a horde of school friends and other girls, mostly a little younger than herself. Billy, now over 15, had enjoyed easy and generous friendships with all these friends of his sister without arousing any resentment on the part of his sibling, ever since he was twelve. In return, all Natalie's girlfriends had enjoyed his company.

Billy was the brains in the family and was already a precocious and highly talented mathematician. Mathematics is known to be a subject where the greatest talent can often appear in the very young. This was not quite the situation where Billy was concerned. His Maths was of high-quality and he had already produced some creative ideas; but in the end, he was hardly a budding academic genius. On the other hand, well before his sixteenth birthday, he had already obtained a major open scholarship to study pure mathematics at Oxford at Christchurch College. The College was already filled to capacity with all the military men returning after the end of the war to take up their promised places. Billy was granted a scholarship, one of the most prestigious of all the university scholarships, when he came far and away ahead of everyone else sitting the entrance exam that year. However, the College made it a condition that he could not take up his place until he was 17 or at least close to it. So it was that he was due to go up in October 1950.

During the summer months of 1948, with Conrad back home waiting to start at University in the autumn, what Billy was to do before going up to Oxford became a major topic of family conversation. The year before, Harry had insisted that he was to continue at school for a further year, until he was 16, even though there was little he could now learn from his maths teachers. He could only leave school after his sixteenth birthday in the summer of 1949, and then they would face up to the question of what he might do for a year before taking up his place at Christchurch the following year. But meanwhile, Harry felt that the discipline of school would be good for him. Conrad was delighted to find himself back in the old Avakian-style family discussions and came up with a whole series of the most exotic solutions for Billy's immediate future.

Billy had not seen Conrad since he was nine years-old. To begin with, he was rather shy around this so-phisticated, experienced man, who had returned from five years of responsibility and situations fraught with danger. But Conrad had not changed. He never pulled rank with his little brother. Within days Billy was at ease with the brother he loved, and he became just as cheeky as ever. Now that he was older, Conrad couldn't simply get the better of his little brother by simply sitting on him as he had in the past. He was neither as quick or as sharp as Billy, so couldn't compete on that level, and thus found it more difficult to rely on his natural maturity with the boy. However, Harry and Olga, perfectly ready to 'pull rank', often intervened, insisting Billy defer to his elder brother whenever it became necessary,

Billy was just discovering classical music – an art form which often accompanies a talent for mathematics. Conrad regularly took him out. The lunch-time concerts of Dame Myra Hess at St. Martins in the Fields were still continuing. The great London orchestras were getting back into their stride again. Conrad had money and never stinted on paying for his brother. Olga sometimes, rather clumsily, tried to suggest to Billy that he shouldn't always accompany Conrad on these excursions to the Theatre, the Opera and Concerts, but Billy countered that he never pestered Conrad to take him anywhere – Conrad always simply offered. The last conversation between them on this matter took place towards the end of August. Olga said –

"Billy, my darling, I do think that you ought to let Conrad go out with someone else – a girl friend for instance – rather than hanging on to him so that he only considers taking you."

"Mama, we've had this out before. It's not fair – I never ask Conrad to take me out to a concert. He always gets two tickets, grins at me and simply tells me when we are next going out and to what."

"I know – but if you were to say 'no' sometimes. He might take someone else out."

"Oh mother, for heaven's sake, Conrad is, what, 24? He doesn't need me to help him to invite a girl out and…"

"A little more respect please Billy," interjected Harry who had been listening rather than concentrating on the newspaper he was reading.

"Olga, I do think that in this instance Billy is being fair, selfish little scamp though he may be. I don't think it's his task to refuse Conrad's invitations, if that's what Conrad wants, Billy has every right to go along with him. It is clearly giving both of them a lot of pleasure. You worry unduly my dear."

Olga sighed and never raised the subject again, though over the next few weeks, before Billy went back to school, he and Conrad went out almost every night. Conrad was actually 25, he had soldiered for almost six years in North Africa and Italy – what was she thinking about? Perhaps Harry was right and she did worry too much. As it happens, however, although Conrad was not a novice when it came to sexual experience, until his recent relationship with Zipora in Kfar Etzion his experience had been limited to short rather unsatisfactory one-night liaisons. At the start of the war, an attempt by some of his military colleagues to sample the sexual delights of the old town, when they were first in Cairo, had left him feeling cold and unfulfilled, and the experience had been an unmitigated disaster. He had normal, uncomplicated heterosexual fantasies as a youth, but he was sexually reserved if the girl in question was of his own class or education. His dark and smouldering good looks won him the attention of most girls he met, but he always backed off at the last moment, avoiding any real commitment. Throughout his wartime placement in Rome, Giancarlo, and the PCI toughs with whom he shared accommodation, were forever introducing "il Inglese molto simpatico" to as many girls as they could find. He loved the company of these girls – and they loved his. Nevertheless, at the door to numerous apartments, or family homes, there might be a kiss, even a passionate kiss, but the invitation in for a cup of coffee or a liquor would be refused. It was always done with such charm that it never rankled with any of them.

Olga had intuitively divined a shyness and reserve in her eldest son, which she worried could cause him difficulties as he grew older. At the same time, she could see that Billy, the younger of her sons with Harry, had no such problem. He was not shy, nor the slightest bit reserved. She failed to see that Billy had the almost completely opposite problem – open, unreserved and bursting with hormones, ready to fall in love with everyone – a budding Cherubino.

Billy was at school at Westminster and was there now as a weekly boarder – at his own request. Olga had put her foot down at the start, refusing to accept the current English upper class attitude that required boys to be sent away to live in the company of other boys of a similar age, rather than with their parents. So it was that Billy, who easily passed the common entrance exam, started at Westminster as a day-boy. But when he reached his fourteenth birthday, he began to press for the right to be a boarder, craving the camaraderie and close friendships which he thought he was missing by the daily commute. Olga would not agree, but here at last Harry began to take a hand. After carefully checking on Billy's motivation, he argued the matter out with Olga and eventually they compromised with Billy becoming a weekly boarder, which was an option at Westminster. So Billy would come home on Saturdays and go back to school on Monday mornings.

After consultation with the Mathematics department at Christchurch, it was accepted that in his last year at school, until he became sixteen, Billy was to switch from the Maths sixth form and go instead to the languages section, where he would take up French and Italian. At the same time, he would go twice a week for a whole afternoon to a private Mathematics professor, who would keep him on top of the subject, and well ahead of any maths instruction available at the school.

Where Conrad was all dark good looks with a natural charm and dignity, Billy was all wide blue eyes, fair hair and a naïve and cheeky, somewhat immature outlook on life. Within the family, all the girls – Natalie's many friends, four or five years younger than Conrad – almost all had a deep secret crush on the handsome and inaccessible elder brother, but none of them had ever touched him, or been touched by him. Then, when he was nineteen, he had gone off to the war, not to be seen again for several years. But these same girls, continually in and out of the Bridgeman house, and two or three years older than Billy, had had a completely different relationship with him. Billy was naïve, trusting and a little naughty. They enjoyed teasing him with sexual inuendo – and he enjoyed teasing them back. Natalie was never jealous or resentful of the bantering attention given to her younger brother by her friends. The war had ended, and while there was as yet no sexual promiscuity, inhibitions were loosening. Billy, unlike Conrad, was touched by these girls and he touched them back. He was kissed and was taught how to kiss. He did not have the sort of sexual fantasies that Conrad had had at fifteen or sixteen because he was meeting and enjoying the company of girls – a little older than himself admittedly, but with all of whom he had a very easy-going relationship. Olga saw all this, of course, and so had no worries where her youngest was concerned, though perhaps she should have.

But, of course, none of this playing around amounted to 'love' in any sense of the word. As the summer ended, Billy began his weekly boarding at Westminster. Although only 15, he was in the sixth form and in a senior dormitory. There really was no need to analyse quite why or how it occurred – it simply happened. Billy fell deeply in love with another boy, Barry – almost a young man really – over two years older than himself. Could it really be called love? Certainly, as far as Billy was concerned, it did. He had had quite a few adolescent sexual experiences of a fairly innocent kind with Natalie's friends, and he knew that his feelings towards this young man were quite different.

But Billy was quite perceptive, even if a little naïve and immature, and could see that the object of his love did not return it. If, at first, he fondly imagined that there was a mutual feeling, he soon came to realise that he was being cynically used. There was nothing particularly vicious or immoral about it. The older boy knew that the young lad, not particularly good-looking, but obviously sexually precocious, hero-worshipped him. So Billy was passionately kissed in the squash courts, and there were several episodes of fumbling intimacy between them. This went on for about four months until the young man left school to go into the army. It was never entirely clear who had seduced who. Billy undoubtedly allowed himself to be used by the older boy, but was hardly an innocent victim. He had fallen for the young man and had been as manipulative in the first physical contact as Barry. The difference was that, without being conscious of it, he really craved and sought 'love' from the encounter, whilst the older boy only wanted to satisfy his sexual cravings.

The experience, such as it was, had no lasting or deleterious effect on Billy's naturally optimistic and trusting nature, but it was symptomatic of a problem that would plague him for the rest of his life in all his relationships with women. Right up to and including the final dramatic end, Billy always imagined that 'she', whoever she might be, was as much in love with him as he was with her.

Chapter 12

Conrad and Harriet connect

Conrad went up to Oxford in October. Attlee's first socialist administration, voted in by so many of the soldiers still in uniform in 1945, was in its third year, and Oxford, with its extraordinary mixture of young men, who were mature beyond their years, fresh from the war, jumbled in with those brilliant but immature boys fresh from school, was an exciting place to be. Conrad thought that he would have great difficulty in adapting himself to an academic student life after the excitements of the war. However, the atmosphere was so interesting in those years that he slipped back into the student round with great ease.

Conrad first met Harriet Tate in the winter of 1948. Harriet, through her enormous personal determination, had overruled her mother, and had managed by sheer hard work to get a place at Somerville at Oxford. She was proposing to study Italian. She had been unable to avoid leaving school at 16 at the end of the war. Her mother, Tessa, had not been left particularly badly-off by the death of her husband. He had died, conveniently, whilst still fully employed by Calico Printers, who did not question the death and dealt generously with the pension due to his widow. But she always pretended to Harriet that they were very short of money. Harriet had duly taken a short secretarial course and had gone to work with a firm of Manchester solicitors. While working for them, she applied herself to the study necessary for sitting the entrance exams to an Oxford College. With a single-minded determination and an iron will, she ignored her mother's complaints. She also fended off a series of young lawyers and legal clerks eager for her company; instead studying almost every evening without fail.

By the year Harriet finally sat the exam for the group of colleges of which Somerville was one, she had physically matured into a strong young woman. She was a little on the short side still, but exuded a sensuality such that whoever she addressed was smitten. She wore her dark brown hair long – when combed, it reached down to the small of her back. Hers was not, nor ever would be, a classic beauty, like that of Olga Avakian, Conrad's mother, but her strength and self-confidence was stunning in its own way.

Harriet also took up her place at Somerville in October of 1948. Under the circumstances, it was inevitable that Harriet and Conrad would meet. Worcester College was a college that was one of the closest to Somerville and they both attended many of the same lectures and even shared one of their tutors – in medieval Italian literature. So it was, that one day following on from an animated discussion on the merits of an aspect of Dante's Divine comedy, Conrad suggested a coffee together after the tutorial. Conrad might have been reserved, but he was not shy. He carried his easy charm effortlessly from one milieu to another, and the self-confidence he had achieved as a result of his wartime experiences meant that he was perfectly comfortable with this aspect of social relationships. For her part, Harriet, who had spent over a year fending off the attentions of all the rather brash young men flocking around her in her employer's office in Manchester, was ready for an innocent, or for that matter not so innocent, dalliance.

Their relationship stuttered on in fits and starts. But the more Harriet was attracted to the amiable young man, the more she became frustrated by his restraint.

If it was a question of going out together to a party, or meeting and sharing a drink and an omelette in the Clarendon Arms, or a salad together in the Welsh Pony, or taking a boat out on the river, Conrad was always superbly efficient and attentive. Harriet simply adored every moment of the day or the afternoon with him. But later, when they came to his rooms in the early evening to discuss poetry, or said goodnight in the lee of the Radcliffe Hospital before she returned to college, a fairly chaste kiss was the most they ever exchanged.

Harriet's feelings for Conrad were distinctly physical. She had soon had enough of intellectual conversations about Coleridge and her belated discovery of Platonism. Her body ached to be tightly embraced by him. She wanted his arms around her, enfolding her, with his lips pressing down on hers. Conrad, on the other hand, was looking for what he thought was love. What did he think that meant? He wasn't sure – all he knew was that it was more than the sexual fantasies that he had had as a boy, or the short affairs he had in the army, or even his liaison with Zipora. He needed more than sexual flights of fancy – but what? So the more Harriet devised ways and means of getting Conrad to respond passionately to her advances, the more Conrad prevaricated and waited – but waiting for what he had no idea.

Harriet became a fairly frequent visitor to Conrad's rooms on the staircase in the beautiful main Quad of Worcester College. She was quite stunning in the way she looked, a self-confidence and sensuality in the way she held herself. Everyone on the staircase regularly remarked on her comings and goings and, eventually, the man whose rooms were opposite Conrad's on the third floor, persuaded her, on an occasion when Conrad was out, to join him in having tea together. He too was an ex-soldier of about the same age as Conrad. His name was Jacob Astley and he was a direct descendent of that eponymous Royalist general of the Civil War, in command of the King's infantry. The General's famous prayer delivered on his knees in his tent directly to his God just before the Battle of Edgehill, remains an absolute model of an English gentleman's restrained devotion –

"Oh Lord, in all the turmoil of this day's work, if I do forget thee, do not thou Oh Lord forget me."

Tall and urbane, this Astley, known to all as Jake, had little of the devout nature of his ancestor. In line himself for a hereditary baronetcy, he was wealthy and assured. Harriet was flattered by his attentions. There was possibly also an element of spite in her actions – at least a desire to shock Conrad out of his complacency – though she knew perfectly well that trying to arouse jealousy in Conrad would not work. But in starting this new relationship it was Conrad she was trying to impress, rather than Jake. But once the relationship with Jake began, it took on a momentum of its own.

Astley was at that moment trying to come out of a homosexual relationship with a young music scholar – Michael – who had deferred his national service and had come straight up from school, as so many of those boys who got scholarships did. Michael, whose rooms were on the ground floor of the same staircase, had fallen in love with Jake's sophistication and experience as a war veteran, and was six years younger. The affair, if that is indeed what it could be called, was generally recognised by the rest of the men on the staircase. This was the highly charged period when Oxford was full of ex-soldiers, many returning scarred from their difficult and life-threatening experiences, and a smaller proportion of young, immature but highly intelligent young men straight from school. Socialism, sex and serious debate was all the rage – only a few years later it would all change and would become parties, personality and pleasure.

It did not take more than a few weeks for Jake to give Harriet what she was craving, without perhaps fully realising it herself. Soon, whenever she arrived in the afternoon to see Jake, he would ostentatiously 'sport his oak'. This was the second heavy door which, when closed, meant that the resident was not to be disturbed. On these occasions, Michael, who would of course have seen Harriet arriving, would come up and burst into Conrad's room and pick a quarrel with him. On one occasion, a week before the end of that second term, he began upbraiding Conrad —

"For God's sake Conrad, you brought that bloody woman into our lives – why don't you do something about it?"

"I don't know what you are talking about, Michael. Calm down old fellow – you're over-excited."

"Look, Jake isn't at all interested in women. He's only pretending to be in order to spite me. Your lovely Harriet is going to get hurt, and you ought to do something about it."

"First she's not 'my' lovely Harriet, and secondly she is quite capable of looking after herself. Michael – I don't know exactly what their relationship is, but you have to face up to the fact that the one you had with Jake is currently over. His sporting his oak like that is a very clear message to you that any affair that was between you is over. Oh God… look don't crack up for heaven's sake. I hate tears and this situation doesn't warrant them. He's actually letting you down gently. You've just got to get used to it."

Conrad had long since seen that the young and impressionable Michael was totally in thrall to the dominating Astley. He had also seen that Jake was only flattered by the boy's infatuation, and was not emotionally involved. Conrad, being Conrad, was concerned that the lad didn't do anything silly or have a breakdown. So he spent time and energy seeing to Michael's volatile emotions as Harriet continued to see Jake almost every afternoon, with the oak ostentatiously sported.

As the days passed, whenever they chatted together after lectures or after their one joint tutorial, Harriet would infer to Conrad, that her relationship with Jake was permanent and that marriage was likely – though Jake never mentioned anything of the sort to him. This was still a decade before the sexual liberation of the sixties and whilst liaisons of this kind were more and more common, they tended to be covered by the suggestion of an engagement.

Meanwhile, seeing to Michael's emotional turmoil, and generally trying to soften the blow to the boy's oversensitive psyche, Conrad failed to notice that, despite talk of marriage with Astley, Harriet still seemed to want to see him and continue their chats and meetings. As the summer term ended, Conrad became aware that Michael began to look and talk to him in a subtly different way. Conrad recognised immediately the possibility that the lad was transferring his over-abundant affections to himself. He carefully back-tracked and by doing it gently and with great sensitivity avoided that further pitfall, without causing the young man any more pain, or at least limiting such pain as was inevitable in the circumstances. The term ended and everyone went their separate ways for the long summer vacation of 1949.

* * *

Conrad had now been a student for a whole year and decided that he would return to Italy for the summer holidays. Italy was still in some turmoil, but travel throughout Europe, including Italy, had become much easier. As the summer started Billy who was now 16 was to be allowed to leave school as arranged. He had a year free before he could take up his scholarship at Christchurch. Conrad suggested that once the school term ended, Billy should join him and they could both stay in Florence at the Palazzo Maggi, where his Aunt's mother-in-law resided. Of course this could only be for two months at most, but after, Conrad suggested that Billy could spend the rest of the year with his Aunt Sima and Uncle Nicolai on the Maggi farms in the Veneto. There he could perfect his Italian and have the experience of working on a farm.

Both Harry and Olga were enthusiastic about this plan. Being under Conrad's wing in Florence would keep the boy out of mischief, and having to work on a farm, under the supervision of his somewhat strict and serious Uncle Nicolai, would undoubtedly be good for him as well. So Conrad wrote to the three sisters who lived at the Palazzo Maggi.

The three sisters in question were - Sofia, the Contessa Maggi, the widow of a Count Maggi who had been the owner of a large estate in the Veneto: Varvara, the Countess Berchtold, the widow or some other close relative by marriage of that Count Berchtold who had been the Austro-Hungarian foreign minister at the time of the outbreak of the Great War: and Natalya, the Countess Androvna, the mother of Uncle Nicolai who had married Sima – Olga Bridgeman's elder sister. These three sisters were the daughters of a somewhat impoverished aristocratic family in turn of the century Russia, each marrying well into the inter-connected late nineteenth century European aristocracy.

In the course of all the upheavals at the end of the

Great War – Natalya, Countess Androvna, whose husband had died during the war, had arrived in Constantinople with her son Nicolai, as part of the great White Russian exodus from Sevastopol after the crushing victory of the Reds. The young Nicolai had fallen in love with Sima Avakian, Olga's elder sister and thus Conrad's Aunt. They had married and, in due course, left the city to go to Italy, together with their mother the Countess, in order for Nicolai to take up employment as the manager of the estate of his Uncle and Aunt in the Veneto.

The late Count Maggi had also owned a building in Florence which was known as the Palazzo Maggi. After he died, just before the outbreak of the Second World War, the Palazzo was converted into three apartments – one on each floor – and the three sisters, all now widowed, decided to live there together. During the War, Conrad, while stationed in liberated Florence as an Intelligence officer with the Eighth Army, had frequently visited the three ladies for the two weeks he was in the city.

Conditions in Italy, completely catastrophic at the immediate end of the war, were still somewhat chaotic. The communist threat was dissipating as American aid poured in. However, social reform was in the air and conditions for people on fixed incomes were difficult. Both Natalya, the Countess Androvna, and Varvara, the Countess Berchtold, were in fairly straitened circumstances and welcomed any paying guests that could be arranged. The Contessa Maggi, who still had her income from the estates that Nicolai managed, had the larger of the three apartments, but even she now occasionally took in paying guests. She still managed to retain the services of her full-time live in maid – Giuseppina, who contrived to cook and serve meals and do the cleaning for all three apartments. The cleaning of the entrance hall and the common parts of the building was carried out by local girls. They came and went with alarming regularity. Indeed, juggling with one girl one day and another the next had become one of the main pre-occupations of the three elderly ladies.

Each of the three Contesse wrote back enthusiastically to Conrad and were looking forward to his arrival with his younger brother to live with them through the summer. The Golden Arrow service from London to Paris had begun again within a few months of the war's end. Conrad took that train from Victoria, crossed Paris going across to the Gare de Lyon and then sat on his own in the wonderful fin de siecle station restaurant, reliving his meals with his father there before the war. In due course he took the train across the Alps and on, first to Domodossola – "Panini, Birra. Arangiata" – then on to Milan, and eventually Florence. He was given a large double room in Maggi's flat with enormously high ceilings and long muslin curtains fluttering in any welcome breeze. There were two beds and this was where Billy was also to stay when he turned up in due course when the school term ended.

Chapter 13

Conrad reflects

I have never thought of myself as being at all unusual or different from all my friends. I know that having an Armenian mother does make me only half English, but that has never left me feeling any different. I adored school and never had any difficulty in getting on with everyone. When war came and I went into the army I loved the military life right from the start. I have always seemed to be able to slip into whatever role I have been asked to adopt without difficulty. Perhaps this was why I survived so easily in the nine months when I lived in Rome while it was under occupation by the Germans. I was acting – let's face it – as a spy, reporting back to Eighth Army Intelligence, and it would have been death if I got caught. But it seemed to come easily to me and during those nine months I almost became as Italian as I was English.

I once asked Mardik what language he 'thought in' – as opposed to what language he spoke at any one time. It never crossed my mind to ask the same question of myself. I am clear that wherever I am and whatever language I am speaking I always do my mathematical calculations in my mind in English. But I do remember that within a day or two of living in Rome behind enemy lines I was quite certainly 'thinking' in Italian – not just always speaking it. Nevertheless, even while thinking in Italian I remained myself, with all my English attitudes and inhibitions.

I have sometimes felt that this is a weakness in my character. I adapt too quickly and without thinking to whoever I am with. I took on a Jewish persona when I was with Zipora in Kfar Etzion, yet had no difficulty a few days later in empathising with a circle of elders in a Palestinian village on the road from Tel Aviv to Jerusalem. I have caught myself speaking English with an American accent when I am in the company of Americans. Indeed on one occasion I was taken to task because one of them thought I was poking fun at them. Perhaps this is why I am not assertive enough in my relationships with the young women I become fond of? My wish to adapt to them and to their wishes acts as an inhibition. But then sometimes I may be too assertive – pushing my views on everyone, just like Billy. No that's not fair either.

Ah …Billy, Billy … I must stop treating him as I do. After all, he is his own person and not just my little brother. I must admit, though, I do so love being his elder brother. I can never think of him as anything other than that wide-eyed trusting kid who looked to me to sort out all his boyish problems. Still, I must take greater care as to how I speak to him, instead of assuming he understands everything I am trying to say. Billy has an odd selective memory. Alongside his extraordinary mathematical genius, he lives in a sort of dream world in which all people around him are entirely noble and all of them love him. However he does also have a healthy scepticism and independence of mind. Unlike me, he always shows an admirable refusal to follow the crowd or the prevailing fashion.

* * *

And then there's the lovely Harriet Tate. I really am quite attached to her. Her acute, engaged mind seems to mirror my current interests precisely. She sees and appreciates Italian art and literature in an almost miraculously similar way to my own feelings. And I can't kid

myself that I don't also fancy her in other ways as well
– that body and that brooding sensual look that exudes
a sexuality that elicits a reaction in me and in my head
as well as in my groin. However, I am a little unhappy
to see that she has fallen for Astley. There's nothing I
can pinpoint that is wrong with Jake, but he has aggressively right-wing views and can be quite domineer-
ing towards all around him, particularly those younger
than him. I really don't believe that this is what Harriet
wants. But there it is – she says they are proposing to
get married, so perhaps there is more to Jake than I can
see myself. Pity! I do enjoy spending time with Harriet.
We seem to have a lot going for us, but she is clearly en-
thralled by Jake and talks about him all the time, trying
to get my approval for their relationship. I must stop
being irritated by this – it is surely only the obsession of
someone in love.

* * *

The train from Paris to Milan was very crowded and
I missed the comfort of travelling with my parents on
the Simplon-Orient to Istanbul before the war. I struggled out of the station in Florence with my luggage and
arrived at the Palazzo Maggi hot and bothered. However, I was immediately enveloped by all three Contesse
and warmly welcomed into their home. Giuseppina
was still with them, and even her forbidding features
creased into a wonderful smile. What a contrast with
my first visit during the war. Then, even though I was
only twenty-one, I was an officer in the British Army
which had just liberated the city. I was able to provide
them with some extra provisions from army stores and
on my last day I dined with them in full dress uniform.
Now, a full four years later, I somehow felt younger and
less mature than when I was with them during the war

– more dishevelled – less confident – scruffier – perhaps more jaded.

Sofia, the Contessa Maggi, is a sweet and lovable old lady. Past seventy now and maintaining a sort of grande dame dignity all her own. The aging process has affected her once pretty features, but she is still an imposing figure. She is also rather deaf. Her English is accented but, like all of those from the pre-Great War generation, impeccable. The world of all three sisters is narrow, centred on Florence but leavened by the internationalism of the pre-war aristocracy. I have to be careful, pretending to prefer Churchill to Attlee for instance, and dragging up scraps of information about our royal family with which to regale them. All three are snobs – living in a past which has gone for ever – but I love them all.

They have a friend of Maggi's staying with them – a Signora Coppoli, who comes and stays every so often. She lives in the country but comes to the town to give English lessons. They all speak English well – and believe that it is the right thing, the chic thing, to do. Signora Coppoli is a large imposing and rather selfish grandmother. She wears black bootees which somehow suit her. She dislikes Giuseppina, she dislikes Maggi's two sisters, she appears to me to be a scheming and – I would go so far as to say – diabolical old lady. But from the start she wants to ingratiate herself with me and comes out, when we are alone, with the most terrifying confidences about all the others, except Maggi of course. The most outrageous and banal flatteries set them all into a flutter – with the exception of the Countess Androvna who I think sees through such artificial charm, and is in any case the more intelligent of the sisters.

Varvara, the Countess Berchtold was, I believe, the wife of that Count Berchtold who was the Austro-Hungarian foreign minister at the outbreak of the Great War. She still has Hungarian nationality. I don't know much about it but Billy, in his wisdom, once told me, in his usual cocksure way, that if any single individual could be blamed for the outbreak of that catastrophe, he would be amongst them. When I muttered something about evil old men – he replied, 'Nonsense, brother. Count Berchtold, like most of the others, was a gentle man who abhorred violence, but didn't know what he was doing.' Cheeky scamp! The Countess was, of course, completely dispossessed by the Russians on their entry into Hungary at the end of the war. She has a fund of gracefully Central European diplomatic memoirs which are trotted out during dinner. She doesn't like the Signora any more than the Signora likes her and they tend to be verging on the brink of a row most days – usually placated by the tireless Maggi, who often appears oblivious to the catty snubs and insults that pass between them. Both the Signora and Berchtold are forever getting hold of me to complain about each other.

I don't know whether I am pleased or annoyed at what it is in me that encourages people to confide in me. During the war, I always seemed to be able to get much more information out of our prisoners-of-war than my colleagues.

Of course it is actually the third sister – Natalie, Countess Androvna, who lives on the top floor, to whom I am related. Sima, my Aunt, is her daughter-in-law. However, she does not eat with us every evening like Berchtold, and it is largely round the dinner-table that I interact with these delightful ladies. It is an enchantingly small world! These dear old ladies live in their pasts and in their dreams; getting slightly on each others nerves; ignoring the harsh realities around them; attached to Florence and all it represents in their proud aristocratic way. Here I am, sandwiched between them, spoilt by their kind hearts. How could I not love them all?

And the food is magnificent!

Chapter 14

The summer of 1949

Harry had insisted that Billy was to finish the school term, which went on much longer than the Oxford term. He could go out to join Conrad once school had ended. That summer, like the previous one, was extraordinary throughout Europe. The continent was still only just beginning to emerge from the terrible desolation – both physical and moral – of the devastating last year of the war. The refugees, that great mass of hopeless displaced persons milling about as the great Nazi slave-labour machine ground to a halt in 1945, had by then all been dealt with. An atmosphere of normality seemed to have arrived, while at the same time, on the other hand the Cold War was just starting and the continent remained unstable.

It was one of the ironies of the age that the ghastly slave-labour regime of the Nazis, together with their genocidal policies towards the minorities of Europe, had accomplished a major ethnic cleansing of the whole of Eastern Europe – with the exception perhaps of Yugoslavia. The effect of shifting Poland westwards; of removing the Germans from the East and the Balkans; of throwing the Germans out of the Sudetenland; all this had caused the elimination of minorities everywhere. After the end of the Great War, it was the boundaries of the nation-states that had all been changed in order to accommodate the people. After the Second World War, it was the people themselves who were displaced and moved about in order to accommodate the nation-state.

Billy, armed with more than adequate funds from his parents, took the same trains as Conrad – but, never having had the same experiences travelling with his father, he did not linger at the station restaurant of the Gare de Lyon. When he finally arrived in Milan, he found himself caught up in an enormous Italian railway workers strike. It was complete chaos, and Billy first sat for ages in the station, before getting on the only train that left that day from Milan going south. This turned out to be a slow stopping train that stopped for interminable periods at all the small stations along the North Italian plain. It eventually came to a complete standstill late in the afternoon just before Bologna. Billy was the only person in his compartment – this was an old coach with no corridors. The train simply stood there in the middle of fields of high reed-like stalks of some grain or another that he could not recognise on either side. He had not had the sense to buy any food, not even a panini; he was after all only a 16 year-old who had always had others providing for him. He remained cold and lonely all night. Despite the summer's midday heat, as the night wore on the temperature dropped and the cold got into his bones preventing a moment's sleep.

Meanwhile Conrad had been waiting all day at the bar in the station at Florence, drinking several glasses of Carpano, one of his favourite aperitivos. Getting bored, he decided to try out one by one, a glass of each of the many quinine-based drinks sitting on the shelves at the back of the bar, all with exotic names and garish labels. There were at least 14 different makes. At last after 11.00pm, once it became clear that no train would be arriving from any direction that night, Conrad staggered home, much the worse for wear, just managing to avoid Giuseppina, and collapsing onto his bed fully dressed.

The next morning, he went down again to the station, now nursing a fairly fearsome hangover. Carefully avoiding the barman's eye, he drank copious cups of coffee and hung about the platform as the occasional train pulled in. Meanwhile, Billy's train had finally got under steam and after stopping at every station, eventually reached Bologna. There it was stuck for several hours – then set off again and in fits and starts finally arrived at the Stazione Santa Maria Novella in Florence by the late afternoon. Billy was exhausted, hungry and dirty. He may have been a maths genius, one of the youngest scholars ever to have been chosen for Christchurch, but he was quite naïve and unpractised for his age. Conrad embraced his brother, holding him tight, and Billy began crying from sheer exhaustion and a sense of relief at being at last in the safe hands of his elder brother.

Conrad led his young brother to the Palazzo Maggi. Rescued from his ordeal, Billy's mood changed into that of a febrile and excited boy, chatting nonstop, and highly exaggerating the drama of his experience on Italian State Railways. Conrad knew that Billy would feel humiliated if he appeared before the grand old ladies, in an over-excited, dishevelled and dirty state. He spirited him quickly into their bedroom, after getting Giuseppina's nod of compliance, and a couple of hours later, after a hot bath, a change of clothes and morale boost, Billy was ready to be introduced to the three Contesse in the sitting-room, waiting to go in to dinner. Knowing of Billy's pending arrival, Natalya, Countess Androvna, was present on this evening.

The three Naritsyn sisters were not directly related to Conrad or Billy. However, Natalya, the Countess Androvna, was the mother of their Uncle by marriage – Nicolai, and this made the Contesse think of the young men as family. Above all, they had each come to have a deep affection for Conrad from the moment he had come into their lives during the war five years before. Speaking in impeccable upper-class English they welcomed Billy as he came in with Conrad dressed for dinner – Conrad having provided him with a tie. Without any shyness, Billy went forward, bent down and kissed each seated sister in turn firmly on the cheek – something Conrad had never yet had the courage – or the nerve – to do.

"Ah, Signor William, welcome, welcome. It is wonderful at last to meet you. We have heard so much about you from your dear brother. I am so sorry that you have arrived just at a moment when we in Italy seem to be having so many problems. I really hope that your stay with us will be happy."

The three ladies spoke gently, one after another, without appearing to interrupt each other, as if their lines were rehearsed. Then Contessa Maggi, although the youngest of the three, took over and said –

"Conrad, caro, we understand that your brother has come to Italy for a few months in order to improve his Italian speech. So. today we will continue in English, but from tomorrow Italian only while in the house."

"Certainly, Contessa."

"Now Signor William, will you…"

"Er, please Ma'am call me Billy – everyone does and I am not used to William."

"Very well. Will you take an aperitif? Conrad see to a drink please. I will have a Cinzano, and you – er – young man?"

"No thank you, Madam, my father doesn't allow me to drink alcohol."

And so it was, in this charming but inconsequential manner, Billy came into the lives of the three sisters. Neither the Contessa Maggi, nor her sister Berchtold, ever quite got used to using the name Billy – it seemed too frivolous and perhaps a shade vulgar. In any event, after that first evening, once Italian became the language between them, they did not have to try, as Billy became Guglielmo. While Billy for some strange and inexplicable reason could not abide the name 'William', he had no difficulty with Guglielmo.

For over a month Conrad and Billy explored the art treasures of Florence, both together and separately. They would meet at lunchtime at the same café in the far corner of the Piazza Signoria and would then spend the afternoons together – the Uffizi, the Academia, the Ponte Vecchio, Santa Croce, the Palazzi. Billy came to know the town better than he knew London. Conrad had retained contacts with all those he had known during the war and as a result they also travelled to other towns nearby. Fairly soon after Billy's arrival, Conrad went on his own for four days to Rome and reopened his friendship with Giancarlo and his ardent Communist circle. Conrad, mildly left-wing like so many of his wartime contemporaries, never had any deep political convictions himself, and allowed their political arguments to wash over him. He was suspicious of their disciplined and authoritarian beliefs, but his innate love for people, particularly those with whom he had shared wartime experiences, prevented him from entering into any arguments.

While Conrad was in Rome, Billy met a couple of English art students from Cambridge who started chatting to him from the next table in a cafe. There had always been something about Billy which made people think that he was older than he was. It was certainly not his looks. Taking after his father, rather than Olga, he was admittedly tall for his age. Nevertheless, from a purely superficial point of view, he was usually taken for an 18 or 19 year old. Something similar had happened to him when he was only seven and had been presumed older by two 10-year olds in an unfortunate incident that took place in Istanbul before the war, which had landed him in trouble. So it was again here in Florence, that the two students, looking on him as about the same age as themselves, introduced him to their own mixed group of Cambridge students who were living on the southern outskirts of the town beyond the Palazzo Pitti. While Conrad was away, Billy began joining them in the evenings after dinner at the Palazzo Maggi. For the first time in his life, urged on by his new companions, he began drinking wine – the rather nasty cheap red Chianti which the group were drinking.

It was two days after Conrad's return from Rome that he told Billy one evening that he would be going out that night with a friend. Billy had missed his daily excursions with Conrad and had been disappointed that Conrad had had other things to do when he came back from Rome, so that their joint explorations had not immediately recommenced. This recognition that Conrad had his own life and friendships, sparked off one of Billy's fits of jealousy. It never crossed his mind that he, too, had found new friends in Conrad's absence.

For Conrad, everything in life turned round his awareness and empathy for the people whom he loved. For Billy, everything turned round his awareness and anxiety about how or whether other people loved him.

That night, after dinner, Billy went off to see his new friends in the southern suburbs of the town. It was not as if he really liked the cheap red wine which they were all drinking – but somehow he was led into taking glass after glass. There was nothing intentionally malicious about it; they really had no idea that he was only sixteen, or that this was the first time that he had consumed significant amounts of alcohol.

He should really have stayed the night and slept on the floor, but he had no idea he had drunk too much. The fresh air hit him as he came out of the hostel to make his way home. This made him dizzy, but he walked on past the Pitti, across the new bridge and into the main town. By now, in a complete daze, he finally made it to the front door of the Palazzo Maggi. Try as he might, and creating a disturbance, he was quite unable to get the old key into the lock. Totally disorientated he leaned against the door, and then became violently sick, vomiting all over the wooden panels and over his clothes.

By now Giuseppina, whose room was on the ground floor next to the main door, was awake. She pulled on a dressing gown and hurried to the door. Having peeked out to check who it was, she opened the door. Billy was still leaning against it, his face squashed into his own vomit, and as the door opened he fell forward onto the floor with his body half in and half out of the building and passed out completely. Giuseppina could not move him and hurried upstairs, knocking on Conrad's door. He was lying on his bed reading. Billy had not returned, so he was waiting up for him, and had only just begun to get a little worried.

He hurried down. Billy was completely dead to the world and was stinking. Trying to make as little noise as possible, Conrad bent down and with Giuseppina's help he threw Billy over his shoulder and staggered up the stairs, Once in the flat he thanked Giuseppina and told her to go back to bed. He undressed his brother, getting no cooperation at all, and then carefully washed him with a flannel and a towel and put him into bed. Then taking a pail of warm water into which he put a bar of soap and Billy's stained shirt, he went down to the front door. There, again working as quietly as he could, he washed down all the vomit before it dried. When he had finished, he threw the now filthy shirt into the dustbin. Making sure that Billy was breathing properly in his sleep, he finally got to bed himself as the faint hint of dawn was showing in the window. The next morning, Billy did not wake up until midday. Conrad, meanwhile, had already gone out after breakfast and purchased two new shirts in Billy's size.

Conrad never knew whether the Contessa Maggi ever found out what had happened. Certainly, Giuseppina never referred to it, either to Conrad or to Billy, and so he could never tell whether the Countess had awoken during the night, or whether Giuseppina had ever told her. Billy loved his older brother, there was never any doubt about that; but somehow he accepted everything that Conrad ever did for him as his right – as something natural. So the only thanks Conrad usually got was a cheerful grin and a kiss on the cheek.

Three days later, Nicolai and Auntie Sima arrived, having driven down from the estate in their new Fiat. They stayed only two days in their mother's apartment at the top of the house. It was now the end of September and Conrad was due to return to Oxford for the new term. The morning that he was due to leave, he at last embraced each of the three sisters, having been emboldened by the example given by his younger brother, and was taken to the station by Nicolai and Billy. On that same afternoon that Conrad left on the train to Milan, Billy piled into the back of the little car and the three of them drove back to the estate in Veneto, where Billy was going to spend the next eight months with his Aunt and Uncle working on the farm.

Chapter 15

Billy's narrative

I suppose that those two months that I spent in Florence at the home of the Contessa Maggi in the summer of 1949 was one of the most exciting and formative periods of my life. I lived every hour in a fervour of pleasure. Every day my eye would feast with wonder on some new sculpture, some new painting or some new building. All this was carefully and lovingly introduced to me by my brother Conrad, who patiently pointed out to me one marvel after another.

I arrived in Florence after an exhausting train journey, which due to the Italian Railway strikes took several days. Even though I already had a scholarship to read Mathematics at Christchurch starting in September 1949, my father had insisted that I had to remain at school until I was 16. After leaving school in July, it had been arranged that I would go to Italy to live for six months on the farm managed by my mother's eldest sister Sima, and her husband Nicolai. I suppose the idea was that I should learn Italian and get a bit more practical experience about 'Life' – uttered by all my elders and betters with a capital 'L'.

That last summer term at my school – Westminster – my Maths teachers had given up teaching me from the syllabus. Instead, I was studying twice a week with a retired Professor of Mathematics who lived near the school. He introduced me to the problem of the fifteen schoolgirls, postulated originally by a Victorian mathematician – Thomas Kirkman. This was one of a series of mathematical puzzles raised by this fascinating clergyman that I explored during the summer – problems largely about combinations. I wrote a long dissertation on the man and his puzzles for my professor. You have 7 friends whom you wish to invite to dinner in threes. How many times can you issue your invitations before 2 of them must come together for a second time. Easy-peasy! But then apply that to the 15 schoolgirls, a problem set out in a mathematical journal of the time. Fifteen schoolgirls walk out 3 abreast for 7 days and it is required to arrange each day's walk so that any one particular pair walk only once in the same row during the week. Well Kirkman worked it out and applied for the prize that had been offered by the journal. I have to say that I did too, though of course separated by a hundred years and aided by new developments in mathematical knowledge in between. Still I was able to work it out and provide the formula pretty quickly.

Conrad tells me regularly that I shouldn't be so cocky. He claims that to be 'cheeky and cocky' is the worst possible combination. But because he is so often right and reasonable, it makes me want to do something outrageous to shock him out of his complacency whenever we are together. During those eight weeks in Florence, he led me through so many experiences of art and architecture that my brain was reeling by the time he had finished with me and we parted. I felt free and liberated in a way that I had never felt before. On top of that, I found that in Italy I could be much more expressive and enthusiastic about everything I saw and everybody I met, without once having to worry about what all my English friends might think.

What was it about Florence when you are 16? What was it? Chi lo se. It was perhaps that you learned to look and see things with greater intensity. It was what made one aware of the symmetry of a curled grape-stalk, a fig and a peach stone placed on one of Maggi's wonderful china plates, even while trying hard to concentrate on the Italian conversation flowing around you. It was that moment, standing behind a group of tourists milling around, that your brother pointed out to you a Ghiberti angel gazing in stupefaction over their heads. That extraordinary moment, when gazing at the Byzantine bas-reliefs on the Santa Maria Maggiore you saw the exact same gesture echoed by the policeman directing traffic at the nearby crossroads.

Conrad took me everywhere. After almost six years of separation while he was at the war, I remembered again how much I loved him and felt once more how much he loved me, though he never ever said so. Why can't people say 'I love you' when they so obviously do? I also recalled how he would always look after me regardless of where we were or what we were doing. But then – why not? Isn't that what elder brothers are for?

When September came to an end, Conrad returned home for his next term at Oxford, while I went to my Aunt's home near Padua.

Uncle Nicolai and Aunty Sima arrived in a small Fiat. We all saw Conrad off at the Stazione Santa Maria Novella. Then it was time to say goodbye to the three old ladies, confounding them a little because I not only kissed each of them but gave them each big hug. Then, perched in the back of the little car, with my Gladstone bag beside me, we drove back up to my Aunt's home near Padua.

Uncle Nicolai manages the land and estates of the Conte Maggi, his own uncle by marriage. This old gentleman died before the war, leaving his widow, in whose apartment I had been living with Conrad, as the sole owner. Most of the tenant farmers had bought out their lands and farms, but Nicolai had taken over those that had fallen into the estate and managed them on behalf of his widowed Aunt. The main estate where they lived is set in beautiful countryside, not more than about three or four kilometres from a small town – Galzignano. This town was about 15 kilometres from Padua.

The house itself, known as the Villa Maggi, was not a farmhouse, but a small Palladian-style villa. Set on the side of a low hill, it was surrounded by cypresses and other dark evergreens. There was a drive which curled up from the road below and ended at the front. There was not much of a vista due to the amount of shrubbery and well maintained hedges encircling the villa. Dotted around the gardens was statuary of all kinds – the cherubim and seraphim type of thing. There were fountains with yet more rococo statuary. However, Uncle Nicolai never had them working – at least never while I was living there. I found the heavy green trees and hedges rather oppressive and gloomy. But then I was never there during the heat of high summer when the shade would have been really welcome. I arrived in October, after the heat of high summer had passed, and I left to go home the following May.

The Villa was at the centre of an estate containing four separate farms, each carefully specialising in a different produce. Uncle Nicolai had an old pre-revolutionary Russian title and was referred to by some of the older employees as 'Il Signor Conte Androv'. He was fairly strict, and, to be honest, was fairly humourless. I think that he had been told by my Dad that I was not to be indulged in any way and to treat me just like any other of his employees. From the start, I had to be at work by 7.00am. On the very first day I was given a bicycle in order to be able to get from one farm to another.

I would ride down the wonderful little lanes that wound their way round the farms. During the month of October 1949 it was always in glorious morning sunshine. I had to be at the dairy farm by 7.00am at the latest. I would arrive to help with the milking and feeding of the cows and deal with the cleaning out of the stables. This farm had the highest concentration of labour – having, as well as the herd of cows, several pigs and other animals. After the first two hours work, I would have breakfast with the farmer and the other workers, served by his wife, with all of us sitting round the big table in the kitchen. I was on duty with this farmer, doing whatever jobs were required until about 11.00. I would then cycle to the next farm. Throughout the whole seven months that I was there, I always started my mornings at that dairy farm, which was about a ten minute walk from a tiny hamlet called Castelnovo. The second farm that I would have to go to each morning changed according to Uncle's requirements for extra hands.

I would work at the second farm from about 11.30 till about 3.30pm. There, at one of the three other farms, I would have my lunch with the others – usually in the fields, or in the case of the farm producing wine, in the vineyards. That farm, which concentrated on producing an excellent local wine, was further away on the slopes of the Monte Vanda, the highest hill in the area. It was quite a tough ride to be able to get there in time. The food for lunch would usually be brought out by one of the girls employed on that farm.

I was always finished by 4.00pm at the latest, though sometimes a little earlier than that. I would cycle back to the Villa after which I was always free for the rest of the day. On good days, I would cycle round the countryside. Several times I went into Padua. There I would go into the Scrovegni Chapel to look at the Giottos – a painter to whom I had first been introduced by Conrad in Florence. One could just walk in and out of the chapel quite freely then. I would always have my evening dinner with Uncle and Auntie. My Italian improved by leaps and bounds. However, the language I spoke with all my work colleagues on the farms was rather different to that spoken at the Villa or that which I had been laboriously learning in Florence round the dinner table of the three Contesse. I'm not sure if it was dialect like the Venetians speak, or just local and rough. Either way I had to be careful at dinner, as Uncle Nicolai was quite sharp in correcting me if I came out with any slang.

There were two lively sisters who worked at the dairy farm. One was 18 and the other 19 years-old. They were not the daughters of the farmer but lived with their own family, in a house in the nearby hamlet of Castelnovo, and came to work at the farm every morning. They were always already hard at work before I arrived at 7.00. One of the sisters – Maddalena, the youngest, had a local boy friend who held a job in Padua. Although there was no formal engagement, it was generally accepted that they would soon be married. The other sister did not have a boyfriend so far as I knew.

From the start, I was teased mercilessly by both of them. They laughed at my attempts, clumsy at first, to join them in the milking. They taught me words which when I first repeated them caused my Aunt to tell me off. I soon learned not to trust them and would check with one of the men at the farm if they taught me a word or a phrase. Maddalena was small, pretty and mischievous with short jet-black hair. Paulina was tall – taller than me. She too had jet-black hair which was long, though she tended to keep it tied up under a scarf when she was at work. She was not very pretty, but she had stunning long legs and always seemed to have a sultry, angry expression.

I wasn't overawed by them – at least I don't

think so. Once I had got used to the accent of the area, and got over my initial shyness, I gave as good as I got. Conrad would have said that my natural cheekiness came to my aid. All the other workers at the dairy farm were much older men and married, so I was the only available young male around. The teasing gradually became more provocative without any actual contact. I felt sexual feelings coming on. I really liked them both, but it seemed to me, at first, that it was just harmless flirtation – nothing like what I had felt for Barry.

I know that Barry had not loved me – not even for one moment. He used me simply to satisfy his own urges. He never ever considered what I might have wanted out of the affair. He simply threw me a look whenever he wanted anything and I followed him and did whatever he wanted. Why did I do it? Well I think I loved him. It was not just sexual; I wanted to lie with him, kiss and hold him. But I also wanted him to be proud of me if I won a race or a game of squash, and I always excelled in any sport if I knew he was watching. I wanted to hear him say 'Well done Billy'.

This was different at least at first. I could feel that Paulina wanted something from me, and to be fair I realised that I wanted something from her, though I wasn't really clear as to what. The critical moment came within a month or so after I had started working there. One morning, after the milking was done, Paulina and I were alone together in the cowshed raking the hay in the loft above the cows. The gentle, but provocative, ribbing that went on between us suddenly changed into a charged silence. Paulina rather deliberately put down the rake and came up to me, taking my rake out of my hands and setting it aside. I knew that this was a special moment. She leant forward and I felt her lips on mine. I was not taken by surprise, I simply didn't know for sure what to do. Her hands came round the back of my neck and she pressed hard on the back of my head pushing me forward towards her as I felt her tongue exploring my mouth. I don't know whether she then fell back on the hay, pulling me down on top of her, or whether I pushed her down. It doesn't really matter how it happened; it just happened and there we were.

The memory of the earthy smell in that cowshed has gone, but the sound of the soft chewing of the cows below has remained with me ever since. This was not my first kiss. I had already kissed several girls – mostly Natalie's friends, all of whom thought that I was older than I was. Barry too had kissed me, but with a violent almost sadistic passion that literally took my breath away. This was different again. I became aroused as I had never been before. Above all, it was deliciously tender. I was overwhelmed. I had no idea what to do on that first occasion in the cowshed. I only knew that I had to follow her gentle instructions communicated to me only by the movements of her body. Throughout the whole proceedings, we hardly said a single word to each other. Paulina undid my buttons, she did whatever she had to do to her own slacks, she guided my hand to where she wanted it to go. Of course it went no further, on that occasion than our hands and lips, but she did it all with a patient kindness which I had never experienced from anyone before.

After that first half-hour we spent together in the loft, I began to fall in love with Paulina. I simply could not imagine, experiencing as I did that gentleness and consideration that she had shown to me and continued to show, that her own feelings were not that of 'love' also. But it turned out that I was mistaken.

As the days and weeks passed, Paulina would tell me where and when we would next meet. I would duly cycle down to the appointed spot – her house if her parents were away – an empty barn – a hayrick – a spot in the woods. Recalling that half year I have no idea what it was that really motivated her. I am sure it was not just 'sex'. This was 1949, more than ten years before the sexual liberation of the sixties. It took a few meetings and sexual experimentation between us, but eventually the moment came when we fully consummated our coupling. How, in the Italy of the late forties, she got hold of the thing that she slipped onto me, before she guided me into a full sexual union, I really don't know.

At Christmas of that year, Uncle Nicolai's mother – the Countess Androvna – came from Florence to stay for a few days. I went with Uncle Nicolai in the little Fiat to pick her up from Padua station. I knew that my brother adored all three ladies at the Palazzo Maggi, but I always had the feeling that he preferred Maggi and Berchtold. I, on the other hand, found I had a soft spot for Madame Natalya right from the start. Of the three sisters, she was the only one who had had sons. I had a feeling that she saw through all my social stratagems. But I was equally sure that she was amused, rather than irritated by them. Whenever I came out with a grin and a bit of outrageous flattery, she would give me a look with those deeply intelligent eyes and would give me a knowing smile, which never failed to bowl me over.

I was not given much time off over the Christmas holidays. The cows still had to be milked every day. However, for three days, I was no longer required to go on to the second farm and was, instead, allowed to return home for Christmas lunches with the family. Paulina and I were at the height of our regular meetings, and I would cycle away in the afternoons after lunch to her selected rendezvous – much to my Aunt's surprise as my explanations were pretty feeble. I know that neither Uncle Nicolai nor Auntie Sima had the slightest suspicion of what I was doing. However. I twice saw the Countess give me one of those special smiles which both worried and thrilled me so much, when I returned in the afternoon.

I was committed to Paulina – I really was fully committed. I knew I was in love. I wanted to do everything for her that I could. I longed to be with her and listen to her endearing words. Surely this was real and mutual love – but once again, as if I was fated, I began to realise that Paulina was not in love with me in anything like the real sense of the word. I suppose I could say that she liked me. I was 'simpatico' for her. But that was all. She had a practical side to her character that saw that our relationship was going nowhere. I was a foreigner – I would soon leave – it was in a way a safe affair for her that could not in the end cause any complications. There was never, never, any contempt or condescension in her attitude – but the fact that I was only sixteen slowly became more apparent to her, or so I believe. She continued only because it was exciting and enjoyable, and because she was an affectionate girl and knew that I was in love with her – and I think that this gave her a feeling of sexual power which she enjoyed exercising.

In the end, our last meeting alone was in that same hayloft. She knew that I was going home two days later and that I was now going the rounds to the four farms just to say goodbye to everyone. We simply stood and stared at each other. In the last six months I had grown physically and I was now as tall as her. I took the lead, as I had rarely done before. I held her in my arms and she arched back. I kissed her with a depth of real feeling – but in the end that was it. I had come to know what she wanted just by the movement of her body, and I knew that she didn't want to go beyond a kiss on this occasion. She smiled at me as we parted, gave me a further peck on the cheek, and then, without another word, she clambered down the ladder and away. Returning home the next day, I did not see her again before I left.

Chapter 16

Oxford

Billy returned home in May – it was now 1950. He was due to start as a Maths scholar at Christchurch in the October term. His Italian had become almost as good as Conrad's, though he never achieved Conrad's complete fluency in the language and always had an unmistakeable English accent.

The year before, on his return from Florence for the new term at Oxford, Conrad had drifted back into a somewhat desultory and careful relationship with Harriet. Harriet had spent that same summer on a tour of Turkey and Iran in a old, ramshackle car. She had made the journey with an old school-friend and the friend's older brother. It was 1949 and well before the coming heyday of young westerners touring in the Middle East. Everyone with whom she had discussed the trip was adamant that it was absolutely necessary to have a male escort - hence the presence of the brother.

When the new term began, she was back, eager to see Jake and to look up Conrad. She poured out all the details of her trip, the wonderful sights and the occasional disasters, on separate occasions to both men. She found that she had greater pleasure recounting her adventures to Conrad than to Jake. Conrad was always interested and attentive, appreciating the importance to her of the experiences that she had gone through, where Jake's mind was, or seemed to be, solely on her physical attractions. Convinced that Astley and Harriet were in love, Conrad maintained a polite reserve with her. Perversely, the more Conrad kept his cool, the more Harriet's interest in him increased. She was much more used to fending off the eager attentions of young men, rather than being the one attempting to extend a friendly and satisfying relationship into a more loving and physical one. She was undoubtedly falling in love with Conrad, at least in so far as she was capable of love at all.

Conrad was still in the same rooms in the main Quad of Worcester College. Jacob Astley was also still there on the same staircase and with the same rooms directly opposite.

It would not be easy to analyse with any assurance Harriet's feelings and her motivations towards the two Worcester College men. She had many followers throughout the University – this was still the period when girls were in a very small minority in the University. She dealt with all these admirers with sophistication and aplomb, but her relationships with Conrad and Jacob were different. She liked Conrad a lot and loved every moment that she was with him. But, despite his easy charm, he always retained a reserve towards her which was irritating and challenging. On the other hand, she was excited by Astley's sexuality, challenging her in exactly the opposite way. She was also a little afraid of him. Accordingly, despite wanting above all to be wooed by Conrad, she tended to drift back to Astley. Harriet was not a virgin. She was sexually mature and her liaison with Astley had very quickly been fully consummated. Meanwhile, she had never exchanged more than fairly chaste kisses with Conrad.

Still present on this Worcester College staircase was Michael, the boy who was still deeply in love with the indifferent Jake. The whole ménage was typical of the Oxford of the late forties – an extraordinary period when two-thirds of the student population consisted of young men battle hardened by five or six years of war, who had returned to take up places offered to them years before. The other third were clever young boys of 18 or even less, who came straight from school, who, by dint of scholarships, had been accepted before having to do their national service. Conrad at 25 and Jake at 26 were facing Harriet and Michael, both only 19.

Over and over again, in order to keep her hold over Jake, Harriet had to put up with Michael. She often had to swallow her pride and had to tolerate his presence, cruelly insisted upon by Jake, even though he was well aware that the boy hated her. Conrad remained uncomfortably in the middle, having to listen to Michael's rage whenever Jake 'sported his oak', if Harriet was visiting him in the afternoon. Harriet of course was not allowed to be in the college after 6.30pm so there was never any question of Jake sporting his oak when Michael crept up the stairs and into Jake's rooms at night. As for Jacob Astley himself, he had long since ceased to worry himself about the complicated emotional feelings of either of the two 19 year-olds.

In her happier moments when Harriet was enjoying conversations with Conrad, he enthused about the days he had spent in Florence the previous summer. Harriet asked for the address of the Contessa Maggi and told Conrad that in the coming summer she too wanted to go to Florence to perfect her Italian. She duly wrote, mentioning Conrad's name. The Contessa replied enthusiastically that she would be happy for Harriet to come, and in the letter discreetly referred to her terms.

By the start of the summer of 1950 Harriet and Astley had become a recognised couple. There was an implied suggestion of an engagement. This was the sedate fifties; there was no hint of the coming sexual liberation of the sixties. Liaisons like those of Harriet and Astley were acceptable in the university's closeted atmosphere, but only if an engagement was seen to be in the offing.

Conrad's feelings were complicated. He enjoyed Harriet's company, and he found her attractive and sexually stimulating, but he had an easy relationship with Jake, too, and believing him to be in love with Harriet, he loyally kept his distance, much to her distress. At the same time, Michael's increasing hysteria and complaints worked on him and somehow prevented him from recognising Harriet's own complicated feelings. Once the first glow of passion was over, she actually preferred to be with him. But Conrad, faced with his own internal inclinations towards loyalty, failed to recognise the true nature of Harriet's feelings towards him.

Jake had a deep respect and admiration for Conrad. It was Conrad who helped him in the continuing saga of Michael's hopeless infatuation. But Conrad never ever realised that Jake was continuing his liaison with Michael at night. He assumed that Jake was in love with Harriet, and more to the point that Harriet was in love with Jake.

He was wrong on both counts.

It was not just the thought that Harriet had decided herself to go to Florence over the coming summer, that contributed to Conrad's decision to return to Florence as well. He wanted to revisit the pleasurable surroundings of the previous year. So he asked Billy, who was moping at home, working on ever-more abstruse mathematical puzzles, to join him. Having nothing much else to do Billy enthusiastically agreed. And he was in fact the first to make the trip out to Italy.

This summer, the arrangements were to be different. Harriet had already been given the large room in the apartment of Sofia, the Contessa Maggi. Conrad had been allocated the much smaller single room in the same flat. But Billy, no longer able to share with Conrad, was to stay in the apartment of Natalya, the Countess Androvna, in her only spare room. It was however arranged that all the evening meals would be taken in the elegant dining room of the Contessa Maggi.

It was to be a momentous summer for everyone.

Chapter 17

The summer of 1950 – Florence

Billy was the first of the threesome due to arrive in Italy for the summer. He had decided that he would visit Nicolai and his Aunt Sima at the Villa Maggi in the Veneto before going on to Florence. He planned to stay with them for at least three days, and of course wanted to renew his acquaintance with Paulina if he could. After his arrival, he discovered that Paulina was no longer working at the dairy farm, and none of the afternoon staff seemed to have any idea where she might be. However Maddalena was still there and Billy cycled down the following morning to have a word with her.

It seemed that Paulina was now engaged to a young legal clerk from Padua. Maddalena herself was now married. She admitted to Billy proudly that she was pregnant. She was loath to let him know the date the baby was due, though she confirmed that the actual marriage had been only a few months previously. Billy was still very naïve for his age and failed to appreciate why she was so evasive.

Billy asked after Paulina and Maddalena said that she would let him know when he could arrange to see her, if he came again the next morning. So Billy cycled down again the next morning and Maddalena arrived with the news that Paulina was taking that very day off and would be happy to see him in the afternoon at her home in Castelnovo. Billy returned to the Villa Maggi, and then after lunch, in a frenzy of boyish excitement, he again grabbed the old farm bicycle and cycled down to the village.

"Ah mio caro Guglielmo," called out Paulina the

moment she opened the door. She smiled with such a welcoming warmth in her eyes that Billy's heart turned over. He smiled back at her with an uncomplicated feeling of sheer joy, so special an attribute of youth. Paulina beckoned him in and then to his disappointment gave him a kiss – on both cheeks! She then ushered him into the formal front room of the house, rather than into the cosy kitchen where they used to sit together the year before, when he was only sixteen. But that was indeed when he was sixteen – now he was seventeen. He was taller, more robust and, above all, more masculine, and she was engaged to be married to another man. They sat down facing each other.

Billy was not feeling shy and Paulina was perfectly relaxed and clearly happy. Accordingly their conversation was neither stilted nor embarrassing. However, within only a few minutes Billy became aware, in the pit of his stomach, that their liaison of the previous year had meant much more to him than it had to this cool and self-possessed lady. Though only a rural farm-worker, she had a poise and self-awareness that Billy totally lacked.

It was not that Billy imagined that they would pick up where they had left off, but he desperately wanted some mutual recognition of what had taken place between them, only six months ago. After all, their affair had gone on day after day for months on end. Poor Billy, it was no use his having told himself time and again that for Paulina, two years his senior, it had never been love, when for him, he had felt deeply every kiss, every touch and mutual caress. He may have been a Cherubino in respect of all those stolen kisses with Natalie's girlfriends – but with Paulina he was convinced he had felt real love for a woman, above and beyond the natural affection and kindness she had shown him. He held tight to the hope that her feelings for him were deeper. Caught in a complete quandary, not until this new meeting had he finally known for sure what to think.

And now, facing her cool detachment – what actually did he want from her? He did not know. And it came to him that, after all, it had not been that different to his adolescent crush on Barry when he was not even 15. Paulina had been kinder, gentler, more considerate and, from his point of view, considerably more rewarding. But in the end, and in both cases, he was left with a memory of passion and love on his part, while having to accept that to both these objects of his love, he had left no impression at all. Barry had undoubtedly forgotten the incidents within days, while Paulina would probably have completely forgotten him within a year. But for him, the memory – or at least the narrative that he had created for himself – would stay with him for ever.

Tea was brought in by her mother, who remembered Billy well from the previous year. Paulina had no hesitation in inviting her to sit with them. They chatted together easily, largely about the coming wedding and the forthcoming arrival of Maddalena's baby. Billy might well be in a turmoil of emotion inside, but his natural extroverted character allowed him to play the role expected from him in most social occasions, and this attribute did not fail him on this occasion. Eventually, long before it became dark, Billy made his excuses and cycled back to the Villa Maggi.

La Fenice in Venice was still closed, but the Scala in Milan was open and thriving. Uncle Nicolai worked his contacts over the telephone and got a ticket for Billy who stopped in Milan on his way to Florence and went to a performance of Rossini's "Il Turco in Italia". Being used to the then more sedate performances at Covent Garden, he was bowled over by the enthusiasm and rowdy admiration of the Italian audience. It happened to be an early appearance of Callas, who had already re-fashioned herself as a Milanese. This particular Rossini opera contains two competing sopranos, who at one moment, in most productions, almost come to blows in the second Act. As it happened, on this particular evening the other soprano was a well-known Napolitana diva. Each lady had their 'claquists' in the audience. And each claque shouted 'bravo' and clapped enthusiastically as their particular heroine came to a Rossinian climax at the end of their arias – each claque trying to outdo the noise made by the other. Callas, of course, with the bigger more demanding part, and with the Milanese audience behind her and, in fairness, much the better actress, unquestionably got the better of these exchanges.

Billy came out into the soft summer night in a state of excited Inglese-Italianato bliss. But that night, not knowing either of the two sopranos, he thought, to his future embarrassment, that the Neapolitan girl had got the better clearer voice.

Eventually Billy arrived in Florence. Neither Conrad nor Harriet had as yet appeared. He settled quickly into the little room he had been allocated in the third floor apartment of Nicolai's mother - Natalya, the Countess Androvna. The Countess Androvna, despite being the eldest of the three sisters, had kept her elegance and good looks much better. Well into her seventies, she nevertheless still exuded a pleasurable old-world charm which thrilled the ever-susceptible Billy, who could not hide a sort of submissive, boyish attraction towards her. From the start, the evening meal was always taken in the large dining room of the Contessa Maggi, where Giuseppina continued to do all the cooking and serving. Until the arrival of the others, they all spoilt the young man shamelessly. Then Harriet arrived and two days later, in a reversal of the situation the previous year, Billy went to meet Conrad at the station.

Conrad expected this visit to Florence to be fairly un-eventful. His feelings towards Harriet were complicated both emotionally and sensually. But as he was still con-vinced that she was in love with Jacob Astley and that they were going to live together and would be getting married in the near future, he intended to keep a cer-tain reserve in all his relations with her. But from the very start, from that very first evening when they were all seated round the dining table in the Maggi dining room, his design began to unravel.

That first evening when all three guests were in the dining room together for the first time, the Contessa Maggi opened the French windows which led onto a balcony with steps into the lovely small garden at the back of the building. She led them all down into the gar-den – then holding Harriet's hand fiercely she pointed and said "Ecco Signorina" and proudly pointed to her two tortoises standing and chewing at some leaves.

"There are in fact three, my dears," she said, "but for some reason we never ever seem to see more than two at a time."

Up to this point, the conversation had been in the im-peccable English of the three old ladies. But with a sort of nod, Maggi indicated that all conversation should now be in Italian as Harriet in particular had come to Italy to improve her spoken language.

Conrad remembered the tortoises from the previous year, and felt again how they were as ageless as the three Contesse themselves. However, there was not always sweetness and light between the three sisters. That very first evening Varvara, the Countess Berchtold, came out with the comment that the Hungarian national football team had won a title, and rather archly pointed out that the Italian team had come very low down. The remark was clearly directed straight at Sofia, the Contessa Maggi, who began murmuring wrathful replies. A first-class storm now ensued between the two old ladies, neither of whom scarcely stopped to take a breath, as they tore into each other. Eventually Natalya called out "Basta, basta – sorelli". She then turned apologetically to Harriet and Conrad who were sitting side by side and said –

"Oh dear – one day my sweet sisters are going to have a row."

Harriet's face puckered up into a sort of twisted grimace, as she made a huge effort not to burst out laughing. She felt Conrad beside her, also trying hard to control his reaction. Her hand went down and to the side where it came in contact with Conrad's hand. She squeezed hard and he squeezed back. That squeeze – that moment of shared understanding – was the start of a month of increasing intimacy; an intimacy not only stoked by their romantic visits to the artistic treasures of the city, but also wrapped up in the unfolding events, funny and endearing, surrounding the three sisters of the Palazzo Maggi.

Day by day, the little dramas and discussions round the dinner table, gave Conrad greater insights into Harriet's mind, which seemed to be attuned perfectly to his own. It was only a few days later that Berchtold was again in full flood –

"Ah, Conrad caro, you have read some Freud then. Poor man – he thought that all those reminiscences of the young girls he treated, all from impeccably good families, were just dreams. All their recollections of abuse by fathers or uncles were, he thought, all make-believe – fantasies. He gave it a high-faluting name – the Oedipus Complex. Rubbish, I was there in Vienna at the time – most of these so-called fantasies were completely true, but no one would believe it, least of all the mothers."

"But Contessa it was not only Freud. What about Dostoyevsky, he understood the…"

"Ah Dostoevsky. I admired him when I was young, but now – no – no – I want a more positive art, not all that negative pessimistic stuff. Besides, he was Russian, and they are and always were unhealthy, nihilist and irreverent."

Harriet glanced anxiously at Natalya as Berchtold came out with this attack on her people and said –

"Come, come Contessa, that's a bit sweeping isn't it. After all, they saved us from a Nazi future, and whilst they might…."

"Saved us – saved us! Communism is about to sweep us all away and you say 'saved us'. A barbaric people who ruined my husband's family's estates in '49."

Conrad, thrilled by Harriet's intervention on behalf of the Countess Androvna, and forgetting, as was easy to do, that Varvara herself was born a Russian, did a quick mental double-take. What was the Berchtold woman talking about? '49'? That was last year wasn't it? Nothing particular had happened last year to justify this particular complaint, or had it? Then he remembered – good heavens the woman was talking about 1849, not 1949, when the Russian Tsar had poured his troops into Hungary to help the Austrians crush the Kossuth re-volt. His hands crept forward and took Harriet's. He was rewarded with yet another squeeze.

Each day Conrad and Harriet went out together exploring all the beauty and fascinations of Florence. Sometimes Billy would go with them, but increasingly, as he saw how the relationship was developing, he be-gan to avoid doing so. Billy had often been childishly jealous of Conrad's friendships with others in the past.

However, he sensed that this was different, and to that extent, he had undoubtedly matured. He did not think about it consciously, he simply instinctively left them to themselves. But of course every night they all met in the dining room of the Contessa Maggi. Day by day went by – Conrad and Harrriet walked round the city; then in the evenings the three sisters and their three guests all sat round the dining table and almost always started by discussing what they had seen during the day.

One day, Billy discovered that there was going to be a performance by the Magio Musicale Fiorentino under Tullio Serafin of Donizetti's "Lucia di Lammermoor". Callas was coming down from Milan to play the title role. The part of her brother was going to be taken by Titto Gobbi, and the part of her lover – Edgardo - by Giuseppe di Stefano, then at the absolute height of his powers. Tickets were simply unavailable. A very few of the cheaper seats were to be put on sale at 10.00 am of the morning of that evening's performance. Billy was determined not to miss it and went to join a queue that had already been formed at 8.00 pm the night before. He had already explained to Natalya, who passed it on to Giuseppina, that he would not be at dinner that night. Conrad and Harriet thought that he was mad, but the three Contesse were enthusiastically behind the boy's decision. They arranged for Giuseppina to prepare some sandwiches and demanded that Conrad should take them down to where Billy was queuing. They also insisted on providing one of their satin cushions, on which he could be seated during the long night.

To posterity that performance remains the perfect, the defining, performance of the opera, captured as it has been by the wonders of recording. So exceptional was that evening, that Billy heard something very rare in Italy. At the end of the second Act, after the incomparable Sextet and the final despairing cry from di Stefano of "Ah mi disperde", as the curtain came down on the final chords, there was a moment of complete silence, before the audience erupted in an ecstasy of applause. Normally Italian audiences are shouting their appreciation even before the final chords are played – but on this occasion, Billy experienced that rare magical moment of a total silence followed by a huge roar of applause.

For Harriet and Conrad, the magic of Florence took them daily further and further into another world – a dream world where all that mattered was love and truth and beauty. Conrad could not deny what was happening, nor could he fail to see the signs of love in Harriet's eyes. But he was well aware that Harriet had regularly slept with Jake and that they were, as far as he believed, to all intents and purposes engaged. The subject of Jacob Astley was somehow always avoided in their many otherwise very open conversations. For they discussed everything – subjects even married couples sometimes shied away from in those days, but Harriet's relationship with Jake was never examined. Conrad shied away because he still had a strong sense of loyalty towards a friend; Harriet because she could not bring herself to admit that her sexual relationship with Jake had arisen largely as a reaction to the Conrad's seeming indifference to a more physical relationship.

One day, walking down the Via Ricasoli, as the two of them walked hand in hand, they stopped at a second-hand bookstall at the side of the road. They started rummaging through the books on display. Harriet picked up an old but intact edition of the Fioretti of St Francis. Conrad smiled with delight at her find and he urged her to buy it there and then.

"Well Conrad darling, I will have it and keep it with

enormous pleasure if you are prepared to buy it for me and to sign it."

Could anything really be more innocent and free of any complication. But for Conrad the word 'darling' hit him like a rapier thrust. He looked at her and imagined to himself that she too was as devastated as he by having used the word 'darling'. He said nothing but immediately bought the little book, borrowed a pen from the old bookseller, signed it there and then with a flourish and added some suitable words.

How could he have come to such a conclusion? Living as he did as part of an Anglo-Armenian family where words like 'darling', 'my life', 'my soul', 'my loving father' were in constant use. What was it that made him believe for a moment that there was something more behind Harriet's use of the word. Despite his age, despite his wartime experiences, Conrad was really a complete innocent when it came to his relations with women. He had no idea what motivated Harriet. There was a clear, even wonderful, meeting of minds and hearts, but not of bodies.

They walked all day and every day. At the fountain near the Porto San Gallo, they leaned together over the fountain's edge, rippling their arms in the water, warm from the afternoon sunshine. They walked up the Porto San Giorgio and down the small road outside the walls. They stared at the fresco on the gate by the Bicci di Lorenzo. They sat and had a coffee and stale cake at a café by the side of a road, and turned to each other simultaneously to remark on the beauty of the creased features of the passing old lady – and laughed at how they had both thought of the same thing at the same time.

For Conrad these were magical moments of unalloyed pleasure; each one embedded in his memory as signs of a burgeoning love – a love which left in him a mixture of joy and of anxiety. Why anxiety? Impossible to analyse, nor did he try – it was simply there, an unavoidable part of his joy.

One evening, one of the Contesse mentioned that there was to be a popular gathering at the Porto San Niccolo that night, the evening before the Feast of the Madonna. Conrad and Harriet decided to go with a group of Americans they had befriended. Once there, realising that they wanted to be alone together, they ran off in the middle of some fireworks, holding hands and laughing with delight. Lost in the milling crowds, they stood together on the steps of a fountain. Harriet, desperate for a touch, for a physical proof of the love she seemed to see in Conrad's eyes, leaned forward in the midst of the yelling crowds, and turned her face towards him for a proper kiss on the lips. Conrad's head turned a moment too soon and the proffered kiss became a chaste peck on the lower cheek. Was it accidental – a momentary glance at something happening on the other side of the little piazza – or was it an avoidance that Conrad had really intended? She would never know.

Since first meeting Conrad at Italian literature lectures, and then later in her almost daily visits to that staircase at Worcester College, Harriet had been attracted to Conrad. She revelled in his clear and probing mind, she loved his dark good looks, coupled to that extraordinary mixture of gentleness and certainty. But she had become increasingly frustrated by his puritanical reserve. She was aware that Conrad was worth more than a hundred Astley's, but when it came down to it, she was unable to do without the sexual excitement of the affair with Jake. The fiction about an engagement was just that – a fiction. Society still frowned on unmarried liaisons of this kind, and being thought of as a 'fiancé' was an acceptable smokescreen. But now here were all her frustrations rising all over again – was Conrad never going to respond to her sexual needs and add that necessary dimension to what she was increasingly sure was real love?

Chapter 18

The Contessa's dream

It was a few days after the incident of the failed kiss in the Piazza, that the whole house were sitting at the dinner table waiting for the pasta course.

"I dreamed of Pietro last night," said the Contessa Maggi as Giuseppina brought in the pasta and began serving. The Contessa always told the assembled company about her latest dream over the pasta. Despite the fact that she was already over seventy years old, they always turned out to be very vivid dreams indeed.

"Much too vivid to be really true," was her sister Varvara's comment to Conrad on one occasion, but "one must keep up with the times". Conrad had nodded but had no idea what 'keeping up with the times' had to do with dreams.

"I dreamed of Pietro last night," repeated Maggi.

"Yes, cara,what did he say? Such a nice boy he was," said Natalya addressing herself to Conrad. Then, Contessa Berchtold began talking yet again of the Hungarian successes at the Helsinki games – she was never really happy unless her comments were at the centre of their discussions. Of course Varvara was Russian by birth like all her sisters. But her marriage to Berchtold – who Billy and Conrad believed had been the foreign minister of Austria-Hungary – had changed her allegiance and made her a keen supporter of that antiquated empire, though she could not stomach the Austro-German element.

"The Hungarians are fine horsemen – they always have been," she said.

"Yes, yes, Pietro was on a horse. He looked so hand-

143

some," resumed Maggi, ignoring Berchtold's interruption. "He was dressed in such fine clothes, sitting astride a gorgeous grey horse." Here the Contessa paused and sighed, for at her age, when one is in one's late seventies and starts talking about the dead, one becomes a little sad. But rallying, she continued, now addressing herself directly to Billy.

"You would have liked him – so full of life."

"Now then, cara, tell us then what did he say. What did he do. What happened?"

"Well, now, he leaned down – took my hand and raised it to his lips and then slipped a note into it on which there were written three numbers. He then raised his hat and rode off without saying another word."

There was a deep silence while Giuseppina cleared the pasta dishes and brought in the next course. The first to speak was Natalya – the Countess Androvna - as she began helping herself to the fish; it was a Friday. Without looking up and with her eyes firmly fixed on the slices of fish going to her plate she said quietly –

"You know what they are – they're the winning numbers in this week's lottery."

There was more silence until they were all served, but Harriet sensed this idea, dropped like a stone into a small pool, spreading ripples and sinking into everyone's thoughts.

"That's pure superstition," blurted out Berchtold, who never agreed with either of her sisters on principle.

"But wait – I have the numbers. It must be – it must be," called out Maggi, now convinced. "They must be the numbers."

"Clever Pietro, clever Pietro – coming to you like that in your dreams. Quick, quick, cara, what are they – do you remember the numbers?"

"Well of course I remember them – what do you take

me for – senile or something? But look he showed them only to me – I'm sure I must not divulge them, surely that would be bad luck wouldn't it."

"Yes, I think you are right cara," said Berchtold, now herself fully convinced, despite her initial reaction." But listen you must bet for all of us. How does the lottery work by the way – I have no idea."

Giuseppina was hastily summoned and she explained that this lottery was a weekly one in which five numbers were drawn from a possible ninety, for each of ten principal Italian towns. One could forecast three of them for the town of one's choice. Prominent personalities drew the winning numbers for each town every Saturday. It was now generally accepted by everyone in the dining room – Italians and British alike – that they were certain to win.

"Vinceremo, vinceremo. I shall go travelling and forget about the Russians."

Natalya beamed at her sister and spoke of living in her own palazzo once again. Maggi purred like a cat and smiled at everyone round her table, because she was giving happiness all round. She turned to Conrad, her favourite, and said –

"We will celebrate. We will order champagne. You shall have a 'smoking', and we will all order special dresses. Vinceremo. Vinceremo."

Then came the fruit and the whole table turned to discussing which town to choose.. Maggi said that since Pietro had been a Florentine, he had obviously meant it to be Florence – and besides she had had the dream in that town. Natalya agreed on the grounds that it really seemed to be the only logical choice.

But Varvara's mood of tolerance had cooled a little by this time, so, staring into space and muttering to herself she claimed that she could sense – feel – that it should be Turin. This was really quite ridiculous. Conrad, to whom everyone turned, had to compromise between doubting her powers of clairvoyance or upsetting the other two, and ended up by suggesting Bari. Frankly that was even more ridiculous and consensus was accordingly now reached over Florence. Finally, as it was not considered proper for a lady to enter the 'banco di lotto', Conrad and Billy were chosen to go down and place everyone's bets the next day. Wishing each other good-night and in a mood of excitement, they all parted.

The next day was a Saturday and the day of the draw. Conrad and Billy went round and placed the bets at the local banco, 'that den of thieves' according to the Contesse, together with a sealed envelope, handed over to them that morning by Maggi, containing the three numbers. Having been instructed to think of something pleasant while he was in 'la spelonca di ladre', Conrad contemplated the champagne they would be drinking that evening, while Billy thought of 'Lucia' and the most expensive seats in the theatre. Instead of thieves, however, there were only two bored young girls with rouge and too much lipstick, who smiled and giggled at Billy, handed Conrad the receipts and returned to their 'libri gialli' – their passion paperbacks.

The results of the draw were always announced on the wireless at seven and again at nine on Saturday evenings, as well as being published the next day in the Sunday newspapers. That Saturday evening Signora Coppoli had been invited to come to dinner. This inevitably added to the already electric atmosphere. Berchtold, backed by Giuseppina, had tried to get Maggi to cancel, but the good Sofia would not entertain this for a moment. The Signora duly turned up and made everything worse by loudly pooh-poohing the whole enterprise and blaming everybody, and Berchtold in particular, for giving any credence to the whole matter. To heighten the already unbearable tension in the house, the wireless then failed completely at the first bulletin. As the Contesse had never attached an aerial this was not particularly surprising. Billy fashioned another one out of a suit-hanger and carefully attached it – during which operation Natalya told Harriet all about Signor Marconi, the inventor of radio, whom she had known well.

"I didn't dream at all last night," said Maggi as they all began their pasta. This unusual remark was accepted with complete understanding by the whole gathering. The dinner group was very subdued. Over the meat course, Natalya wondered aloud whether Pietro might not have meant it to be next week. Berchtold looked into space, muttering to herself, and said she was sure it must be this week, but perhaps after all not Florence. As the fruit arrived the wireless was turned on and the news began.

"De Gaspari… Nato… Farouk…'un po dissipato ma sempre un re', muttered Berchtold, who along with the others was biting her lips…the 'flotta inglese' sailing somewhere or other…Guerra e pace…"

Harriet and Billy, now half convinced, eagerly waited for the numbers. Poor Conrad, dreading the inevitable and thinking –' oh if only, if only – for their sakes'. Then came the towns and the numbers – Bari… Torino… Firenze…"

Everyone was watching Maggi closely. They had to – for despite all the pressure, Sophia had kept the numbers to herself. "It won't work if I tell you," she had said. The list of numbers stopped. There was a short silence and then Maggi got up and switched the wireless off.

"Cosi… cosi… E un peccato…Buone notte, cara

sorelli… buone notte."

She shuffled out. Dignity of course prevailed and not another word was said by anyone round the table. They all gave their subdued 'good nights' to each other and the incident was never mentioned ever again.

"I dreamed of President Truman last night," said the Contessa Maggi the next evening as they all settled down to their pasta.

Chapter 19

Myth or Love

Conrad loved music too, if a little less flamboyantly than Billy. But he was a serious reflective sort and he had never shared Billy's love of early Italian opera. Conrad always thought of Rossini and Donizetti, and the like, as somehow frivolous and without the depth of feeling that he saw in the orchestral works of the great German composers. So when Billy enthused about Callas or Gobbi, he extolled Wagner and argued that the Ring Cycle was worth more than the whole of the Italian repertoire put together.

"What do you see in all that tum-ti-tum-ti-tum stuff with all those ridiculous plots," was his refrain.

Billy had never seen a performance of a Wagner opera, though he had heard some excerpts on Conrad's scratchy 78s. He enjoyed the loud purple passages and the heightened drama of the music, but found all the mythology and the storyline tedious and pretentious. Conrad, on the other hand, was steeped in the myths and symbols of the Ring and spent many a fruitless afternoon revealing them to his brother, before playing a record to illustrate what he had just patiently explained.

Harriet, for her part, did not really enjoy music. She was not exactly tone deaf, but she simply did not get the same pleasure from a piece of music as she got from contemplating a beautiful painting or a delicately turned pottery vase. She did not even care for background music, and would get irritated when her mother played the piano, though this might have been more due to their relationship rather than the music itself. However she was happy to join in enthusiastically when the brothers argued over the respective merits of their favourite operas. She always sided with Conrad, not just as a matter of loyalty, but due to the irritation she felt towards Billy as the summer progressed. She felt sure it wasn't jealousy – there was no comparison between the love of the two brothers and the love she felt for Conrad. But it was there all the same and it was more a resentment towards Billy's character, which contrasted so markedly at times with Conrad's.

It so happened that in 1950, Furtwangler was conducting two full cycles of the Ring at La Scala in Milan. Conrad challenged Billy to go with him for two days to try and get in to whatever performances they could. Harriet, clearly, was not going to be left out, though privately, she felt nothing could be more boring. But how were thay ever going to get tickets?

Once again, Uncle Nicolai in the Villa Maggi near Padua was called upon. Down a very creaky telephone line, he promised to do his best. But when he later reported the price of the tickets, both Conrad and Billy agreed that they could only afford to go to one . In the end, Nicolai managed to offer them either 3 tickets together to Die Valkyrie, or three odd singles to Gotterdammerung. On Conrad's advice they plumped for Die Valkyrie, and the question then arose as to where they would stay. Here in the end it was the irritating Signora Coppoli, who came to the rescue. She had a cousin who owned an apartment in the Piazzale Martini with some rooms he let out to students, in a building above a garage, who was prepared to put them all up for two nights at a very reasonable price.

The atmosphere at La Scala when they turned up was electric. Kirsten Flagstad was singing Brunnhilde and this performance was going to be recorded live for posterity. All the way in the train to Milan, Conrad had enthused about the symbolism in the four operas, painstakingly going through the story and the 'motivs' that run through and unify the whole immense work. Harriet listened with admiration as Conrad's critique uncharacteristically went over the top in its enthusiasm. Billy, however, listened with more cynical detachment. Conrad explained how Alberich, the Nibelung dwarf, steals the magic gold and fashions a ring of power from it, having to renounce love as the precondition of achieving power. At some point in the train journey, Conrad went on –

"But Wotan, the head of the Gods, who is on the face of it the good guy, is not actually all that different from the obviously evil Alberich. They were both after power, and Wotan, too, renounces love, despite producing scores of children by different women."

"Oh no," said Billy, "it all sounds hopelessly pretentious and Germanic;" but was immediately reprimanded by Harriet who told him not to be so childish,

Throughout the journey, Harriet was fascinated by Conrad's obvious enthusiasm, a side of him which she had not seen before. Of course, Billy knew the story, but was disinterested in the Germanic philosophy – man sundering himself from nature and his basic animal instincts, guiltily eating of the tree of knowledge and thus achieving self-awareness.

"It's all very well, Conrad, but where is the passion?"

But as they settled into their seats in La Scala, from the very first thrilling notes of the storm at the start of Die Valkyrie, Billy was bowled over. Forgetting all the myths, psychology and philosophy, the love of the doomed Siegmund and Sieglinde tore at Billy's heart. Who cared that they were brother and sister and that their love was incestuous and taboo, who cared about the symbolism, the music itself tore him apart, This was love as he himself imagined it. How could Conrad have spoken at such length without once mentioning the power and passion of the love that poured from the stage and the orchestra?

Then, in the third Act, Billy had to face up to another kind of love – the love of a father for his daughter, and her love for him. The scene was unforgettably poignant, with Flagstad at the absolute height of her powers and Billy came away overflowing with emotion. As they waited for the No. 13 tram back to their rooms, he simply could not keep still, but kept hugging and kissing both Harriet and Conrad and enthusing about what he had just heard and seen.

It was typical of Billy, when they returned the next day to Florence, that he behaved as if it was he who had led them to this great revelation. He seemed to suggest that it was Conrad who had been unappreciative. Harriet was outraged, and endeavoured to remind the irritating boy that he had been the one shaking his head with doubt the day before. She was even more annoyed by the fact that he had presumed to kiss her the night before while they were waiting for the tram, and with more ardour than Conrad had shown in over a year. But when she appealed to Conrad to support her, he simply smiled and nodded at Billy's new-found enthusuasm. For Conrad, the knowledge that he had again added something to Billy's development was enough in itself to give him pleasure.

Back in Florence at the Palazzo Maggi, Billy was still on a high, pouring out all his feelings during the first dinner with the three Contesse, in his halting but exuberant Italian. Each of them indulged him; Maggi with a soft sigh of collusion with the confidence of youth, Berchtold with a wry grin at the naivety of youth, and Natalya, with her secret sensuous smile, which so thrilled him. Once again the scene profoundly upset Harriet. By what right did this scamp – not worth a half of his brother – deserve the affectionate indulgence of the three old ladies so admired by Conrad.

In the end, the Contessa Berchtold inevitably had the last word as she reminisced about life in Vienna during those extraordinary days just before the Great War. Billy had just finished recounting, word for word, Conrad's explanation of the sexual symbolism of the father-daughter relationship in the opera. Berchtold looked at him, smiled and then said –

"Ah well, you know, my dear, that I heard Freud himself once say – 'Sometimes a cigar is after all just a cigar'."

Billy was still young enough to blush deeply and then fell silent, realising he had been talking too much. Harriet giggled, pleased at the way the boy had been discomfited, and the party broke up. Billy always assumed that whatever the three old ladies said was to be taken at face value and must be true. Conrad, despite the affection that he had for each of them, always weighed up their statements more critically, and never quite believed that Berchtold had actually met and conversed with all the famous personalities whose names tripped so easily off her tongue.

Chapter 20

The ever-impressionable Billy

The lazy hot days of summer in Florence shimmered on. The three of them soon slipped into a daily routine. After breakfast Harriet and Conrad would go out on a morning expedition to a museum or palazzo, or simply to take a stroll. Meanwhile Billy would go back up to bed, thinking idly about girls, music and mathematics in that order. They would agree to meet for lunch and share the afternoons together. In the course of his own wanderings about the town, Billy had occasionally met up with other tourists – far fewer on the ground in those days than later. The moment came when he firrst met and started chatting up a couple of girls in a tiny café in front of the Santa Croce, who turned out to be Danish.

The three of them began arranging to meet and sightsee together. Billy always made it clear to the two girls that he was not available in the afternoons, or for that matter at lunch, when he said he would be with his family. Billy revelled in their company, and became devoted to them and their rather immature but very charming enthusiasms. They were very alike, though not actually related. They were not conventionally pretty, but they were tall, had fair hair and blue eyes, and both were eye-catching for all the young Italian males in the streets, who made their appreciation known vocally. Billy, whose Italian was now perfect, understood their comments and asides and took a sort of pride as he walked the streets with a girl on each arm.

The girls were some years older than him, but travelling to Florence on their own, they had been taken aback by the attentions of those Italian young men, for whom women were all either 'angels' like their mothers and sisters, or 'whores' like all the foreign girls flocking to the city. The somewhat unwelcome attentions paid to the two girls as they walked in the street, had on occasion even included some touching and had been causing them some distress. Once the girls began going round with Billy, his presence shielded them from the physical attentions, though not the unsolicited comments, of these young men. The girls gratefully accepted him as their protector – thinking he was older than he really was.

Billy never thought of introducing them to Conrad, nor had he fallen in love – at least not like he had with Paulina. But sex was never far from the surface, in much the same way as his escapades with his sister's girlfriends. Both girls liked holding him and being held by him. Soon enough, their farewell kisses exchanged when Billy left them each day for lunch with his 'family', moved from chaste kisses on the cheeks, to increasingly passionate ones on the lips. Billy had always been highly susceptible to kissing and being kissed, and his groin stirred rather obviously on such occasions, and both girls were aware of it. However, from their point of view, it was far better than being pinched in the rear by unknown local boys, and there was always the safety net by virtue of their being two of them together.

The regular meetings with Conrad and Harriet shortly after lunch would usually take place at the same café at the far end of the Piazza Signoria away from the loggetta. Billy usually arrived first after saying goodbye to the girls further away from the square. On the day immediately after the drama of the Contessa's dream, a little incident, known only to Harriet, occurred. For a change, Conrad and Harriet had arrived first at the café. They were seated at a table in the piazza on an outside table set in the square, sipping their coffees. It so happened, on this occasion, that the girls had accompanied Billy almost as far as the Piazza down a side street before Billy turned to say goodbye. Young and impressionable though he might be, he could be firm in making his own desires known, and he had been adamant that he did not want them around when he was with his family. The girls were under the impression that 'family' meant a strict mother or father. On parting, their kisses were long and passionate, with both sides clearly enjoying themselves.

Looking straight down the same side street that Conrad's chair backed on to, Harriet watched as Billy lingered over the kisses with each of the girls. She made no comment, nor did she say a word to Conrad, who carried on chatting, oblivious to the little drama going on behind his back. Watching Billy, Harriet felt a flickering of her own desire, a mixture of irritation and sexual stirrings. By the time he joined them, both Billy and Harriet were in full control of themselves, and Harriet never mentioned to anyone what she had witnessed.

* * *

The next day Billy decided to go off to Sansepolcro and to spend the day looking at and trying to commit himself to Piero della Francesca, originally introduced to him the year before by Conrad. Billy, as always, was in the good books of the Contessa Maggi. On the previous evening, during the evening meal, she had shown them all a knot in her handkerchief which was there to remind her to do something. She had now forgotten what it was for, and appealed to the visitors and her sisters to see if anyone could help. Billy was the only one cheeky enough to come out with a host of suggestions, one of which finally hit the mark. Maggi approved of the trip he was proposing and arranged for Giuseppina to give him up-to-date train and bus timetables.

Billy was up at 5.00am and made his way to the station, already bustling with activity even at that early hour. The businessmen on their way to Rome for the day; families going off to the countryside for lunch with grandparents; as well as on this particular morning, many 'cacciatori' with their double-barrelled guns and their outlandish and faintly ridiculous clothes, all in a state of great excitement because the season was only just starting.

He caught the train that he had planned to take, but within the first few minutes it was already running later than scheduled. Arriving at his destination, Billy found that he had missed the bus he had intended to take. He wandered about looking slightly lost until he was helped by a couple of friendly policemen –

"Lei va a Sansepolcro?"

"Si."

Then a 'grazie' as he was directed to another bus a little further away, that was due to leave shortly. In what other country, he thought to himself as he clambered aboard, would a local policeman act in this way towards a young tourist who was simply looking lost, guessing exactly where he was wanting to go.

Billy was already in a state of joyful delight. He loved – that was the right word – this sort of drift into the beautiful unknown. The streets of Florence and his life there was becoming rather predictable – the stroll round the streets – being lectured on all he was seeing by Conrad – the stately meals with the three Contesse in the evenings. He looked out as the bus zigzagged up the hills on a road carved out of the sheer rockface, leaving a curving scar on the face of the countryside. Tall pine trees; well tilled fields; terraces where the ground was steep, that had clearly been moulded and worked on for centuries; men getting on and off at remote stops going to work; peasant women with huge bundles going to market, all with a cheery greeting and a few ribald words with the driver.

As the bus veered and swung back and forth in tune with the twisting road, two women in front of Billy complained loudly that they were feeling sick, Windows were opened and everyone hurriedly changed places so that the two could lean out and throw up out of the windows as the bus chuntered on. Billy felt a great sympathy for the two women, whose groans were met by encouraging pats on the back.

Alongside Billy, now sitting on the aisle, was a sort of open leather bag with a narrow opening at the top. Sitting in this bag was a duck. Every so often this jack-in-the box fowl would stick its head out of the small opening and be patted back by the woman sitting on the other side of the aisle, who directed her great toothy grin at Billy, making different remarks each time.

Eventually, the bus arrived at Sansepolcro, and Billy alighted at the little walled city set in a lovely valley. In the early morning sunshine, he strolled directly to the Palazzo Communale where the Piero fresco was situated in splendid, solitary glory. It was a moment of sheer wonder for Billy as he sat for over an hour staring at the mathematically perfect fresco set against the simple white-washed walls. Never again would Billy experience such exultation and peace as he experienced at Sansepolcro. And there was the deep satisfaction in having found this marvel entirely on his own. Conrad had never visited this particular site. It was probably the only piece of famous Tuscan art to which Billy had not first been introduced by his elder brother.

Determined to press on with his explorations, Billy

decided to take a bus to the village of Monterchi on the other road back to Arezzo. At Anghiari, a large red-faced farmer hauled himself up onto the bus. Walking unsteadily to the back, carrying a small bundle, he managed to tread on almost everyone's toes, eliciting curses and cries as he passed. Sitting comfortably next to Billy, with his large hips spreading into the aisle on one side, and pushing firmly into Billy's legs on the other, he opened and spread out his cloth bundle and proceeded to press on Billy a share of his copious lunch. A great loaf of fresh bread, cheese, pepperone, thick slices of ham and the most delicious looking fresh figs. Billy who, as usual, had completely forgotten about providing anything for himself, was famished. Billy always assumed throughout his life that someone – usually Conrad of course – would provide for him.At first he politely demurred, but when pressed, began to tuck in. Conversation with the jolly farmer flowed easily with gales of laughter from the man in response to Billy's opinions, which the man found incredible. However, when Billy asked whether the man knew the way to the 'cimitero', he suddenly became solemn and full of sympathy, asking Billy if he had someone buried there. When Billy replied 'no, no', he was only going to see a Piero fresco in the chapel of the cemetery – the rotund man roared with laughter at the incongruity of Billy's trip, and, for the rest of the way, regaled Billy with increasingly risqué stories – patting him up and down his bare thigh and knee for emphasis.

On arrival at his destination, and following the fat farmer's directions, Billy began the four-kilometre walk to Monterchi itself – and what a lovely walk it was. Dry dusty road; women in bare feet smiling at him as they passed; grapes beginning to appear and ripening between the leaves of the vines by the side. Billy soaked it all up, his mind full of Piero who he discovered had married a girl from Monterchi. It was not just that Billy knew that Piero della Francesca was a mathematician as well as a great painter, he could see and feel the mathematics in the frescos and paintings.

Soon the little town, a large village really, came into view, and Billy found the cemetery and its chapel. A small ten-year-old girl opened the cemetery gates and led Billy to the mortuary chapel. There, above the altar, was the famous pregnant Madonna with her attendant angels. Billy stared – it wasn't only the pregnant Madonna which so caught his attention, but also the attendant angels – mathematical reflections of each other both in form and colour. The little girl reappeared and began talking ten to the dozen about Piero – the fact that government experts were continually trying to move the picture away to a museum, but, said the little girl, "mama always cries and so it is still here". Billy's heart melted with love for all mankind.

He walked up the slopes from the village into the hills above. There, he had a magnificent view of the road he had just walked up after alighting from the bus; of the ducks swimming in the river below; of the cemetery and the jewel of the village; and of the hill above it on the other side in Umbria – the borderline between Tuscany and Umbria passing right through the cemetery. Everything was very still and peaceful. Billy dozed and thought of Piero della Francesca, thought of all the men and women who had worked over the centuries in this countryside to create the benign scenes which artists like Piero depicted with such emotional finesse. He thought of his family and of their love for him and his love for them; and of his feelings which went beyond his family embracing other people and places, loves of many different kinds. Surely this was happiness!

Chapter 21

Siena

It was only a few days after the drama of the lottery numbers and his return from the trip to Sansepolcro that Billy declared that he was beginning to have enough of the 'magic' of Florence. He suggested that they all went off for a day or two to Siena. The annual Palio race was due and it was only a two hour train ride away. Harriet responded enthusiastically. Conrad who was in love both with the magic of Florence and now with Harriet, was not quite so sure, but, anxious to please her, he agreed.

Consulting the three Contesse at the evening dinner it transpired that only Natalya had ever actually seen the Palio. She commented –

"It is increasingly becoming a tourist attraction – but for the moment, the Siennese are still passionate about the race and the flag-waving contest."

"What is it all about Contessa", said Harriet.

"Well, my dear, Siena has been divided since medieval times into several – I think the correct word would be 'wards'. I believe there are 15 of them – or is it more – I'm not sure. Each ward has its own flag and they are all fiercely competitive with each other. The town has a unique main Piazza – most irregular in shape and sloping down fairly substantially to the Town Hall at the bottom. This building has a very tall and thin Campanile, and ... er ... where was I? Oh yes! Thank you, Varvara my dear, I can manage quite well. Well each year they have a festival day when they arrange a horse race run around this Piazza. It's very dangerous as the roadway is narrow, dusty and there are sharp corners; in one case, less than ninety degrees. It is a no-holds barred race. They whip each other and cut across each other ruthlessly. Riders fall off and the population, mostly gathered in the centre of the square with a view round the whole course, goes wild.

"Is that all – all that fuss – surely it can only take a few minutes?" said Berchtold.

"No, no. The race itself is quite short but they go around three times. Then, before the actual Race is run, they have a parade in the square, when each of the competing wards march round the Piazza with drums and flutes and there is a spectacular flag-waving contest performed at regular intervals, but with particular care when in front of the mayor and some judges."

"What's that then – just waving their flags around."

"More than that – they are really large flags. They twirl them, throw them up in the air wrapped round the pole in such a way that at the top they unfurl and float down, fully open, into the hands of the flag carrier. The different flags are very colourful so it really is quite a spectacle as each ward will have more than one flag bearer. Very picturesque and photogenic – I have no doubt that in a few years it will end up as a pure tourist attraction."

"But at the moment?"

"Well when I was there last year, there were no foreigners at all as far as I could see, and the population went wild with enthusiasm, indeed with real passion. There was almost a riot – but perhaps that simply reflects my old-fashioned view of what is proper and orderly behaviour."

In fact, whenever any of the Contesse mentioned the word 'popolare' or any of its derivatives, there was always an ever so slight hint of disapproval – particularly when referring to their enthusiasms. In any event it was all clearly far too exciting to miss. But the Palio was due to take place the very next day in the evening. Neither Harriet nor Billy could understand why Conrad was wavering.

"Where are we going to stay?" he wondered.

"Oh nuts, brother. We'll get up early tomorrow. Siena is only a couple of hours down the railway line. We arrive in the early morning – we find a couple of rooms and spend the whole day on the streets, and most of the night. I heard that they party all night on the day of the Palio," said Billy.

"Yes, yes" confirmed Natalya, "If you are in the area of the winning ward I believe that they actually have the fountains running with wine. Pretty cheap wine you can be sure – but still wine."

Conrad still hesitated. It was understandable. When it came down to it, it would be he who would be responsible if anything went wrong. Furthermore, now he was thinking of Harriet as well as his usual concern for Billy.

"Look here Conrad – even if we can't get a room, we can wander down to the station and get the first train back to Florence, and meanwhile we can sleep on the station benches if we are too early. You don't mind sleeping rough do you Harriet?"

"Good heavens, no. Yes, yes, let's do it."

The next day was a gloriously clear summer day. There was a gentle breeze all day dispelling the heat haze that often hung over the city. They did not get away quite as early as intended. Indeed Natalya had quite a job getting Billy out of bed. But in due course, and with a lot of cajoling from Conrad, they finally got away and were in Siena by midday. They struggled up the hill from the station in the heat of the midday sun and began looking for somewhere to stay for that night.

As anticipated there were no hotel rooms of any kind available anywhere in the town. However, by dint of calling in at one local bar after another, by ordering, and sharing between them, one Campari, or one Carpano, or one Cinzano at each bar, they eventually found a barman who could help them, before they were too drunk to continue their search. This last barman - they had consumed more than nine drinks by then – had a cousin, whose grandmother's nephew's cousin let out rooms.

"Very simple, very small, no running water in the room and only two beds you understand Signori."

"Yes, yes – no problem – no problem – we'll take it for tonight."

A celebratory round of drinks was ordered, and they finally had the pleasure of drinking together, each from their own glass. Meanwhile, a little boy was summoned who took them through the streets to the cousin's grandmother's sister - or was it the grandmother's nephew's wife – they were past being able to differentiate. After showering their host with flowery compliments and thanks, they were duly shown the room. It was indeed very small, containing two small beds one against each wall with just enough space between them for someone to lie down on the floor. There was no running water, no cupboards, and only a tiny window high up in a corner near the ceiling, which clearly could not be opened. But it was clean, and there was a tiny bathroom at the end of the corridor. They paid the outrageous price demanded without a murmur – took a key to the front door of the house, dumped the one small bag, containing toothbrushes, pyjamas, change of underwear and one or two other absolute necessities, which Conrad had been carrying, and sallied out into the town.

The rest of that day passed in a whirl of excitement.

Already well primed by the number of bars they had visited before finding a room, they found themselves offered even more glasses of wine by complete strangers as they wandered through the winding streets. For some time this kept them away from the more public parts of the town, and particularly from the central sloping piazza itself. But as the afternoon wore on, they began to make their way, with the rest of the crowds, to the great Campo. Surprisingly, they already felt a sort of tribal connection to the locality where, quite by chance, they had found a room and already recognised their own ward's flag.

Is it any wonder that people living together in a particular locality can get so passionate about their village, their town, their football team, their nation-state? It had only taken a few hours for Billy, Harriet and Conrad to have developed a loyalty to their team, after booking a tiny room, in a miserable little house, on a narrow cross-roads, with a fountain in the middle, for just one night. Yet for that one night it was their only point of reference, it constituted their one piece of personal territory. Thus it was that they felt a warmth towards all the friendly people pressing around them as they all made their way to the Campo – not just because of the glasses of red wine cheerfully thrust on them, but because of this territorial imperative. They already recognised their ward's flag – an easily distinguishable yellow and black chequerboard – and eventually happily followed one group gathered round one of these flags, flowing into the great square surrounded by all their new-found friends.

They stood, hemmed in by the crowds, but, because of the sloping ground, with a good view all round. The parade by the eight wards that were competing that year, went round the Campo carrying their huge flags, dressed in their medieval finery. The two flag bearers in each team were accompanied by several drummers and pipers. Every so often the parade would halt and the flag-bearers would do their stuff, throwing up their flags, twirling them and generally showing off, to the accompaniment of the musicians. On each halt, one of the eight teams would end up in front of the judges and would be particularly athletic and daring. It seemed to go on forever. The wine continued to flow though Billy lost track of where it came from. Unused to drinking so much, and without having had much food, he began to get a little dizzy. But ever since his disgrace at the door of the Palazzo Maggi the year before, he did now have some idea how far he could go, and stopped accepting any more offers.

Harriet was flushed and in a state of great excitement. On one side of her she had Conrad, who she was now convinced was in love with her, even if he had yet to prove it. On the other side she had the irrepressible Billy, as excited as she was. It felt good having two males in attendance. Billy was not nearly as good-looking as Conrad, but he was getting a lot of attention from the 18-year-old Italian girls for his fair hair, his blue eyes and a sort of shy but robust sexuality, emanating from him, completely unconsciously, due to his youth. Harriet too had not eaten. Even though she had a greater tolerance of alcohol, nevertheless she, too, had not been sparing enough in accepting the many proffered glasses of wine.

At last the parade finished. All eight wards had now performed in front of the judges at the top end of the square, and the prizes had been given out – the top mark being awarded to the ward with a flag that looked like three red stars on a green and blue background. Everybody around them groaned and complained bitterly about the undoubted bias of the Judges, who were undoubtedly all either Papal lackeys, Communist bandits, or Fascist beasts, according to the political views of whoever was complaining. The three young Brits agreed – it really did seem to them that the black and yellow chequerboard flag-bearers had performed far better than any of the others. More wine was passed round.

Then, taking the trio entirely by surprise, the starting gun boomed out.

Starting from the top left-hand corner of the square, the horses came thundering down towards the first corner. Billy yelled out "We're in the lead;" and indeed the black and yellow colour was the first to the corner. A bugle call rang out and some horses slowed and stopped, while one or two others went on for some time. It was a wonderfully Italian chaos, with much cheering and shouting. Eventually it transpired that the Start had been flawed. It seemed that one of the horses had started off before the gun went off, due to a sharp whip that had been administered a second before. There was a long and excited confabulation of the Judges, well out of sight of this part of the crowd. Then the news flashed round the crowd – there was no public address system – that the offending horse had been disqualified and the rest were to start again for a second start. Which horse was it? Oh no! It was the horse of the black and yellow chequerboard flag. Billy and Harriet began shouting and yelling in unison with all the crowd around them. Conrad, not quite so overwhelmed by the emotions of the crowd, saw a little boy who had been standing up on a bollard set in the square in order to see better and held tight by his father, actually with tears running down his face.

The Judges were no longer Papal lackeys or anything

so polite, but were called names which neither Billy nor Harriet had ever heard – though Conrad had. It was crystal clear to everyone around them – but somehow not clear to the judges – that the whip had surely been administered by the rider of the horse alongside. This was a saturnine young man dressed in the colours of a flag with a red and green double diagonal on a white background. This was a flag sported by a crowd just alongside and below them in front of the Town Hall. Noisy altercations broke out on the fringes of the two crowds where they converged.

But even in Italy chaos cannot last for ever, order was finally restored and the race began again. It was undoubtedly very exciting. The horses raced round, swerved round the sharp corners, bumped into each other, whilst the riders slashed away at the other riders and the other horses. All three shouted along with the rest but, for Billy, with the disqualification of the black and yellow rider, a bit of the tension and excitement was missing. After three circuits, the riders galloped to the finishing line. During the race, as the crowds shuffled about to get a better view, the black and yellow crowd, containing Harriet and the two brothers, had been slowly shifted down to the bottom of the Campo and towards the front of the Town Hall. It was not possible from there to see the end of the race or who had been the winner. The winner was announced to a huge roar. Even then it was still not clear down below who had won. But then the winning flag was raised – it was the red and green double diagonal on a white background.

From this moment on everything happened so quickly and so violently that neither Billy nor Harriet could quite piece together what was happening. On the other side of the roadway/racetrack, just below where they were standing, was a very large contingent of grey-clad

Carabinieri. As the winner came round and past them with his fists raised in triumph on his victory lap, the whole of that wonderful friendly crowd around them erupted with a roar of anger and surged forward, and, of course, the little British group was carried forward with them. Heaven knows what the crowd intended – indeed whether, as a critical mass, they had any intention at all. The horseman himself galloped on and out of any danger. But the crush barriers came down and the Carabinieri across the street pulled out their truncheons and ran across the road to confront the advancing crowd. It was frightening and it was ugly. The crowd had no 'will' as such; by now it was surging forward mindlessly. The Carabinieri were supposed to be disciplined and well-trained. It was, however, immediately obvious that they were not. They panicked and began viciously hitting out with their truncheons at the front line of people, who were being pushed forward by the crush of the crowds further behind.

The sound of hard wooden truncheons on backs, on chests and above all on heads was sickening – and all the time Billy and Harriet were being carried forward towards the flailing truncheons. There were screams and shouts all round – the noise was terrifying in and of itself. Billy felt completely helpless. His hands were pinioned to his side by the crush of people round him. Harriet too seemed to have lost any will to struggle free. Helplessly they were surging forward ever closer to those terrible truncheons rising and falling with stomach-turning crunches.

Then, miraculously, Conrad was right beside them. Having faced far worse experiences than this before, he took in the situation immediately, from the moment that the crowd surge began. He was quite ruthless in forcing his way through the milling, panicky crowd and to the side of the two people he loved. They were fortunately to one side of the crowd, and the line of Carabinieri in front of them did not extend much further to their left. Conrad saw this and as the crowd continued to move forward – the momentum had not yet worked itself out – by sheer dint of his physical strength and without any concern for the other people around him, he literally pushed Billy and Harriet sideways and to their left. They too, once they saw what he was doing, came out of their helpless stupor and began making their own efforts. By now, too, the violence of the Carabinieri had communicated itself to the crowd which was at last losing some of its forward momentum. Clinging to each other, and helping as best they could in the direction Conrad was pushing them, Billy and Harriet finally emerged from the edge of the crowd to the left beyond the line of Carabinieri. But Conrad, who was further into the crowd, was too late and got a crack across the head, before he, too, emerged, dazed and bleeding in the now open space beyond the line of truncheons.

Harriet in a state of shock had squatted down in the first open space she could find. Billy, no longer quite the helpless piece of flotsam tossed about by the crowd, turned back and, holding Conrad tightly, led him to the upper fountain and began bathing the wound on his head, which was bleeding profusely. Everything had happened in a great rush – much quicker than the time taken to describe it all. From the moment that the crowd surged forward and the Carabinieri panicked and began lashing out, to the moment that the incident fizzled out, could not have been more than four minutes. However, during that four minutes about thirty people had been struck and there were twenty men still bleeding and moaning on the floor, in clear need of attention.

By now, the Carabinieri were themselves under control, with two officers running up and down, shouting at their men. The crowd was beginning to melt away. Incredibly, the music and the dancing at the top end of the square had continued unabated throughout, and no one at the top of the Campo seemed to have noticed what had happened at the bottom end. It was another five minutes or so later that the first of the ambulances arrived. They nosed their way through the crowds, beginning to disperse through the little streets leading into the Campo, and stopped in front of the Town Hall. Once there, the several paramedics jumped out and began checking on all the wounded men. Some less badly wounded had wandered off but there were still about twenty mostly sitting on the ground in shock and bleeding.

To Harriet, it seemed that she had been trapped in the middle of a large mindless crowd, threatening and passionate, but in fact the whole affair had only involved a small section, the yellow and black chequerboard crowd, and not even most of them. As a riot, it did not rate more than one short sentence in the next morning's papers. Even then, looking around, Harriet wondered why it was that only men seemed to have been wounded. There were plenty of women in the crowd, and she had seen several being driven alongside their men towards the police line and those striking truncheons. Discussing the incident later, Conrad, who was and remained a convinced lover of everything Italian, claimed that even in that short burst of unprofessional panic, the Italian carabinieri instinctively stopped themselves from striking out at a woman. The Contessa Berchtold's comment on that suggestion, when it was raised round the dinner table later, was a shake of the head and a short sharp and rather rude word.

Several of the wounded men were being treated on

the spot there and then, but Conrad was bleeding badly and the medics said that he could not be treated by first aid and that he should accompany twelve of the other wounded men in the ambulances to the hospital to have it dealt with there. The ambulances were full and Billy and Harriet, having checked on which hospital Conrad was being taken to, had to follow on foot. By the time they arrived, Conrad had already been given a sedative and had had a couple of stitches in the side of his head. He was arguing vociferously with the nurses as they came into the ward in which he was sitting up in a bed. The staff were insisting that he was not in a condition to leave and that he had to stay overnight at the very least. The two nurses and the young doctor were relieved when Harriet and Billy came in. Assuming that Harriet was a wife, they turned to her for support. They explained that there was no problem, no danger, as Conrad was well, strong and healthy, however a blow on the head severe enough to require stitches could cause concussion, the effects of which could be delayed. Conrad needed to be somewhere where he could be continually monitored for at least the next twelve hours.

Conrad argued that he had experienced far worse situations and had gone on regardless. But with Harriet and Billy now backing the professionals, his will began to waver. Harriet clinched the discussion by pointing out that in any case he would be far more comfortable in a hospital bed for the night than in their miserable little room in the house on the crossroads, where, if he came out, one of them would have to sleep on the floor.

"Fine – ok, ok – but you two are to leave now and not hang about in this depressing place. If you don't promise to have a great evening and join the celebrations – I will insist on leaving. I'll see you here tomorrow morning at 9.00 and then we can be off. I'll get a good night's sleep and you can tell me all about it - listen you can hear the sounds of revelry even from here."

The mood was cheerful. Everyone was smiling – the young doctor shook hands and hurried out – the nurses shooed Billy and Harriet out with kisses on both cheeks, and three different narratives of the incident were already being formed. Harriet and Billy left and merged into the cheerful crowds now in full celebration all over the city.

Chapter 22

Billy fails the test

Memory or narrative – it is impossible to be completely objective about trying to separate the two. When recalling the past, everyone believes that they are simply reporting what their memory is telling them truly happened – but so often this is not a true memory of what occurred but the narrative that they started constructing in their minds from the first moment the incident occurred. I think I remember every moment of that summer's day in Siena vividly – but then I begin to wonder how far the recollection is true as the edges of memory blur. Was the crowd's surge forward really as terrifying as I seem to remember? Were the Carabinieri really quite as vicious as I seem to recall? Did the whole incident, as the crowd surged back and forth, really take the ten minutes of my memory? One fact does stand out, as I did subsequently check it – namely that there was no mention of the incident in any newspaper the next day. On the other hand my brother did get a blow on the head and he did have to stay in hospital for the whole night.

I had been the keenest of the three of us in favour of making an expedition to Siena for two days and I was pleased to have been supported by the Contesse. I really liked all three sisters, but I was not quite as besotted with them as Conrad. He was fond of all three of them, and his opinion was leavened with a sort of nostalgia for the vanished glories of old Europe. He was probably most taken with the proud but gentle Sofia – the Contessa Maggi; but he had almost an equally soft spot for the acerbic Varvara – the Countess Berchtold, and was caught between them when they bickered. Varvara, the Austro-Hungarian aristocrat, could not quite get that Austrian Imperial contempt for the Italians out of her mind. So it was that to her sister's irritation she would always take an Austro-Hungarian view – even rubbing in the impressive victories of the Hungarian football team as against the poor showing of the Italians at the time. Neither she nor Maggi knew much about football, but that didn't stop them arguing about it passionately. As for me, I preferred Natalya, Nicolai's mother, and was very pleased to be staying with her on this occasion.

Memory plays tricks with us. I remember my first kiss. I was nine years old and I used to take piano lessons together with a girl a little older than I, who was a neighbour. We would walk to our piano teacher's house together – people were a good deal more relaxed then about letting their children out on their own on the streets. She was a lovely girl, pretty, with a delightful birthmark on her cheek. I remember her name – it was Nanette, though I can't remember her surname, if I ever actually knew it. Our piano teacher was a dried-up wizened old lady – or so it seemed to us – who was very strict. She did not hesitate to rap me over the knuckles with a ruler if I got my scales wrong, or if it was clear that I had not practised since the last lesson. We had our lessons together and she was harsh to both of us, with a sharp sarcastic tongue, but she never touched Nanette. I remember well – or do I – this particular occasion when she had been particularly hard and had struck me several times. I was close to tears and my eyes were damp, though I managed not to cry as we left. Outside the house, before we got to the street and still in the front garden, Nanette stopped and, holding my hand, squeezed it hard in sympathy and kissed me on the cheek. To this day I can feel her cool lips as they kissed and lingered.

I was too young to get an erection, but I was not too young to feel aroused and to sense a real love for this fellow human who had witnessed my valiant attempts not to cry – boys were not supposed to cry in those days – and who wanted to comfort me. As it happens, some days later I saw her again with a big red-headed 12 year-old boy from the neighbourhood, who was a bit of a bully and gave all us 9 year-olds a hard time. They were in the woods behind our houses and I saw her being kissed and clearly enjoying it. It was my first disillusionment in the world of love.

Nanette's father was an RAF pilot. He died that year and the family moved away. I never ever saw her again – but the memory stays with me.

That was completely innocent – but I remember it more vividly than the more carnal kisses I exchanged with Natalie's girl friends when I was 14 or 15. None of this had anything to do with 'love'. I did however fall in love with Barry and once again memory is unreliable and distorted. I recall only my overwhelming feelings of guilty love – a mixture of platonic hero-worship for this strong popular masculine figure who clearly desired me, combined with my wish to be loved – loved by anyone. But what about the kisses and fumblings – I have very little memory of those at all, partly, I'm sure, because I was quickly aware that they meant absolutely nothing to the other young man.

Finally there was last year's affair with Paulina at the Villa Maggi. I had fallen in love deeply and without reservations. Paulina's warmth and gentle instruction, as we made love, touched my heart over and over again. But it turned out that for her, too, as if I was fated always to disappointment, I had meant nothing to her at all.

When we came out of the hospital on that summer evening in Siena, we were both at first a little subdued. However, the celebrating crowds won us over and we soon began 'carousing', as I think Shakespeare might have called it. We wandered the streets and drank many glasses of wine. What the Contesa had said was true – some of the fountains, certainly the smaller 'acqua potabile' ones, were actually spouting red wine. I've never seen it before and I have never seen it since. But even there I could be mistaken.

Could it be that my mind, already befuddled, saw the water running red. We were handed paper beakers of red wine by young men standing alongside these fountains. Perhaps the wine was served from barrels at their feet, rather than from the fountain itself. Could it be that. primed by the Contessa's words about fountain's spouting wine, a combination of memory and narrative sees the fountains running red.

I was only 17, while Harriet was over 19. There was only two or three years difference between us, but at the time it seemed more to me. Harriet was a sophisticated Oxford undergraduate who had captured my brother's heart. Her conversations with him were intellectual and often way above my understanding. She was cool and collected in all she did, whilst I was still just a boy in nearly all senses of the word. So what was it about that evening; why did I start seeing her differently as the night wore on. We were surrounded by the revelry of the happy Italian crowd, letting their hair down probably for the first time since the end of the war in which they had suffered so much.

We wandered round the town, drinking and supping on the various foods sold by street vendors, giggling like the teenagers we were, with not the slightest interest in high 'art' or architecture. At midnight the crowds were still thick. In order not to lose each other, Harriet had taken my hand and whenever I flagged or thought of resting, she would pull me along. Her eyes were shining and even at 17, I sensed a warm sensuousness emanating from her. Italian men are not noted for great reserve when it comes to recognising and appreciating beautiful women, and Harriet was the centre of attention wherever we went. They looked at her very frankly and I was aware of an undercurrent of sexual excitement in the air. I don't think Harriet was aware of it, or perhaps she was, but coped with it all as easily as most Italian girls did.

I lost all sense of time but by the early morning I was exhausted – or I thought I was. I have never been as physically strong as Conrad, and the early morning rise and the day spent continually walking was proving too much for me. Several times I said to Harriet that we really had to go 'home' for a rest. Every time I raised this, Harriet would wrap her arms round my neck, kiss me and laughing out loud said –

"Home – home – oh you mean that miserable little hovel on the cross-road. What do you want to go there for, when 'here' is so much more exciting?"

Nevertheless the moment came when I could be persuaded no longer and said that I could not continue. I insisted that I now had to go and rest and that she had to come with me as otherwise Conrad would never forgive me for leaving her alone on the streets. At this pathetic attempt to be a bit more assertive, Harriet gave an ironic laugh – but agreed to follow me, that is if I could find my way. As it happens I have a good sense of direction and in fifteen minutes had arrived at our destination. Conrad had given me the old iron key to the front door and we stumbled in and made our way up to our little room.

I flopped down, still fully dressed, onto one of the beds. My head was going round and the act of lying down seemed to make it worse. My own narrative of this night in Siena has always been that I was completely inebriated and no longer knew where I was or what I was doing. But guilty memory sharply reminds me that though I was indeed very dizzy, I did consciously turn my head to watch as Harriet took off her blouse and stepped very deliberately out of her summer frock. But that very use of the word 'deliberately' is surely inter-pretation again, isn't it? How could I really tell whether it was 'deliberate' or not? The final incontrovertible fact is that Harriet stood in the space between the two beds, in only her black lace underwear. She stood look-ing down at me. I could not have been as drunk as I thought, because I immediately began to be aroused.

I had never seen a girl in her underwear in quite this way before. Somehow Paulina had always been more discreet in our many encounters. My loins stirred and stretched and it was, I suppose, pretty obvious what was happening and it was clear that Harriet saw it all. I could see an excitement in her eyes. I had always as-sumed that Harriet did not really approve of me, large-ly because I suppose I was too young and too cheeky for her. She seemed always to feel triumphant whenever I was told off by anyone – and her smile on those occa-sions was not always very pleasant.

I knew it was vital that I should get up and quietly leave the room. I knew it absolutely and with complete certainty. Everything depended on my having the will-power to act. All I had to do was to get off that bed and go out to the bathroom at the end of the corridor. I had 'taken' from Conrad one way or another all my life – what had I ever given back to him in return. This was such a small – such a little thing I could have done.

But I did not move. My age was no excuse, no excuse at all. As Harriet stared down at me, instead of smiling and turning away – I stared back. Neither of us turned our eyes away and then Harriet sat down at the side of my bed. God help me, I actually shuffled over a little towards the wall to make room for her.

I lay there frozen – that much I think is absolutely accurate and not just self-justifying narrative – but then passivity can be as sexually stimulating as rough grop-ing. Either way, I do not cite my passivity as any sort of excuse for my behaviour that night. I cannot speak as to Harriet's feelings or motivations, but one thing I have to accept is that at any moment I could have stopped the progression of events with a single word. I did not do so – not because I was too young to know how, but because somewhere at the back of my consciousness, I didn't want it to stop.

The long moment passed and still staring down at me, Harriet's hand, as if accidentally, passed over my straining bulge. It lingered and then she leant down and shifting herself on top of me she kissed me with a force and a passion that took my breath away. She then began undoing the buttons on my pants. From that mo-ment I was lost. We twisted and turned, tumbled onto the floor and staggered back up again – locked into each other's arms. One way or another it went on almost all the rest of the night with only three intervals whilst we got our breath and strength back, and during which I experienced moments of great joy and tenderness as we clung to each other. Yet throughout that whole night, not a single word was said between us. At last, now ly-ing together on Harriet's bed, entwined in each other's arms, we finally fell asleep.

But I slept for only about forty minutes. I was com-pletely spent – physically and emotionally. I rose, disentangling myself, careful not to wake her up. We were both completely naked by this time. A touch of light was just beginning to show from the small window near the ceiling. I sat for a time on the edge of my bed and in a slow trickle tears began to form in my eyes and ran down my cheeks. I didn't sob; I made not a sound. But inside me I was contorted with guilt and self-loathing. How could I have acted as I did? My Dad had always said that I was a selfish scamp. But this had been worse. As if I was still a small boy, I craved punishment. I had to get out of that room, but of course I couldn't just abandon Harriet. I scribbled a note saying that I was hungry and had gone out to get something to eat. I wrote that I would meet her at the hospital after she got up. I had only the same clothes from yesterday to think of and I bundled them all together and went out quietly to get changed in the bathroom. I left the key and the note on my bed.

Once outside I wandered round the town in the early morning – but I was not actually hungry at all. In any case, relying on Conrad as I always did, I had no money with which to buy any thing, even a coffee. Stupid – stupid – stupid! What had I done? In the end I had nowhere to go so I drifted back to the hospital. This was the 1950's – one could not just walk into a hospital ward and expect to be able to see your brother at any time you chose. There was such a thing as strict visiting hours. I sat in a miserable waiting room and thought about my betrayal. I had no idea what Harriet thought or what I was now supposed to do. For me the experience was devastating – and to make it worse I still felt the sheer sexual excitement when I recalled the details of that long – but probably in reality fairly short – night.

What had been in Harriet's mind? Did she love my brother – I had to admit that I had been thinking that she did over the last few weeks, and I was pretty sure that Conrad was in love with her. Oh God, what would she say to me, how should I react? Surely I wasn't in love with her was I? But if not, then what had I been playing at.

Then Harriet came in. It was still not yet 9.00 am, the time we were supposed to pick up Conrad. I looked up at her, fearful as to what my reaction ought to be. She was looking cool, though as sensuous as ever. She simply smiled at me – waved a sort of friendly but highly chaste kiss in my direction and began chatting to the receptionist at the desk who was on duty. It seemed as if nothing had happened between us at all. I immediately felt a deep shame come over me – I could actually feel my face blushing. I felt that the two to three years actually separating us was more like five – that I was sixteen and that she was over twenty. I felt humiliated and ashamed.

She had made it quite clear, without having to say a word, that whatever had happened between us the previous night was already forgotten as far as she was concerned. That friendly wave and the gesture of calmly touching her lips and waving at me showed she had taken complete command of the situation, making it clear that nothing that had happened the night before concerned her or gave her any emotional problems of any kind. Furthermore, that laconic wave and friendly smile clearly indicated that it did not need to concern me either and that there was nothing to discuss, nothing to explain between us. Whatever it was, was over.

It seemed that yet again I had gone through a deep emotional experience which would remain with me for the rest of my life, but which appeared to have had no meaning at all on the other party.

Chapter 23

Billy decides

Harriet had been an only child and she had had no experience of a younger brother. She had had plenty of dealings with those older than herself, all buzzing around her like bees round a honey-pot. She had never had the slightest difficulty in fending these off and had always been in complete control. Her liaison with Jake had been mutually satisfying – an affair which suited them both. While there was talk of an engagement, for public consumption, both of them knew that there was no real prospect of a more permanent relationship. Harriet soon saw that Jake was as happy with the situation as she was herself. It was not simply 'lust' – but it was certainly not love for either of them.

So for Harriet, what took place on that night of the July Palio was basically meaningless if physically satisfying, and certainly a good deal less significant than her couplings with Astley. She felt nothing for Billy. In fact, on the whole, she somewhat disapproved of him. He may have been a whiz-kid at mathematics and one of the youngest ever scholars going to Christchurch, but for her he was just a boy. She knew that she had led him on, glorying in the sexual power that she had exercised – but so what? She owed him nothing. The combination of drink and the sexual energy of the streets had made it inevitable, and in the end she had got exactly what she had been craving. The boy had fulfilled the role in which she had cast him, with, she had to admit, flying colours. In addition she felt a certain thrill that she had manipulated and dominated the only other person who commanded so much affection from the man she loved.

183

She knew that the man she wanted to marry was Conrad. She also knew that he would not go to bed with her until either they were married, or until the future had been irrevocably agreed between them. Conrad's reserve, and the slowness with which he was moving to commit himself, had left her frustrated and in need of physical release. Billy was available and turned out to be easy prey. In fairness, Harriet had no conception of the turmoil that she had caused the boy. Even if someone had pointed out to her that her actions might have left Billy in a state of guilt, even of fear, she would have repudiated the suggestion completely. After all, nothing had as yet been agreed between her and Conrad. Above all, she would have pointed out – and pointed out quite fairly – that though he might be only 17, Billy had participated willingly in the seduction, with a physical forcefulness that was entirely his own, and not just as a result of her manipulation.

So it was that she smiled at Billy when she arrived at the hospital – blew him a kiss and received what she thought was a shy smile in return. She was aware of his blushes, but assumed that they were caused simply by his recollection of the previous night. As for the possibility of 'shame' or 'guilt' – that was ridiculous, and did not cross her mind for a moment.

Conrad appeared in the waiting room very soon after 9.00 a.m. There was no luggage other than the one small bag that Conrad again carried. They wandered round the town again, visiting the severe black and white Duomo and getting into the Palazzo Publico to see some of the rooms that were open to the public. Conrad, who had had a good night's rest and was completely refreshed, was bubbling over with enthusiasm, and Harriet picked up on his mood. They walked hand-in-hand as Conrad enthused about Siena and they recalled together the excitement of the Palio. With the beautiful weather adding to his pleasure, the still electric atmosphere of the city, and Harriet beside him, Conrad did not notice his brother's unusually subdued behaviour.

Back in Florence at the Palazzo Maggi, life was due to return to its normal tenor. On the very first of the evening dinners in the dining room of the Contessa Maggi, Conrad was excitedly going through the whole incident at the Palio. Natalya commented –

"Yes, yes, one of the extraordinary things about the Siennese contadini is that they tend to have a great rivalry with one other particular ward – and consider it almost as bad if their rival ward wins as if they lose. It sounds to me as if the winner on this occasion was the main competitor of the other ward."

"Well gentlemen," said Maggi, "what are your plans?"

"My dear Contessa," said Conrad, "do you mean our plans during the next few days in your beautiful city – or do you mean our plans for the rest of the summer."

"No, no, I know your plans for the rest of the summer – you will continue to steep yourselves in our warm Mediterranean culture – either here or in other parts of our lovely country. No, no, I mean when you all return home."

"Well Contessa, you know that Billy is starting his first year at Oxford as a mathematics scholar at Christchurch. I will still be there at Worcester for my last year – and Harriet will also be there in her second year. So, can you imagine, we will all be up together for a whole year. Incredible is it not how the war has created this situation. I am nine years older than Billy – but the combination of my late entry into university due to the war, and Billy's early arrival due to his brilliance, means that we will all be there together for one whole year."

This was greeted by a silence during which the Pasta

185

course was removed and some meat and vegetables appeared. Then into the silence Billy said quietly –

"Ah Contessa – I did tell the Countess Androvna this evening earlier, before coming down to dinner, that I am leaving tomorrow. I promised to return to the Villa Maggi and do some more work for Aunty Sima and Nicolai on the farms. I also need to get back home for… er…er …"

"Nonsense Billy – you can't leave now, just a day after we've got back. There are weeks before the end of summer or having to prepare for university."

"No, sorry Conrad – I have to go. I would have loved to stay longer – but it's impossible."

Conrad argued for some time, but was eventually convinced by the fact that Billy was going to go to work for a week or two at the farms in the Veneto like the previous year.

The next day Billy left. But on arrival at Milan station he did not switch to a train going to the Veneto but returned straight home to London. Billy was now 17. As an Oxford scholar, he had deferment papers enabling him to complete his three or four years at university before doing his National Service. Deferment for scholars was almost automatic. But Billy, his mind still in a turmoil, now had other plans.

On his third day at home Billy approached his father on his return from work in the afternoon and asked to speak to him. Harry, although now over sixty, was still working at the Admiralty. They walked into his study together.

"Well, Billy, what is it – what's this all about?"

"Father, I need your help."

"Billy, my love, what's with all this 'father' business. Come, hokis, give me a hug. You've been totally self-absorbed ever since you got back. Come. Come. There, that's better. Now my son what do you want."

"Daddy – I'm sorry but I want to do my national service now, before going up to university. Can you swing it for me."

"Good heavens – whatever for? Conrad is still up and has another year to go. I know that he is looking forward to you both being there together. What's happened?"

"Nothing Dad, nothing. I just feel that I will get more out of university if I am away for a couple of years. I feel I am too young at the..."

"Oh come on Billy – you have never in your whole life ever felt that you were too young for anything. Look – did you have a quarrel with Conrad? Olga tells me that you came back earlier than expected."

"No Daddy no. We had a marvellous time. Countess Natalya is a lovely lady. No, believe me, no, it's nothing like that. It's just...well... difficult to explain."

Harry had always been stricter with Billy than with Conrad for deep-seated reasons that were too complex to analyse. But whereas he was never quite sure what Conrad was ever thinking, both he and Olga had always been able to read Billy like a book. He knew Billy was holding something back – but he also knew that he meant what he was saying, and that this was not just a whim.

"Have you said anything to your mother?"

"No, Dad, no you are the first person I have spoken to about my decision."

"So that means that you haven't consulted Conrad either."

"No, Daddy."

"Hm...Well Billy if you are sure and if you have really thought it through – then we will see if we can do something. I can see some sense in the idea. Do you want to go into the Navy – I can certainly get you in, even on National Service."

"No, Dad, no – you know I get seasick. Anyway I want to go into the army."

"Funny – ironic – I can feel your grandfather shouting down from heaven – or up from the other place – rooting for you all the way."

"Will the university make things difficult?"

"No, not at all – on the contrary, as a matter of policy they all prefer taking students after their National Service. Come on Billy, my love, cheer up. I'll sort it out for you. Come, you could be off very soon, so I'll warn your mother and we can all go out tonight for a slap-up meal together."

Harry was as good as his word. He had sorted out Christchurch and the local army board within a week. Billy did his infantry 'square-bashing and even before Conrad returned from Italy, Billy had left England, posted to Malaya where the army was involved in containing a communist insurrection.

Chapter 24

Conrad and Harriet

On the day after Billy left Florence, Conrad and Harriet went for the day to Fiesole. In the bus going up the hill there were two English girls sitting in front of them flirting mildly with a couple of young Italian men. The girls could speak no Italian – the men had little English. Conrad and Harriet giggled together as they listened in to the stilted conversation. Asked what they did one girl turned to the other and said in a cockney drawl "We're artists aren't we Maisie". Neither group could really understand the other – the two English girls imagining some innocent romance, the two Italians imagining the easy acquiescence of foreign girls.

On arriving in Fiesole, Conrad and Harriet bought some bread and salami and wandered into the country-side, eventually settling down on the grass by a shrine on the side of a dusty unpaved road. The weather was hot and the skies clear. Harriet urged Conrad to pick some of the grapes from the vines in a nearby field, Conrad demurred muttering something about the farmer's livelihood. Eventually, however, he relented and went to pick some berries instead, pointing out that the grapes were not yet ripe. Harriet started sketching and brought out her watercolour paints while Conrad lay back, munched his bread and contemplated her sensuous figure and handsome features. Two little boys – the children of the local farmer or so it seemed to Conrad – came down a lane leading up the hill and stood staring at the two 'stranieri' with fascinated curiosity. Conrad sat up and watched as the two little boys came and knelt patiently beside Harriet watching her paint, while the sun shone, a slight wind lazily stirred the olive trees, and Harriet sketched on.

Conrad suddenly had difficulty breathing. His eyes misted over and he had a vision. The two little boys had become angels kneeling by Harriet's side like two cherubim from a Renaissance painting. Harriet herself, in white dress with blue flowers, white sandals, blue scarf loosely knotted round her neck just covering her bare shoulders, was a Quattro-cento Madonna. The whole scene blurred and Conrad turned away and looked into his own soul where, for the first time, there was no longer any doubt or anxiety about his feelings.

When his vision cleared, and he looked again, the two little boys were gone and Harriet was looking at him and smiling. This calm and gentle smile, full not only love but of real affection, flooded over him, and he smiled back. From that golden afternoon on, Conrad had no more doubts – the distorting image of Jacob Astley was buried once and for all.

That same afternoon, when they got back to Florence, they found that they were too late for the Fra Angelico museum, where they had intended to go. Instead they wandered hand in hand into the Botanical Gardens. The inevitable moment came – Harriet leant back against a large tree. Conrad leant against her and holding himself up with a hand against the trunk on each side of her, he kissed her again and again, more and more passionately, as Harriet opened her lips to let him in. But as this was Italy in the 1950s, he soon felt a tap on his shoulder as one of the garden keepers muttered "non si puo…non si puo". Scandalised women, dressed head to toe in black fluttered past as they disentangled themselves.

Now, there was no holding back, but this time it was Harriet's restraining hand that kept passion from boiling over rather than Conrad's sense of propriety. It was as if the physical urges, which had left Harriet so frustrated, had been assuaged by that night with the unfortunate Billy in Siena. A more open relationship could now develop. Harriet was not the type to bother analysing her own reactions. She accepted that in one part of her mind she had always been in love with Conrad – or at least had always desired him. She therefore found a great release of her spirit in Conrad's uninhibited sexual advances. As for the night she'd shared with Billy, and any influence it might have had on her, she never gave it a moment's thought. Nor for a moment did it cross her mind as to what it might have done to the young lad. Perhaps after 17 years, without realising it, Billy had without realising it at last given something back to his elder brother.

By comparison, Conrad, could no longer keep his hands off Harriet. Art was no longer enough. In the Uffizi, one afternoon, at the end of a long corridor they embraced, locked in each other's arms. People passed and re-passed but Conrad was oblivious. Again a tap on the shoulder. A friendly Italian youth whispered that a ridiculous man had been scandalised, and had gone to fetch the Uffizi security police. "E stupido quest'uomo," he said. Conrad agreed, but Harriet nevertheless broke away and taking Conrad's hand, they moved on.

As the summer days passed, they had quite by chance found a little neglected spot on the banks of the Arno – a little fortress of broken walls between two of bridges with a lot of rubbish piled up nearby – the river itself slow and sluggish. A stunted tree, in full leaf, gave a bit of shade and a lot of privacy. They bathed in the river and dried themselves, and then, shielded from any prying eyes, they finally consummated their love. Conrad found that he no longer gave any thought to Astley or worried that he might be mistaking the joy and beauty of Florence for his love for this woman. He had at last learnt how to fulfil that love without any guilt or reservation.

It would of course all take time. Conrad had to finish his final year at Worcester – Harriet her two more years at Somerville. But the issue was decided. Conrad and Harriet would in the fullness of time be married and no one else mattered.

Chapter 25

National Service

Billy may have been a maths genius, but emotionally he was still a boy, and a fairly immature one. However, he was quite clear in his own mind over what he was doing. He was going into the army rather than taking up his place at Christchurch, due entirely to what had occurred in Siena. He could not face the thought of being up at Oxford at the same time as Conrad and Harriet. He may have been 'a selfish scamp' as his father believed, but he had been aware, during the course of that summer, that his brother was in love with Harriet. Of course he had no idea how far, if at all, their physical relations had matured, but there was no mistaking the fact of Conrad's love. Accordingly what had happened, what he had been a party to, could only be described as an act of unpardonable, self-centred betrayal.

Billy was uninhibited about his own sexuality, and the ease in which a kiss gave way so quickly to desire, Also he ruefully accepted his father's strictures on his character, namely that he was egotistical and thought only of his own feelings. But the closeness to his brother that he had experienced the previous summer in Florence, followed by his eight months on the farm in the Veneto, had given him a new insight into the feelings of others, and in particular those of his elder brother. He had become aware that he had taken his brother's love and protection entirely for granted all his life.

He had given what he believed to be 'love' to many people, but had ended up by being disappointed, realising time and again that his love had not been reciprocated. Now, following on that night in Siena, he became aware that, perhaps, he had been equally guilty in not returning the love – albeit of a different kind – that had unstintingly been extended to him all his life by his brother.

Billy was not naturally prone towards feelings of un-redeemed guilt, and Siena had introduced this complex emotion for the first time. In his childhood, Billy had been a rumbustious and fairly naughty boy. But his parents were strict, and childhood guilt for such misdeeds, had been quickly assuaged by the physical punishment swiftly administered by Harry and Olga; and as parental love was always abundantly present and openly shown, there was never any residual resentment, even on those few occasions where there might have been elements of injustice. So it was that Billy psychologically craved some sort of punishment. As a belief system, Christianity coped with this problem of the human psyche better than many, but for Billy a father confessor and a few 'Hail Mary's' was never enough, even if he had been a believer.

Like most other boys and young men in the very late forties and early fifties, Billy grew up with an anxiety about having to do National Service. The six years of war that dominated the childhoods of this generation, was immediately followed by the occupation of Germany, Palestine, the start of the Cold War, Malaya, Egypt and many other trouble spots where the declining British Empire was involved. The government of the day, aware of the mistake that had been made at the end of the Great War of demobilising the army too fast, had let the wartime army run down more slowly. But, by the end of 1948, there was – or seemed to be – a man-power problem. Accordingly at the beginning of 1949, against all the traditions and history of the British people, peacetime conscription was introduced for the first time. Continental Europe had had conscription, of one kind or another, for centuries, but it had never existed in Great Britain. Aware of the national prejudice against any sort of standing army, the government never referred to it as 'conscription', calling it National Service instead.

The ever present anxiety experienced by boys of all social classes was not the fear of 'death' – teenage males generally don't fear death in the abstract – it was because of all the stories that circulated, all highly exaggerated and some completely untrue, of the bullying and horrors of military life. So it was that Billy thought of National Service as a sort of punishment, even though he came from a military background.

Less than a month after Billy had had his heart-to-heart talk with Harry and been given the 'go-ahead', and before Conrad had returned from Italy, Billy walked gingerly through the gates of Ladysmith Barracks to begin his National Service. Having spent some time in an English boarding-school, he was not quite as unprepared as most of the other boys coming through that gate; those who had never left home, never gone abroad, never known anything but the security of the family home. But, like most of them, he had heard all the exaggerated horror stories. Furthermore, at an odd visceral level, he wanted them to be true.

When Billy arrived at the barrack room to which he had been directed by a large beefy lance-corporal on the gate, he found himself in a long line of anxious newcomers all waiting their turn to be interrogated by two hard-faced sergeants. As the line shuffled forward, more young men - boys really – joined from the back of the line. There were in fact eighty new entrants on that particular day.

Throughout the next three months training – square-bashing it was called – Billy had no difficulty in managing the physical side of the course, if such it could be called. He easily managed the early mornings, the marching and counter-marching, the relentless cleaning of boots and brass buckles, the assault courses and all the other paraphernalia of infantry training. What he found difficult was the shouting, the intention to take over the minds of the recruits by continual efforts to de-humanise them and to produce, instead, robots trained to immediate and unquestioning obedience to any order. The fact that his father was a Naval officer, that his grandfather had had a distinguished army career, and that his brother had been a respected soldier for over six years serving in the recent war, did nothing to bolster Billy's morale. If anything, the opposite was in fact the case. He remained forever fearful that he would not live up to what were likely to be his family's expectations.

It should be said that during those twelve or so years that National Service was fully in operation, the training of all those boys for the infantry was extremely hard. It was not at all like the tough training meted out, say, to the Paratroopers or the Marines or other regular soldiers. They, after all, had chosen their profession; they were there of their own free will and usually were entitled to leave at any time during those early months, with the option to buy themselves out. But for the National Serviceman, the only alternative was prison. Of course the training had to be hard, but the regular soldiers who administered it had a residual feeling of contempt and resentment towards these soft civilians forced by law to become soldiers. That contempt was played out in the difference in their attitude to training volunteer professionals, soldiers like themselves, and the way they dealt with these despised civilians.

There were people in society who did complain

about the harsh treatment meted out to the infantry national serviceman, who were of course largely from under-privileged backgrounds. But these complainants were thought of as 'namby-pamby pinko-liberal MPs' according to the blue-rinse brigade, though even a Tory madam would have difficulty in describing the redoubtable Bessie Braddock, the main critic, in quite those terms. However, in the end this was not the Russian army, and the death of a few young men here and there, was deemed an acceptable loss in view of what seemed to be the perceived benefits of the system.

Having been to an old-fashioned English boarding school, Billy had little difficulty coping with the harsh regime. Furthermore, he found companionship amongst these young men facing the same problem of adjustment. These were men he would never have had the chance even to meet, never mind understand, without the system of national service. It was therefore without any hesitation that at his end-of-training interview for what 'they' referred to as "potential officer material", he made it clear that he did not wish to go on to the officers training course, though it was made abundantly clear to him that it was likely that he would be selected.

Once it had been established that he would remain an infantryman, Billy was destined to go to Malaya.

For the jungle patrols of Malaya!

Palestine had been an Imperial war that had been entirely covered by the regular army. Korea was a sideshow for the British, with only a few national servicemen involved. But Malaya was different. Malaya was and has remained the National Serviceman's war par excellence. It was also the war, during the long and patchy years of the decline and fall of the British Empire, that was the dying Empire's greatest achievement.

Chapter 26

Malaya

Most of the troops that went out to Malaya travelled on heavily loaded troopships, passing through the Mediterranean via Malta, through the Suez Canal, still guarded by British troops, again largely national servicemen, and past Aden. But in some cases, the trip was done by air, and this was the case for Billy. It took almost a week to fly to Singapore and the plane had to land in Brindisi, and then in Istanbul, where Billy had no difficulty in recognising the landmarks from his childhood holidays. But then the plane stopped in Ankara, Baghdad, Karachi, Delhi, Calcutta, then a long hop to Rangoon, Bangkok and finally Singapore. Some of the stops were overnight when a coach would pick up the fifty national servicemen and take them to a hotel or a camp and then back the next morning.

Billy had never flown before – the previous annual trips with his family to Istanbul were always by train. He found it very exciting. The plane never flew very high and he was lucky to have a window seat all the way, with a bird's eye view on everything passing below. They were still in their civilian clothes as they were due to join different regiments and would be kitted out in uniforms different to those they had during square-bashing after they arrived. The heat which hit Billy when they finally landed in Singapore was like nothing he had ever experienced before, even in the height of summer in Tuscany. But if it was hard for him, it was even worse for most of his colleagues, none of whom had ever set foot outside Great Britain.

Billy was to join the Wessexshires, stationed in Ipoh

in the north of the country. Together with seven of the new arrivals he was to take the early morning train to the north immediately after arrival. They loaded their kit onto the waiting truck which was transporting them to the station. First, however, still in their civilian clothes, they were driven to the transit camp's armoury. There, each boy, for that is certainly what they were, was issued with a Lee-Enfield rifle and a full ammunition clip of .303 bullets.

"What's all this about, Billy? Why have we been issued with these rifles before we've even properly arrived?" asked one of the other seven anxiously. From the start, the boys in his group tended to turn to Billy for information, even though he was actually the youngest by several months, and despite also being the butt of the most teasing.

"Well..um..I really don't know for sure, but I think that the insurgents sometimes ambush the trains as they go through the jungle."

"Bloody hell – what the fucking hell do they expect us to do about it."

"We could always get Billy to go out and posh-talk them out of it, whatever the fuck 'it' may be," said another.

"It, you moron, means shooting your fucking bollocks off," said a third.

When they reached the station and moved onto the platform, Billy found it strange walking in ordinary clothes through a normal railway station with ordinary people going about their daily lives, carrying a modern rifle over his shoulder. But no one else seemed to take any notice or find anything unusual in a group of eight teenagers walking though the station fully armed.

They strolled up towards the front of the train but, before walking very far, were hailed by a soldier leaning out of a window, clearly another national serviceman like themselves, who advised them to get in right there. They stopped and looked at him questioningly – so he said.

"Look, if the bloody CTs blow up the track and there is any ambush – it's always the front of the fucking train that gets the worst of it."

"Billy, what are CTs?" said one of the boys as they all hesitated.

"I don't know – I'll ask him. Er.. sorry.. but what exactly are CTs"

The soldier laughed and answered –

"Communist Terrorists. They are the ones who will be shooting at us if we get ambushed. Don't worry it happens very rarely nowadays."

So, they all clambered in to the coach alongside which they were standing and settled down. Remembering the old family tradition of how he and Conrad would always go with their father to inspect the engine, whenever they took a train journey, Billy got out and walked to the front of the train. There he stood and inspected the large steam engine, fitted like a Western movie set with a cowcatcher at the front. In front of that engine was another smaller engine pulling a small coach, both of which were heavily armoured.

"Why the second engine?" Billy asked another soldier who was standing smoking and also looking over the two engines.

"Well it runs a few hundred yards ahead of our train as a sort of protection against mines or breaks in the line."

Billy must have looked a bit anxious at this, but the soldier, much older than Billy, muttered that it was now nearly a year since the last train was ambushed and attacked, and there was nothing to worry about. At this point the whistles started and Billy went quickly back to his coach.

It took the whole of the day but at last, long after darkness had fallen, sixteen hours later, the train finally arrived at Ipoh station. Even at ten o'clock at night it was still swelteringly hot. Billy and the others got into the Bedford truck that was waiting outside the station and were driven to the camp which was to be their home for the next eighteen months.

It was hot! Sticky and hot. It took several weeks for the average national serviceman to get acclimatised, and the 'jungle' training that they now went through took the temperature into account and was not too rigorous. They trained for over a month, learning the difference between warfare in a European environment and warfare in the jungle. Eventually, the moment came for their first jungle patrol. Most of the men, including Billy, had no idea what the theory was behind the patrols – they just went and soon came to realise that their foremost enemy was the jungle, not the CTs.

The amount of gear that these young men had to carry, quite apart from their rifle and ammunition, was enormous. On this, their first patrol – still part of the training – they were only going for three days, but nevertheless had to pack in an immense amount : three days' food boxes; a small fold-up metal cooking stove; a pack of twelve fuel blocks; a mess tin to cook in; eating irons; a cup and water bottle; a machete to hack through the undergrowth; a water bag - a large rubberised bag like a pillow case, which you filled with fresh water and 'hung' on a tree near where you had settled yourself.

Then there was the change of clothes you would need and a waterproof cape which you would hang over your sleeping arrangements. But that was not all. You

201

had, in addition, to pack your allocation of all the extra equipment needed for the unit as a whole – spades –radio – batteries – ammunition for the Bren guns and so on and so on. All this, usually comprising well over one hundred pounds, had to be carried up and down hills covered in jungle in temperatures of over 100º Fahrenheit.

This was the daily reality behind all the theories about how to deal with a Communist insurrection. In the end it only worked because these young men stuck at it, continually winding each other up but getting the job done. And it was all accomplished without the use of napalm bombs or fleets of armoured helicopters, thoughtlessly destroying any innocent villages along the way, the system employed by another country facing a similar problem in similar circumstances a few years later.

The one positive factor that applied to the way the whole National Service System operated, was the camaraderie and support that these boys gave to each other. In all the patrols, Billy and the stronger members of each unit unstintingly helped the frailer members in difficult circumstances, or when the load being carried proved to be too much for them. Despite all the teasing and the wind-ups, there was absolutely no evidence of any bullying or abuse between the national servicemen themselves.

Chapter 27

The Jungle Patrol

This very first training patrol into the jungle was almost identical to all the other patrols Billy went on, except that it was for only three days rather than the seven or more days that was usual. Early in the morning, while it was still dark, in the coolest part of the day, the patrol members would collect their weapons and ammunition after loading all their kit onto the transport, and clambered up into the ubiquitous Bedford trucks that accompanied all national service experiences. Dressed in jungle green, sitting side by side at the back of the truck with their rifles between their knees, they stared into the silent darkness, with no other traffic on the roads, due to the strictly enforced curfew placed on all native residents. They listened apprehensively to the constant drone of the insects all around them, drowning out even the sounds of the lorry itself.

Then, eventually, in the middle of nowhere the lorry would stop and they would clamber out. All the kit would be handed down and everybody would load themselves up, with attempts to keep up the group's spirits by light-hearted banter. No matter how hard you trained, there was never really a moment when you were completely fearless. But there was a deep atavistic understanding that you relied on each other, and therefore it was a matter of personal survival, not just heroics, if you could bolster the courage of those around you. Tens of thousands of years of pre-historic hunters and gatherers had fashioned the group courage of the ancient ancestors of these boys. They had known that their puny bodies, armed only with fragile sticks topped with

203

sharp stones, could only conquer the huge woolly mammoth, or the raging wild boar if you could rely on every member of the circle holding together once the animal was cornered. It was not being 'macho'; it was not male arrogance; it was a survival instinct that not only should you hold onto your own courage but do your bit to reinforce the courage of the man on either side of you. Natural selection then did the rest.

Once loaded up with all the kit they had to carry, the soldiers – throughout the emergency their average age was not much more than 18 years-old – would walk through the plantations and along paths until suddenly they stepped out of the bright glaring light of the early morning sun into the darkness of the jungle. It was always the same on every patrol. Enormous trees, slanting at impossible angles; parasitical greenery hanging down from all the trees, big and small; the clinging, sucking vines that everywhere blocked the way and reduced your visibility, some thicker than your arm, others gossamer strands. Above all, with all the kit one was carrying in the rising heat, and the sheer energy required to hack your way through the undergrowth, the sweat was soon pouring off and staining your clothes.

The dark green foliage and the huge trees, rising sometimes to heights of over one hundred feet, meant that not much sunlight could penetrate down to all the stubby undergrowth on the jungle floor. The floor itself was usually soft and spongy, covered with years of rotting leaves and vegetation. In some patrols, the unit involved might walk along fairly well-worn tracks; but at other times the front section of the unit would be hacking away with their machetes and knives in order to clear a way for the rest of the patrol to follow. This made for very slow going, but it had the advantage of relative safety over the well-worn tracks. where there was always the danger of ambush or being blown up by booby-trap land mines.

It was a never-ending vicious cycle – the less you cut away the more the shrubbery clung to you and impeded your progress; but if you started violently hacking away at everything in your path, the more you sweated, lost water and energy.

Of course these patrols did not involve walking on for mile after mile and then simply stopping for the night and going on the next day. The system was that the patrol would find a suitable spot early on the first day and set up a camp near to one of the abundant small streams. First you settled down and brewed yourself a cup of tea, using a cupful of the precious water you had carried in your water bottle all the way. From the start – that is from the training patrol onwards – you would always work in pairs. On that very first patrol, Billy's partner, older than him, but still just 18, began hopping about and yelling the moment he had finished his tea and tore off his sweat-stained shirt –

"What the hell's the matter with you?" shouted Billy.

"Oh Christ - oh fucking hell – just look at the damn little things… what the hell do I do…"

Billy stared at his half naked friend, and there, stuck fast on his lower chest, were four or five slug-like creatures – leeches! Suddenly the whole camp seemed to become aware of them with a fair number of boys yelling and jumping about flailing their arms. Billy, hastily removing his own shirt, found he had none on himself and so was able to keep calm. Warning his partner not to try and pull them off, he hastily lit a cigarette – took a couple of puffs and then one by one touched the glowing end to the slugs, which dropped off without tearing the skin.

Leeches were always a problem on the jungle patrols,

as the men were traipsing through swamps and across rivers. Billy rarely felt them when they first clung, but once he saw them after he got back to camp – black slug-like creatures with their heads buried deep in his body, sucking at his blood – he could not help but feel a disgust which would often turn to panic. He tried to keep calm, but he would fumble with his matches and often drop them before applying the heat which would cause the head to pop out and the leech to fall away.

Setting up the camp in the jungle was a ritual and a skill, which, subject to the slightly different conditions nevertheless worked in the same way every time. As the weeks went by, they all became more and more efficient and faster at the task. First you cleared the flattest little piece of ground you could find in your allotted area, between a couple of smaller trees. Then pulling down the right-sized vines to use as ropes you would fix a stout branch between the two trees. Then you would hang your waterproof capes – using your own and your partner's – across the branch hanging down on either side, stretching the sides out to either side with the use of the vines as ropes. The waterbags would be filled from the stream and then hung from another tree alongside what had now become your cosy corner.

The Sergeant or section commander would then go round making sure everyone had managed and needed no further help. He and his second-in-command would then lay a perimeter wire all round what was now the camp. Of course this was not wire, but a thicker version of the ubiquitous vines that were freely available everywhere you looked. It never ceased to amaze Billy that when the patrol first arrived at a spot in order to set up a camp for the week or more that they would be 'on duty' in the area, it would look like thick, almost impenetrable, jungle. It was always impossible either to see the first arrivals at one end or the rearguard at the other if you were in the middle. However, within only a couple of hours after each pair had finished cutting down the vines, creating their curious tent-like structures, digging pits and using their spades, you could often see right across the camp.

The camp was always situated alongside or very close to a stream, of which there were an innumerable amount in the jungle. A 'water-point' would be established and marked out at the up-stream end of the running stream, from where you could fill your waterbags. A 'washpoint' would also be established further downstream. Finally, at a point towards the downstream end of the camp, a thick vine would be attached to the perimeter vine leading out about 20 to 30 yards into the jungle. This was called the 'latrine vine' and led out to the toilet. This would consist of a deep hole dug into the ground to a depth sufficient to last for the length of the operation, always at least a week, but sometimes longer. Over this would be fashioned a primitive seat made with thick stakes driven into the ground with cross supports, strategically positioned over the hole. When the camp was struck and the patrol was due to go back to base, this contraption would be dismantled, pushed back into the now half full hole, which was then refilled and covered with earth.

One regular army officer, a radio operator, a couple of locally recruited Malay guides and a Chinese liaison interpreter would usually accompany a full-size patrol. During the week-long patrol operation, half the unit would always remain in the jungle camp on guard and doing such maintenance work as might be required, whilst the other half went out on patrol covering the area allotted. The section remaining in the camp would mount guard and continue on guard duty when the patrolling section returned. This would include a guard by the waterpoint and also one near the end of the latrine vine, not only to defend against outside attack, but to ensure some privacy for whoever might be using the latrine in the middle of the night.

And so it went on, week in and week out. There were no helicopters, no home comforts when they got back to the base camp, no supplies of Coca-Cola, no Hershey Bars, just day in day out patrolling through the jungle, showing themselves as the defenders of law and order to the remote villages and plantations, making it increasingly difficult for the insurgents to operate, and occasionally having to fight and sacrificing their lives.

But why did they have to do it? What was the plan behind it all? What was it all for?

Chapter 28

Malaya - the Communist Insurrection

In order to understand why Billy and countless other national servicemen had to traipse into the jungle day after day and face innumerable weeks of sheer boredom and discomfort, interspersed with those occasional days of gut-churning fear and violence, when they faced an actual enemy, it is necessary to look at the background to what became known as the Malaya Emergency.

There were several different ethnic groups living in the Malaya peninsula at the time. The first group, constituting the clear majority, was the indigenous Malays. They made up the largest proportion of the population, though they always remained a distinct minority in the city of Singapore, the largest city stuck right down at the end of the peninsula – a totally British creation of less than 150 years' origin. In general, the Malays, who were Moslem, accepted British rule though their true loyalty was first and foremost to the nine Sultans who ruled over the states comprising the Malay Federation.

The next largest ethnic group was the Chinese population. These were the many Chinese who had arrived as refugees as a result of the Japanese attack on China, together with the smaller group of second generation Chinese who had been born in Malaya. On the whole, the loyalty of both groups was to China, with which they identified culturally. They were separated into two very distinct groups. First there were the long-term residents – mostly in Singapore, but also dotted all over the cities of the peninsula. They were merchants, business men, and small shopkeepers – all hard workers. But secondly, and much more numerous, were the squatters, numbering well over half a million, who had fled from Japanese-occupied China during the War with their families and had settled on any available patch of land they could find, just outside the towns and squeezed in between those towns and the surrounding jungle. They were insecure, having no title to the tiny plots of land on which they lived and which they cultivated, and they provided the main recruiting ground and support for the communist insurgents.

Indians were also well represented in Malaya. They constituted most of the hard labourers on the rubber plantations where the wages were much higher than in India.

Then finally there were the British themselves and other Europeans. These numbered about fifteen thousand, being mostly Civil Service bureaucrats and advisors to the Sultanate governments, police officers, doctors, and above all the rubber planters and mining engineers.

The Malayan emergency was not a colonial conflict where a down-trodden people were rising up against an oppressive imperial power. Independence for the nine sultanates of the Malayan Federation was already assured in one form or another. This was an insurrection aimed more at the Malayan political establishment than at the British who were in any case on the point of departure. It was an attempt by one particular group – the Malayan Communist party – to get control of the state, ahead of, or in conjunction with, the departure of the former colonial power.

The biggest problem facing the Malaysian government following the end of World War II was the restoration of civil government. Because the Japanese had surrendered and not been forcibly removed with any great violence, Malaya had suffered little loss of life or damage to its towns and cities. However, many of its tin mines and rubber plantations had been destroyed to prevent the Japanese using them, so the Malayan economy was in the doldrums with large scale unemployment. The Japanese occupation authorities had favoured the Malays while persecuting the Chinese, who were strongly anti-Japanese due to their occupation and despotic rule in parts of China. Chinese guerrillas, armed and aided by British agents, had been operating against the Japanese occupation forces throughout the war, during the enforced absence of the British. The peninsula was accordingly awash with fighters and arms, motivated and ready to turn against any occupying force.

It was argued at the time that the Malayan Insurrection was part of a wider communist plan to gain power throughout South East Asia. But apart from the fact that the Malayan, almost exclusively ethnic Chinese, communist leaders attended some international communist conferences, there is little evidence to support the view that it was part of any co-ordinated plan.

The surprising fact is that the Malayan communist party was actually on the verge of collapse, having failed in any legal attempts to gain widespread popular support. An armed insurrection was their last hope, and it really was a case of now or never. The former popular leader of the party - Loi Tek - had disappeared, taking much of the party's funds with him, and his successor Chin Peng was still in the process of trying to make a name for himself. Fearful of the effect on party morale, Chin Peng kept the fact of Loi Tek's defection a secret for many months. As it happens, Loi Tek's vanishing act was not just because of stealing the party's money, but it was also because he was and always had been a British agent, and his cover was about to be blown. If a novelist ever suggested, in a work of fiction, that the British had

211

in effect run the Malayan communist party for years, he would be laughed out of court – but this was in fact the complete truth. Loi Tek duly disappeared with all the party's funds and was never heard of again.

Chin Peng, however, was quite a different proposition. He had learnt his jungle warfare skills from the British. The fall of Singapore to a much smaller Japanese force in 1942 was then, and is likely to remain forever, the greatest defeat and surrender of British armed forces in history. That the guns were facing the wrong way must be one of the most ridiculous excuses ever thought up by the military, regardless of its probable truth. Over 200,000 men, well-armed and entrenched in a perfectly defensible island position, surrendered to a much smaller enemy, which, while having air support, had no naval strength at all. Nevertheless, despite this extraordinary catastrophe, several British officers remained in Malaya operating from the jungle, and harassing the Japanese occupation forces. Supported by the Chinese, the guerrilla force they created swelled to over 5,000 and was known as 'The Malayan Peoples Anti-Japanese Army'. The British trained them in jungle warfare and gave them modern weapons, knowing full well that they were mainly communist supporters, but reckoning that the enemy of my enemy is my friend; and also, of course, secure in the secret knowledge that the party was ultimately controllable through Loi Tek. However, once Chin Peng took over, this provided the insurgents with a handy striking force that simply changed its name to 'The Malayan Peoples Anti-British Army'. The fighters were to be paid out of money extorted from the local population by the infliction of a harsh campaign of terror.

Chin Peng described his overall plan to a conference of local communists held deep in the Malayan jungle.

He explained that in the first phase, his little army of guerrillas, hardened by their fight against the Japanese, would raid isolated British-owned rubber estates, tin mines and police and government buildings deep in rural areas. This he claimed would drive the British out of the countryside and into the cities.

Once that was accomplished, and Chin Peng was certain that it would be, the areas thus abandoned by the British would be renamed 'Liberated areas' and guerrilla bases would be established within them to train new recruits drawn from the rest of the Chinese population as the Guerrilla Army expanded. This would eventually result in the forced withdrawal of the Imperial power and the creation of a communist Malaya.

The attacks started at 8.30am on 16th June 1948 in the northern state of Perak, with the shooting of a planter, Arthur Walker, on his estate. This was followed by other attacks on the same day and for many days thereafter on other estates. By their very nature, these rubber plantations were often isolated and in remote parts of the country and almost impossible to defend by any central power. Murders became more frequent both of the British planters and of the Indian workers – the tappers on the rubber estates. Often these tappers constituted whole families, with wives working alongside their husbands, helping with the delicate task of cutting the trees and tapping the rubber. Chin Peng's strategy was clear – the planters would eventually flee, then the Indian workers would melt away demoralised by the brutal killings and the departure of the owners, and finally the areas would be declared liberated. The rebels would continue to target other mines and plantations, causing the Malayan economy to collapse, after which the Imperial Power would depart and the country would soon fall into their hands.

Communist insurgency was rife all over the world, and it all might have been successful in Malaya if it was not for two intervening factors. First, there was the sheer stubborn bloody-mindedness of the intrepid planters. Isolated and vulnerable though they were, they refused to be run off their plantations and move to the towns, for their protection. The suggestion was that they could then effectively commute to their plantations each day. This was of course exactly what Chin Peng was expecting. But the planters scornfully rejected the administration's suggestion, and issued a joint official statement pointing out that the government's proposal "offered no protection for our Asian staff and workers, who are as much entitled to protection as are the Europeans." Almost to a man, having issued this statement, they stayed on their estates and often arranged to mount their own guard with the help of their families and some of their Indian overseers.

The second factor, which had a vital influence in containing the insurgency, was the appointment at the end of 1948 of a new High Commissioner – Sir Henry Gurney. The calm unflappable Imperial Mandarin, who had just presided over the end of the British mandate in Palestine, sitting stiffly upright in the Administration's black Rolls-Royce as it drove out of Jerusalem for the last time, was appointed only a few months after he left that troubled province. The decline of the British Empire was already apparent from its failure to deal decisively with the humanitarian crisis clearly brewing in an area for which that Empire was ultimately responsible. The expectation was that Gurney would now be presiding over yet another scuttle.

Chapter 29

Sir Henry Gurney

Sir Henry Gurney was appointed High Commission-er of Malaya in September 1948 shortly after the departure from Palestine. When Mrs. Golda Meir had stated that no one in his position as Chief Secretary in Palestine had the right to remain so unruffled in the midst of all the horror and violence raging around him, this had, perhaps, said more about her own character than Sir Henry's. However she had put her finger on an essential quality of the man.

He was a small man with receding hair and wore round owlish spectacles. He was a keen tennis player, believed in the virtues of daily exercise and insisted on his regular round of golf on the days set aside for it. In many ways, he gave the outward impression of being a fussy little man. Both in Palestine, and also here in Malaya, where t-shirts and shorts were fast becoming the fashion, he continued to dress formally even when off-duty, always wearing a jacket and tie and carrying a walking stick. Cool and reserved, perhaps even aloof and distant, he appeared to epitomise a type of Impe-rial official that was fast becoming obsolete.

But his diffidence and calm unruffled manner hid a keen intellect and an instinctive understanding of what motivated people to act as they did. Giving way to any kind of panic or over-reaction was for him the greatest personal failure of all. The very phrase 'stiff upper lip' is likely today to result in hoots of laughter, but it encapsu-lates an attitude that could be very useful in certain con-ditions. It is not a question simply of 'suppressing your feminine side', of not showing your emotions, or of not

215

bursting into tears when faced with shocking situations. There is nothing wrong with tears or emotions and Gurney undoubtedly had his share of these, as his close friends would attest. But tens of thousands of years of human history had conditioned the male hunter that in the face of any stressful situation the best survival technique was to remain as calm and steady as possible, or at the very least to appear to be so.

Almost immediately upon his arrival, Gurney made two major decisions that changed the whole conduct of the war. Long before it was postulated by others, he was clear in his own mind that the insurgency could not be defeated without the support of the majority of the people. On the other hand, he understood that such support would not be forthcoming until there were signs that the war was starting to be won, and that enforcement of law and order was successful. Gurney insisted that this was a political war as well as a military one. What was required was armed support for a political struggle – not political support for an armed struggle. At first sight, the difference might have seemed a matter of semantics, but it was in fact fundamental, and it was a difference that another power failed to grasp when facing a similar problem in Vietnam some years later. Had the military view prevailed over Gurney's, the result would have been similar to Vietnam. More and more bombing, more and more firepower thrown at the insurgents in the jungle, resulting in less and less support from the ordinary people being bombed and dying as 'collateral damage'.

It was the classic problem of having to show that you were capable of winning the war and imposing stability as a prerequisite for getting popular support. But in order to do that, you had to take the risk of alienating the very people whose support you were seeking by inflicting death and destruction on the enemy.

Gurney saw soon after he arrived in Malaya that Chin Peng's guerrilla army had been deliberately designed to be immune to traditional military power. No amount of helicopters, gunships, tanks, bombers and the rest would dislodge him. After all, those intrepid British officers, who had stayed on after the fall of Singapore, had helped create this Chinese guerrilla army to fight against the Japanese with precisely this in mind. He knew this was a different kind of war involving a small proportion of the population. One bomb well directed by his military commanders might kill ten of this small active group – but one bomb dropped on a village and killing one small child, could create a thousand new enemies.

Arms alone could never win this kind of guerrilla war. However, before a political resolution could be effected, normal government activity had to be seen to be working. The vast majority of the population, bemused and bewildered by the turmoil of a terrorist/freedom fighter war, could only rally to a government seen to be governing. If bombing and destroying the villages would not work, then the next best thing was to provide the equivalent of a 'local bobby' to go regularly round in the rural districts and be seen to be policing. That was where the national servicemen's boring daily patrols into the jungle came in. Chin Peng could never create those 'liberated areas' he wanted, because day in and day out Tommy Atkins, with his outdated WWll rifle and his voluminous kitbag, went into the jungle on foot, policing the remote estates and villages, rather than destroying them from the air.

It took Gurney some time to argue his case against a purely military solution in Malaya and in London, but once he had brought them to his way of thinking, he then had to produce a political plan. He came up with a quite extraordinary and radical solution. Chin Peng's guerrilla army, not much more than 14,000 or so at its very largest, operated only by dint of the support it received from the half million or more Chinese squatters living on the fringes of the jungle, on land to which they had no specific title. They cultivated this land and lived off its pigs and vegetables, selling to the nearby towns, but all without the security of ownership. Gurney decided to uproot this whole population and to resettle them into villages and onto land to which they would be given full title. Wherever possible, this would be as close as possible to their current locations. The intention was to achieve two things. Firstly to give them a permanent stake in what had become their country; secondly, of course, to be able to protect them from the depredations and intimidation of the guerrillas.

There were some in this section of the Chinese population who were dedicated communists and who supported Chin Peng regardless of their circumstances and who would never change. However, the vast majority were not, and only helped the CTs because in one way or another they were forced to. From the start Chin Peng had launched a violent campaign of intimidation against these squatters, murdering women and children and forcing the men to pay up and provide the support he needed. Gurney had seen it all in Palestine – whether you called them terrorists or freedom fighters – he was sure that his plan was the only way to combat them.

But to give the squatters title to the houses in the villages and the lands to which they would be resettled meant that the land itself would have to be given up by those who currently owned it. In practice, this meant the Malay Sultans. Once he had persuaded London, Gurney started work on this at once. It was his 'unruffled' patience and tactful diplomacy which eventually persuaded these owners to part with their land on the basis that it was in their own long-term interest to do so. Gurney may have lacked the sort of charismatic charm, exercised only a year or two previously by Mountbatten, to woo the Indian Princes into the Indian Union; but what he had in its place was a cool quiet logic showing the Sultans how much better it was for them to have on their land a hard-working secure population with a real stake in the country, than an insecure population of squatters, open to any terrorist wishing to intimidate them.

All this needed patience and took a long time, and Gurney himself would be gone long before it all came to fruition. It has become known to history as the Briggs plan, but it was Gurney who thought it out and started it all. For it to work, Billy and his national service colleagues would have to continue to go, day in and day out, into the jungle and patrol the new villages wherever they were sited, making it clear that the government was as committed to law and order as the insurgents were to creating mayhem. Furthermore, this was to be established by the presence of foot soldiers, rather than by remote firepower and indiscriminate bombing from the air.

These young national servicemen had to grow up pretty fast if, for instance, one of their sergeants was suddenly killed on a patrol. These boys had to face, within days of their arrival, the normal psychological terrors of the jungle: the heat, the leeches as they floundered through stinking swamps, the insects and disease. But on top of all this there was always at the back of their minds the knowledge of the existence of terrible man-made booby traps that could blow off one of their legs at any moment as they traipsed round the area allotted to them, showing themselves openly as protectors of the people, not their destroyers.

A final piece in the tragedy that was to follow was put in place by Chin Peng only a month or so before Billy went on his first patrol.

One of the difficulties faced by the communist insurgents was communications between the different jungle groups. With British help, the original anti-Japanese guerrillas had set up a courier service with secret hiding places dotted about the jungle at intervals, with runners acting as a sort of jungle post office. It required speed and efficiency and Chin Peng decided to appoint someone to oversee the system. He chose a young and very pretty Chinese girl called Lee Meng. She was already an experienced and dedicated fighter with a reputation as a ruthless organiser. Chin Peng sent her to Ipoh to coordinate the courier system, giving her enough money to get a small room and take a casual job as cover.

As Billy went on patrol after patrol, as soldiers died from stepping on land mines, as the occasional full-scale battle broke out between a patrol and an ambushing guerrilla force, 1950 gave way to 1951 and the winter turned to summer.

Chapter 30

Billy falls again

The whole basis of Gurney's counter insurgency plan was to put the presence of British soldiers into the jungle areas where Chin Peng wanted to operate. This was unutterably boring and occasionally dangerous for these young men. But it worked in the way that bombing, and napalm, and hundreds and hundreds of helicopters simply did not. However, these teenagers were not robots, and the army made no attempt to prevent them from using their time off to get some relief, in the normal way any teenagers would, from the tedium of never-ending patrols.

So it was that there was always a daily bus that left the Wessexshire camp each afternoon to take those who were off-duty, when they could afford it, to the night spots of Ipoh, This was not to suggest that Ipoh was full of bright and breezy night-clubs or enormous palaces of entertainment, but in its quiet and provincial way, there was undoubtedly enough to entertain these teenage soldiers. In particular, there was the so-called Chinese Concert Hall, above which was a cabaret where a live band would play dance tunes non-stop from mid-afternoon until curfew.

This was a particularly favourite haunt for Billy. The cabaret girls employed there were all very pretty and wore tight, close-fitting dresses which were both exotic and very sexy. They were all good dancers and had just enough English to appear to be holding up one side of a conversation. The boys would buy a booklet of tickets, like raffle tickets, and each ticket was enough for one dance with one girl. Although by any other nor-

221

mal standard the tickets were very cheap, the British national servicemen, throughout the whole twelve or so years of their existence, were paid such an absolute pittance compared to almost any other democratic army in the world, that the tickets appeared costly. So the purchase of the tickets had to be carefully balanced against their costs in the NAAFI and other payments they had to cover.

Billy was a good dancer and, as he did not consume the enormous amounts of beer and other goodies available in the camp Naafi, was able to afford a tad more of the tickets than his mates. Furthermore, he was bowled over by the demure, lithe and sexy Malayan and Chinese girls at the cabaret. So when he and his current friends went into town on one of their days off, he made a bee-line for the Jubilee Cabaret to buy up as many tickets as he could afford and dance away the early evenings with one pretty girl after another.

Being a natural linguist, within a few months he had learnt to master enough of the local tongue to converse and exercise his natural rather innocent charm on the girls whose names he soon came to know. He never learned any Chinese, but the local Malay dialect was enough. Eventually, he would be dragged away by those of his mates who had stayed the course at the Jubilee. They would then go for a meal, where the local noodle dishes Billy liked would be much cheaper than the thick steaks and chips which his friends, who had not wasted their money on dance tickets, would eat up heartily, paying through the nose for the privilege.

The dancers at the Jubilee were of course strictly regulated, and there was no question of any dalliance – not even a kiss. If they liked you, you could hold them tight as you danced, but if they were indifferent, there was a point of holding them beyond which you could not go. There were also brothels in the town, but despite all their bravado and claims of great conquests, the fact is that scarcely any of them had the courage to sample their services.

The jungle patrols were organised on the basis of at least seven days in the jungle followed by at the most three days rest and recuperation back at the base. Needing at least one full day for a complete rest between patrols, it did mean that you could get into Ipoh about twice a fortnight if you could afford it.

A favourite haunt for many of the British planters and miners who lived in and around Ipoh was the FMS Bar. This was an establishment that had been run by the same Chinese family for about fifty years. The bar specialised in providing good and well-prepared English food produced for all the homesick British families and men living alone in and around the town. The bar was well-stocked and was run by demure and pretty Chinese girls. Whilst not actually being 'officers only' or strictly 'out of bounds' to the national servicemen, they tended to avoid it as it was relatively expensive and seen as being 'posh' and a civilian reserve.

One day, coming out of the Jubilee, Billy got talking to a local planter and his wife and they invited him to join them in the FMS bar. Whilst there Billy, in his usual susceptible way, became struck by the beauty of the young waitress who was serving them. He was being attentive to his host and hostess, but as she passed he could not help but feel the familiar stirring in his loins.

A week later, on the very first day of his rest period, Billy was back at the FMS bar, having, for the first time in his excursions to the city, failed to go first to the Jubilee. The girl whom he had been unable to get out of his mind during his last patrol was serving behind the bar. Billy sat himself down at the long L-shaped bar. Letting his drink last as long as decently possible, he began chatting to her, whenever he had the chance. She gave her name as Lee and clearly enjoyed his attention. Billy was immediately smitten.

For a few weeks this pattern continued. Eventually, the moment came when Billy plucked up courage to ask the girl if they could meet on her day off. Knowing the strict rules at the Jubilee, Billy never thought that she would agree, but in fact she appeared enthusiastic. They arranged to meet on Billy's next rest period and go to the cinema together. Lee spoke good English and chatted easily with him, showing an interest in all his enthusiasms – opera – mathematics – Shakespeare – and the current problems in Malaya.

Lee had a room not far from the FMS bar and at the end of the evening, she invited Billy to come in and have some tea before going back to camp. There, it was she who took the initiative and holding Billy close, she leant up and gave him a long lingering kiss on the lips. Billy, already almost in love or imagining himself to be, completely fell under the usual spell, convinced yet again that this was true love. Despite the great difference in cultures, he felt that there was greater understanding between him and this slim Chinese girl than had existed with Paulina. Their love-making was both tender and passionate. Furthermore it did not just end in the bedroom. Lee seemed to understand him and joined in his enthusiasms, displaying real interest and knowledge.

Once again, and despite all his previous experience, he could not imagine that this gorgeous girl, with whom he had such a rapport, was not as much in love with him as he with her. How often had this happened to him and how often had found himself disappointed, disillusioned and humiliated, when it turned out that the love he had given so openly and freely had not been reciprocated. It seems odd that he had still not learnt to be a little more careful when it came to 'falling in love'. Week in and week out, every day of any rest period, exhausted or not, Billy was in Ipoh meeting with the lovely Lee whenever he could manage it. Their love-making was uninhibited and passionate and Billy once again was 'in love'.

However, in all his previous experiences, no great harm had ever been done to Billy beyond disappointment. His night with Harriet had perhaps done him the most harm – but he was young and the knowledge, conveyed to him through correspondence, that Conrad and Harriet were happy together and were now officially engaged, had done much to assuage his guilt. He was no longer seeking punishment and Siena no longer preyed on his mind as he found both solace and excitement in the enveloping arms of the lovely Lee.

But this affair was going to be different, for this girl's full name was Lee Meng – Chin Peng's dedicated CT courier organiser. She reported regularly to the High Command of the Communist party and Chin Peng was well aware of her developing relationship with the susceptible Billy.

Meanwhile as Sir Henry Gurney's dynamic influence slowly began to take effect, Chin Peng became ever more frustrated by the slow methodical strangulation to which the patient policy of the British High Commissioner was subjecting him. As frustration turned to despair, Chin Peng began to consider more dramatic moves. In his mind, it was the arrival of this old-fashioned mandarin of the British Empire, which was, according to Marxist dialectic, supposed to be in its last death-throes, who was directly responsible for the way the tide was inexorably turning against him. He was sure that his original theory was right and would have worked given time. He was, as so many of the communist insurgents of the time were, rigid in his theories - and so if it was failing it must be due to this one man. He could not conceive that it might simply be a matter of the application of another and superior theory. Due to the foot-slogging patience of all those teenagers, he could not manage to create even one of his planned 'liberated' areas. But Chin Peng could not accept that his theory, backed by all that Marxist historical evidence could be simply wrong. It was only due to that arrogant bureaucratic bastard. There was only one alternative left for him to try.

Assassination!

But how?

He put the problem into the hands of one of his deputies – a ruthless operator by the name of Siu Mah. Siu Mah produced a good plan but it involved the capture – alive – of a British soldier. One would have thought that with all the opportunities for stealthy attack and ambush in the jungle, the capture alive of one solitary British soldier would have been relatively easy. But capture alive in the conditions of jungle warfare is difficult. There, ambush or not, you killed or you died. There was no room or time for surrender and capture. But off-duty was different and, during the course of the next two weeks, several British soldiers, including one officer, were snatched off the streets in unguarded off-duty moments.

Chapter 31

The Disappearance

I was at home on that fateful day when my father came in early from work. It was the 15th September in 1951 – the date is seared in my memory, for it changed my life. My mother, Olga, and I were sitting in the drawing room when my father came in. My mother jumped up as soon as she looked up and saw my Dad as he came through the door. He had said nothing, but she knew at once that something had happened. But it was my Dad who spoke first –

"Oh, my darling – hokis – Olgajanus...."

"Oh my God Harry – it's Billy – for God's sake, what...."

"Wait, wait, listen. No one knows anything for sure at the moment but it appears that Billy has disappeared."

"What do you mean – disappeared."

"I don't know my love, I just don't know. Pethick-Lawrence's secretary came into the Admiralty and simply told me that he had just heard that Billy had gone AWOL. It would appear that he had gone into Ipoh the night before but had not caught the last transport back to camp. At first his superiors just thought that it was some sort of accident and that he would eventually walk back into camp and into a deal of trouble. But this happened a week ago and he has still not turned up and no one has any idea what could have happened. He tells me that the MPs have been out trying to find out what might have happened, but they've not found anything."

"Dad – have you tried the Wessexshires?"

"Of course Conrad, but the CO here says that he has no further information."

"Is there any talk of deliberate desertion?"

"Not yet, son, not yet. Billy was already an acting Corporal and often second in command on the patrols he was always telling us about. I can't believe that there could be any question of desertion. Surely, surely – you all read his letters, he never appeared to be unhappy. Oh heavens, don't look at me like that – the one consistent thing about my younger son is that he could never ever hide his true feelings, and we would have known at once if there was anything that was worrying him."

I telephoned Harriet and told her what had happened. I had introduced Harriet to my parents long before and they were aware that, to all intents and purposes, we were now engaged. I could not contemplate marriage immediately as I had not yet decided exactly what I was going to do with my life. I had enjoyed my life in the army for over six years and had taken pride in the work I did – but in the end, I could not contemplate it as a career like my father. On the other hand I had no idea exactly what else I could do.

After telephoning Harriet, my parents and I talked for most of the rest of the evening, though without getting very far. We all agreed that deliberate desertion was simply not Billy's style. He might have a row with a superior, or complain bitterly about some injustice, or get himself locked up for some reason, but to slink away without telling anyone – no that was not Billy. But if this was the case, it meant that we had to face up to the fact that he had either been abducted, had had a fatal accident, or more likely been killed. However, as after a week no body had been found, there was still some hope that he might still be alive. That night my mother kept breaking down in floods of tears repeating over and over again –

"Oh Billy – Billy – my son – my son…."

We eventually persuaded her to take a couple of sleeping pills and go to bed, while my father and I stayed up the rest of the night talking. It was during those long hours that my dad and I agreed together that I should go out myself to see if I could find out more. The MPs – military police – were not exactly renowned for their investigative qualities, and if the local police had been involved they would have been intimidated by the military presence. My dad pointed out that as I had been fairly close to Sir Henry Gurney during those last days of the Palestine mandate, I could probably get an audience with him that might help my search. I was sure I could find out what had happened – after all, I hadn't forgotten my skills as an Army Intelligence officer.

My student days were over and the 2:1 I had managed was good enough for most professions or the civil service, if that was what I finally decided upon. Harriet had to stay on for a further year, though she would have to leave College and get lodgings in the town. My own thoughts had turned to the airline business, as I felt sure it was going to develop out of all proportion to its current size. But nothing, nothing, was as important as trying to find out what had happened to Billy, even if it only confirmed what I felt was the most likely – namely that we would have to face up to his death.

Dad pulled every string in his considerable bow, calling in all his connections and using up all his accumulated goodwill throughout the military. So, within only two days I was on my way, by grace of the RAF, to Malaya.

The Army seemed to have changed since my time. Everyone seemed to be so much younger – or was that just me getting older. I still had contacts in the Intelligence section even though it was now three years since I had left. On arriving in Malaya, I felt a bit embarrassed to call upon Sir Henry directly out of the blue. He was a bit of a stickler for 'good form'. It seemed rather 'pushy' to press our personal family concerns onto a man facing so many important political problems. Instead, I left a courtesy message with Lady Gurney explaining what had happened and where I was staying and that I would leave for Ipoh the next day. Gracious lady that she always was, she immediately sent a message inviting me to tea that same afternoon. Sir Henry was not there, but I had a very pleasant two hours when we reminisced about those last dramatic few months in Jerusalem. It was obvious that she had already talked to her husband after getting my message and she gave me a letter of introduction addressed to the British Chief of Police in Ipoh. She also absolutely insisted that when I got back from my investigations in Ipoh I was to join her and her husband in a short weekend break they were going to be taking in the resort station at Fraser's Hill. I accepted with pleasure, but said that it would depend on what I managed to find out about Billy's disappearance.

I arrived at the railway station in Ipoh early the next day and checked in at a Chinese run hotel. My first visit was to the local British Chief of Police whom I thought far more likely to have the good information than the CO at the Wessexshires, and indeed that is how it turned out. He extended a warm welcome as soon as I was admitted to his office.

"My dear Bridgeman, I have just read the letter you left for me, from Lady Gurney. Here take it back – it is addressed to 'whom it may concern' and it may come in handy again."

"Thank you Mr. Prendergast." We then exchanged some basic pleasantries until I hit upon the line that opened up the whole situation for me after I discovered that he was a Londoner.

"Oh yes", I said, "I was at school at St. Pauls and I

knew a Martin Prendergast there who was a contemporary. We were in OCTU together. Could there be...."

"Why – certainly, certainly my dear sir – Martin is my nephew, the eldest son of my brother. Are you still in touch, he is married now you know."

And thus, right from the start, the tried and tested oil of the British upper middle classes began to work and I had complete cooperation from my most important contact in Ipoh – one who might easily have resented my coming on to the scene and questioning their own work. Not only was he totally cooperative, but when he learned where I was staying, he absolutely insisted that I should come later and meet his wife and stay with them for the day or days that I would remain in Ipoh.

He had an appointment that he could not get out of, but he insisted that I should get my kit and go to his house for lunch, and we then made an appointment to be back at his office for the task of going through all his papers relating to Billy's disappearance. It was clear that the Wessexshire CO had turned the investigation over to the local civilian police within a day or two of the disappearance, as it had soon become clear that whatever had happened was while Billy was off duty and in town.

That afternoon, we went through everything, all the witness statements and all that Billy's friends had been able to tell the investigating team. It was soon clear that the last person to see Billy alive was a girl called Lee Meng, who worked part-time at the FMS Bar. She had, of course, already been interviewed exhaustively by the Malay police. However, they had not discovered anything untoward. She admitted to knowing the young Billy Bridgeman, but said that he had left her in the evening to go back to camp before curfew. Prendergast had not interviewed her. However, the more we looked

231

through the statements in great detail of other people working in the bar, and from Billy's friends at the camp who usually accompanied him on their days off – the more we became convinced that Lee Meng was the key.

"I suggest that we don't wait till tomorrow. Let's go and interview her again now," said Prendergast. "I'll telephone the FMS and see if she is currently off duty."

Having discovered that she was indeed at her home and not at work, Prendergast and I went, with three duty policemen, to her room. When we knocked at the door, it was immediately opened by a strikingly pretty young girl, whom I thought to be about 23 years old. We began questioning her slowly and gently. Prendergast left it largely to me. I used all the expertise I'd garnered from interrogating Italian prisoners of war.

The technique was usually the same. First, and in the case of this girl proceeding for well over an hour, the innocuous background questions – her childhood – her parents – her school – her friends – her movements. Soon in the course of my sympathetic questioning, her answers began to be contradictory. Prendergast began firing more questions at her in English, whilst the senior Malay policeman followed up in Malay as she began to stumble and failed to reply. I was now convinced that whether she herself was guilty of anything directly or not, she certainly knew more about Billy's disappearance than she had originally let on.

By now, I, too was getting excited and losing my cool as I thought of my naïve trusting younger brother. I too began shouting, which I knew to be very unprofessional. However the girl's evasions, my increasing anger, and Prendergast's sharp examination, had excited the Malay policemen as well, and they began to ransack the room, turning over the mattress and the bed, pulling out all the drawers, banging at the desk. Had Prendergast and I both kept our cool, the discovery made by those local policemen might never have occurred. For there, at the back of a false drawer in the desk, we discovered a cache of Communist Party documents, orders and letters waiting to be despatched by jungle courier. Prendergast told me at once, in the moment of silence that followed the discovery, that there were already rumours that Chin Peng's courier system was being run by a young girl.

The instant this became obvious, I immediately recovered the usual icy calm on which I relied in these interrogations. The girl was now told by Prendergast that she was under arrest – but he waited as I resumed my interrogation and pressed her on what had happened to Billy. After more hesitant evasions, she at last spoke up, speaking with a mixture of genuine confusion, spite and a hint of self-justification –

"The little fool – always thought I loved him. I never did... I never did, not for a moment. Perhaps sometimes... no I never did not for a moment, the poor deluded idiot."

"Very well, very well – so what happened?"

"I told him to leave me alone. He left in some distress and was shot outside the house by some gangsters ... For God's sake, I don't know who they were. I had been suspicious of some types that I had noticed hanging about the house before. I think that they had been watching the house for days. I saw him die from the window. He was shot in the head at point-blank range as he left the building. I watched from behind the curtain as they took his body away. I didn't love him... I swear that I didn't love him... he was nothing to me... nothing...nothing... brainwashed capitalist lackey!!"

The girl then burst into tears as she was led away by the policemen. I went ice-cold, feeling a violent anger and deep sadness. I didn't believe a word that the girl was saying. All my instincts as an interrogator reinforced that belief, but I had to recognise that one thing seemed certain – that Billy had been shot and was dead. 'People she didn't know' – that was a nonsense, of course. Either Billy had discovered something, or he had in some other way become a danger to the CTs. In any event, he had clearly been shot by what were likely to have been guards who had been posted to keep an eye on the house.

I spent that night at the Prendergast house in a state of desperate grief for my young brother. I arranged from there to send a telegram to my dad confirming that Billy had not deserted, but had been shot and was dead. I then confirmed to the Gurneys that I would be returning soon and would take them up on the offer to go with them to Frasers Hill for a weekend before returning home.

* * *

But Conrad's first instinct, arising from his years of interrogating prisoners during the war and in Palestine, was right. Nothing, not a single word blurted out by Lee Meng, was the truth; neither her protestations as to her indifference to the young man, nor the shooting in the street by unknown men. Billy was in fact still very much alive.

Chapter 32

Why did he get out of the car?

One of the problems in fighting against a guerrilla insurgency that has some degree of popular support, is the difficulty of preventing the passing on of information about the comings and goings of those in commanding positions. This was particularly difficult in respect of Gurney – the High Commissioner – who refused to abide by even the most basic security requirements. In Palestine, he had insisted on continuing to live the calm and unruffled life of a senior civil servant, ignoring all the threats posed by the terrorists on both sides. So he would insist on his round of golf, or on his arrangements for a game of tennis or his relaxed and free weekends, regardless of the turmoil around him, and regardless of the fact that everyone would know exactly where he was and what he was doing.

But in Palestine the protagonists were out for each other's blood and were not so interested in what the British authorities might be doing. Death threats were part of the background in which the Imperial mandarins worked. So there was a lot to be said for Gurney's approach of ignoring them and on carrying on with his own relaxed life style.

However, it should be added that in Palestine, the British army's Intelligence section was active and highly efficient. Most officers, including Conrad, were fully aware of what was being planned at any one time by the activists on both sides. But here in Malaya, the situation was quite different, and this was perhaps the only area in which Sir Henry failed to exercise his sharp intellect and see the potential danger. In Palestine, the servants, the cleaners, the drivers, the army of locals backing up the administration, were largely Palestinians, leavened with some Jews in the more senior posts. They may have hated each other, but they had little incentive or desire to spy on or betray their employers – the Mandate government. But in Malaya, those same employees were almost all Chinese and inevitably, despite the most careful screening, some were sympathetic to the CTs, and some went further and acted directly on their behalf.

So it was that Sir Henry's plans for recreation were always well known in advance. The High Commissioner's movements were even more certain because of his regular habits, and his refusal to alter anything he had planned simply for security reasons. His weekend trips with Lady Gurney to the hill resort of Frasers Hill were well known and could be depended upon.

Chin Peng was already beginning to get frustrated by the continuing success of Gurney's policy of regular daily patrols in the jungle. But once Gurney introduced the policy of identity cards and civilian registration in the towns and villages, he began to feel despair. Something had to be done, some dramatic move had to be made in order to wrest the political initiative which was slipping from his fingers – and that something, he decided, was to be Assassination.

* * *

It was pointless for Conrad to stay in Ipoh once Lee Meng had been arrested by the civil authorities and taken to prison. She never wavered from her final statement of Billy's alleged death, and she continued to assert, even when she wasn't asked, that she had never once felt anything for 'that crazy boy'. Nothing more could be got out of her, and there was no question of torture being used – the values of a dignified if dying

Empire still being paramount.

So, after sending off the necessary telegrams to London, Conrad telephoned the High Commissioner's office and arranged with Gurney's secretary to meet them on the Saturday morning to take up the invitation to join the Gurneys on their weekend visit to Frasers Hill. Then he arranged for his flight back to London for the Monday after the weekend trip – he planned to meet Harriet in Oxford as soon as possible after he returned.

It was early in the morning on Saturday, the 6th October, when Conrad turned up in front of the High Commissioner's residence. He identified himself to Gurney's secretary – Dave Staples – who was hovering about, seeing to the loading of provisions in the cars parked in front of the house. There were three vehicles standing in the drive, and a small group of men were gathered about. Soon after Conrad turned up, the Gurney's came out. Sir Henry was full of good humour and clearly really pleased to see Conrad again after all these years.

"My dear fellow – my dear fellow – capital to see you. So sorry to hear about your brother, I hope you managed to find something out. A Bridgeman desert – never! – never! – though unfortunately, that may mean that something worse has happened. Ah well, come on, come on; I'm looking forward to some tennis – with you coming we will be able to make a foursome in the hills. Staples – what's the score, how are we all going."

"Well sir, we've got the official Rolls for you and Lady Gurney, and, as usual, I will be travelling with you in the front. It will be Johnny driving today. I've put Major Bridgeman in with Derek and Sergeant Chou in the first car – and.. er... I've put your golf clubs and a second set in with him."

"That's fine. My God, Conrad you better look after the golf clubs, one set is brand new. That's fine, Staples

– what's the agenda for the weekend."

"We should be arriving at lunchtime, sir. Lady Gurney is booked to go to lunch with the Pembertons. I have fixed up for a pre-lunch game of tennis for us – Captain Davis will be joining us to make up a four. Then… er… a late liquid lunch and a round of golf in the afternoon. We can't, I'm afraid, avoid a full formal dinner at night. Major Bridgeman will be spending the night at the guesthouse."

"Capital! Capital! Conrad have you got your togs/"

"Certainly, they're already in the car with your blessed golf clubs."

"Fine – they couldn't be in better company. Let's go. We'll all meet up at Frasers Hill. Come my dear."

And they all got into the cars. Conrad, a driver and a fully armed Sergeant – Sergeant Chou – in the front car. Lady Gurney, Sir Henry, Mr. Staples and the driver Johnny, in the second car, which was the black Rolls-Royce, proudly flying the Union Jack. Finally, bringing up the rear a third vehicle, a large and old converted Land Rover containing 6 Malay policemen with a British officer in charge, all fully armed.

To the sound of cheerful honking, the convoy moved off at almost the exact time that the spies in the Residency had reported it would leave.

* * *

The road to Frasers Hill was, as it happens, perfect ambush country. It was a narrow road that twisted its way up and down the hills after it rose up from the steaming plains. The slopes of the hills were totally covered with thick jungle that came right down to the roadside in many places. There were few villages, though there were clearings here and there, and the odd place also where some enterprising local had set up a tea shop

– usually at a spot where there would be a spectacular view back over the rolling countryside.

This was the area currently allotted by the CTs to the command of Siu Mah, a close aide of Chin Peng, the man who had already outlined a plan for the attempted assassination of the High Commissioner. In all the discussions revolving round Chin Peng's decision to attempt a political assassination, the fact that the Gurneys regularly went to Frasers Hill for their weekend breaks was a deciding factor. But once the idea was mooted, many more advantages were noted. Firstly, the road going up to the hill station proved to be ideal ambush terrain, and secondly, the whole attempt could be handed over to Siu Mah himself, who had come up with the agreed plan in the first place.

The problem, as Siu Mah had explained to his leader, was that despite the narrowness of the road, and the fact that it twisted and turned, the convoys that drove along it always moved fast and this was especially true of Gurney's own car. It was known that he liked being driven fast. Furthermore, it was not clear, nor were they able to find out, how far the High Commissioner's Rolls Royce was armour plated or reinforced. Even if it wasn't, it became a pure matter of luck as to whether a fusillade of shots at the moving vehicle would kill anyone crouched inside. There was therefore only one possibility of success. For some reason or another the car carrying the High Commissioner had to be made to stop.

It would certainly not be enough to put up hastily some sort of barrier, just before the arrival of the car. This would immediately be suspicious – the driver would back away at once, and then there was always the third car filled with armed policemen coming up firing, right behind, as soon as it caught up. Siu Mah had come up with an answer – furthermore it was an answer which might, just might, remove the element of luck involved in just firing blindly at the car itself, even if it was stationary.

* * *

Billy was not dead!

Naked in bed in the arms of Lee Meng he had been overpowered by four CTs who had stormed into the room on receiving her signal. There had been no subtlety, he had been knocked unconscious, then with his hands manacled behind his back and a blindfold over his eyes, he had been carried down the stairs. Whether out of some innate sense of modesty, or more likely so as not to excite as much attention if they were seen carrying a naked man, a pair of ragged blue denim shorts had been hastily pulled onto the body of the unconscious boy. He was bundled out of the building and into a small truck parked alongside. The fourth man brought out Billy's own uniform in a bundle.

For days and days, weak and in a perpetual stupor of pain, Billy had been carried about, beaten with a bamboo cane if he stumbled, dumped here and there in cellars and at the back of lorries. Blindfolded almost all the time, he was fed only irregularly, though he received water on and off whenever he managed to croak out the Malay for 'water' through parched lips. He lost all track of time. After the first day, his hands were tied more loosely allowing him to eat the diet of cold rice and noodles which were handed to him, pushed into his hands, in a bowl. He remained naked from the waist up and he was regularly struck, when necessary, to keep him moving.

At night, suffocated by the continual darkness of the blindfold, he would use his hands to pull it away. The next morning he was viciously kicked and repeatedly struck on the face for having disobeyed. Nevertheless, every night after the second night, after his guards left him to sleep, he would again pull at the blindfold until it came away. The next morning, every day without fail, his guards would again yell at him and he would be beaten across his upper body with the same thick bamboo cane which seemed to accompany him wherever he was taken. Despite this, every night he would again pull away at his blindfold till it came off. Why did he do it, knowing what it would mean for him in the morning. Perhaps it was because he simply could not sleep for psychological reasons with that damned enforced blindfold in place – and he needed his sleep to keep up his strength. But it was much more likely that this was sheer stubbornness – an attempt to keep up his morale. An act of defiance that showed, however feebly, that he still had some control over his life. If he was going to be whipped, he would be the one instigating the whipping, not just at the whim of his captors. But was there also, even at this late stage, a remnant of that old need to be punished for his betrayal.

After several days, or weeks, he had no idea how long it had been, he was delivered into the hands of Siu Mah. Siu Mah had already disposed of three British soldiers, all regulars, who had been collected and sent to him, together with a Ghurkha, all of whom he thought unsuitable. But when Billy, blindfolded and naked above his ragged shorts was prodded before him in his camp, deep in the jungle near Frasers Hill, he decided at once that this boy was exactly what he needed. Why? The others by chance had all been sent before him in their uniforms and with only an odd black eye or two. Billy had arrived semi-naked and bleeding – just what the plan required in a few days time.

It was now Saturday the 6th October. Siu Mah with his elite platoon of about 30 guerrillas set off before daylight from his camp making for that point in the road which he had already pinpointed for the coming attempt on the life of the High Commissioner. Pulled along, still blindfolded and with his hands tied behind his back, in his now ragged shorts, badly stained with all the blood from the beatings he had received, came Billy, now with his feet scratched and bleeding from the thorns and stones over which he stumbled. Siu Mah was not a sadist, but for his plan to work Billy had to be both clearly alive and yet to appear also beaten and bleeding and in total distress. So as he tottered forward guided and pulled along by the rope attached round his waist, he received another series of blows and lashes, each intended to draw blood and show his body covered in lesions and bloody gashes.

Siu Mah's plan required split-second timing. Here the regularity of Gurney's habits was the key. The CTs had timed the passage of the High Commissioner's convoy several times, and it was always at the same time. Furthermore, on each such occasion the third vehicle carrying the armed policemen was always lagging well behind at this point. Arriving at the spot selected, Siu Mah placed his men, carefully hidden behind the vines and the dense undergrowth on one side of the road – at the end of a short straight stretch. Clear of any cover on the other side, stood one solitary tree a couple of feet out from the road, and about 5 yards away from the edge of the hill which fell away sharply giving a view down to the valley. Carefully chosen, this was a spot where he could see far back down the road as it wound its way up the hill.

By now Billy was almost unconscious and could no longer walk on his own. Still protected by the jungle they tore off his now torn and bloody shorts and with much heaving and pulling managed to get him into his army uniform trousers. He was then carried across the road. Bloodied and falling in and out of consciousness, he was tied to the tree facing back down the road and for the moment placed sitting down on the ground with his feet outstretched. They no longer needed to worry what he might do and the blindfold was at last pulled off and thrown down. Siu Mah and four others clustered round the boy watching the road. An occasional car or truck was still driving by. As soon as one was spotted, the men would squat down around the tree, hiding the battered boy as if they were a group of men sitting about smoking and about to have a picnic.

Then at last a red flag was raised from a clump of bushes further down the road. It wasn't really necessary as Siu Mah had already seen the three cars toiling their way up the road towards Frasers Hill. A car in front, followed a short way back by the unmistakeable outlines of the High Commissioner's Rolls Royce, and falling further and further behind, as it laboured up the hill, the truck with the armed policemen.

The men jumped up. Billy was raised into a half standing position and the ropes tightened. For the first time since they had arrived his eyes opened, blinking against the strong light of the sun. He stared at Siu Mah, who was delighted to see the eyes open, making it clear to any observer that he was alive. Siu Mah gave the boy a sharp slap with his open hand across his face to make sure he was now fully conscious. However, he suddenly thought of the possibility of a warning being shouted. He hastily grabbed up the discarded blindfold, forced the young man's mouth open and pushed the cloth down brutally into his throat, suppressing the boy's reflexive attempt to spit it out. Then, with a final sharp blow to the open gash in the boy's chest producing a trickle of fresh blood, he raced back across the road and into the jungle undergrowth on the other side.

* * *

As the three cars of the High Commissioner's convoy began to mount the hill, one of those small usually unimportant accidents took place, which otherwise might have changed the course of what followed. The old Land Rover, modified so that it looked more like a truck, containing the armed police and bringing up the rear began to falter, already well behind the two cars ahead. Had it completely broken down the forward cars could have been alerted by frantic hooting – but as it happened the old Land Rover continued for some time to splutter up the hillside before giving up and coming to a standstill – by which time the cars in front were too far ahead to hear. It turned out to be dirt in the carburettor and, after a bit of fiddling around, the driver managed to get it going again. But they were now almost ten minutes behind.

The two cars in front were moving quite fast as usual, but when Conrad's car came into the short straight stretch, the sight of the body of a white man, clearly a British soldier, with head sagging, tied up against a tree and bleeding from several cuts and lacerations over the whole of his upper body, was clearly visible. It was impossible to see who it might be, but there was no question that they would have to stop. The driver drove slowly past as they all stared out of the window at the body, and it was clear that he was alive. The driver stopped just past without requiring an order. There was silence all round as Conrad got out on one side and Sergeant Chou got out on the other. There was a low wind rustling the trees as Conrad ran across the road to investigate. Apart from the rustling of the leaves, the only other sound was the faint but growing sound of the Rolls coming up behind them still out of sight. Sergeant Chou was an old veteran and was immediately highly suspicious. He crouched down at the back of the car with his Bren gun cocked and ready.

It is impossible to adequately describe the emotions of Conrad as he ran up to the young man tied to the tree and recognised his brother's bleeding and wasted body. But even in that extraordinary moment of conflicting emotions, he had not forgotten the six years of military training that had taken him through the war as a proficient Intelligence officer. He nearly always carried a knife, and acting quickly on a sort of automatic pilot, he pulled it out and slashed with enormous fury at the ropes which gave way almost immediately. Throwing the knife away, he grabbed Billy in both arms as he sank down once the ropes holding him up had dropped away. Billy's deadweight caused Conrad himself also to sink to the ground, where he sat and began cradling Billy, calling out softly over and over again –

"Billy – Billy – Oh God – come on, come on – Billy – Yeghpirus – Yeghpirus."

Meanwhile the High Commissioner's Rolls Royce had now drawn up and stopped immediately behind the first car. At this stage, events happened in such quick succession that it is unclear exactly what happened in what order. The position in the Rolls Royce was that both Lady Gurney in the back and Staples in the front seat were fast asleep. From the back, Sir Henry saw Conrad sitting beside a tree cradling the half naked body of what appeared to be a British soldier and immediately called to the driver to stop. He began to get out of the car. As he got out and began walking calmly over the road a fusillade of shots aimed at the two stalled cars rang out. This first fusillade of shots killed the driver of the first car outright and fatally wounded the driver of the Rolls who sank down beneath the window and onto the lap of the Secretary. Staples who had been fast asleep when the shooting started, woke up with a start to find the driver – Johnny – slumped against him and bleeding profusely, though not yet dead. Although he had no idea what was going on or why the car had stopped, he had the presence of mind to crouch down below the window while holding on to the driver trying to stem the flow of blood. Lady Gurney who had also been sleeping, had no idea what was happening either, but she too had the presence of mind to lie down on the floor of the car. Neither of them could say later why the cars had stopped and why Sir Henry had got out of the car.

Once the guerrillas saw Sir Henry calmly walking towards the tree where his guest was sitting cradling a British soldier, a positive barrage of shots spat out at him from all directions from the other side of the road. He never reached the pair still sitting at the bottom of the tree. As bullets slammed into his body he raised a hand and stretched it towards Conrad. A last shot then spun him round and he fell at the side of the road, dead.

All the guerrillas, thirty of them, had been shooting at the man who had stepped out of the Rolls Royce, but they were all many yards away and during the wild shooting both Billy and Conrad had been hit. Conrad, only superficially wounded, was still sitting up holding on tightly to his young brother, as tears flowed down his cheeks almost crooning the words –

"Billy – Billy – Billy," over and over again and willing his brother to say something – anything.

Billy's glazed eyes never left Conrad's face, and then – oh God – and then, suddenly full recognition came and a great smile exploded over Billy's face, and his eyes shone with an enormous delight that seemed to Conrad to flood the whole world with joy –

"Conrad... Conrad ... my brother" he whispered through cracked lips – "Oh Conrad, where did you come from – you've come to save me as always – Oh God...."

Then the light in his eyes died for ever, as Conrad in tears bent down and kissed his brother on the forehead, and then himself slumped forward in a faint due to his loss of blood.

* * *

The shooting did not immediately stop after Sir Henry's death. Sergeant Chou, crouching behind the first car continued to shoot wildly in all directions though he could still not see anyone in the jungle around him. Eventually a final bullet silenced him. As the shooting died down, Siu Mah came out onto the road. He recognised Sir Henry's body immediately. His plan had worked. He made no attempt on Lady Gurney's life or the secretary, neither of whom had seen anything and were still cowering in the Rolls, now covered with bullet holes

In the cold clear air, the sound of the engine of the police car further down the road, could finally be heard. Siu Mah acted decisively, ordering his men to take up the body of Billy, and the body of his wounded brother, he and his men melted back into the jungle a minute ahead of the arrival at last of the Police van.

247

EPILOGUE

Excerpts from the first report of the Chief Secretary, to Mr.Griffiths, Secretary of State for the Colonies in London, sent before full investigations were made:

"The High Commissioner's car with Sir Henry and Lady Gurney in the back of the car and the Private Secretary (D.J.Staples) in front and with a Malay driver was proceeding to Fraser's Hill escorted by one Land Rover behind and one scout car in front. A van, which was also part of the convoy, unfortunately had broken down short of the ambush position(sic).

Party was ambushed at 1.15pm about two miles short of the Gap. Driver of the car was hit in the head on the first outburst of fire. Heavy automatic fire was directed from the right and rear both against the High Commissioner's car and the Land Rover (sic). It would appear that after the first burst of fire, Gurney opened the door of the car and stepped out and was immediately shot down by heavy automatic fire.* …….. withdrew. Lady Gurney and the Private Secretary remained in the car until the firing ceased when they crawled out and found Gurney's body in the ditch on the other side of the road. …. Ambush position was some half mile long and clearly carefully prepared. Estimated size of bandit party was 20(sic). Full investigation into the circumstances is being made"

It was not known then, or indeed even now so far as the official account is concerned, exactly why Sir Henry stepped out of the car.

Lightning Source UK Ltd.
Milton Keynes UK
UKOW042025281112

202894UK00001B/2/P